SLEEPING
DOLLS

BOOKS BY HELEN PHIFER

SLEEPING DOLLS

HELEN PHIFER

bookouture

Published by Bookouture in 2022

An imprint of Storyfire Ltd.
Carmelite House
50 Victoria Embankment
London EC4Y 0DZ

www.bookouture.com

ISBN: 978-1-80314-405-4
eBook ISBN: 978-1-80314-404-7

Kindness costs us nothing. A smile, a hello, a wave can have a lasting effect on someone who might not have anyone else. In memory of Kath Mutton, who taught me that it's okay to be yourself xx

ONE

Detective Constable Morgan Brookes was the only person left in the newly renamed CID office, now known as CAST, which stood for Crime and Safeguarding Team, though it would be forever known as CID. It was her first week back after her run-in with The Travelling Man, and her absence had been missed, judging by the state of the office.

She collected what amounted to at least a week's worth of stale coffee cups and was about to dump them in a bowl full of soapy water to soak when she heard the thudding of Magnum tactical boots on the tiled floor downstairs, as response officers headed out of the station's rear door to what must be an immediate response.

She paused, wondering where they were going. It took a lot to muster up that kind of energy on a Monday evening.

Putting the cups in to soak, she went back into the large office which housed the CAST team for Rydal Falls. They were a small team, made up of Morgan, Detective Constables Amy Smith and Des Black, and their sergeant, Ben Matthews. Ben had driven Amy home earlier, as she wasn't feeling well, and Des, who was as useful as a chocolate fireguard, was on his day off. Morgan picked up her radio, turning up the volume to find out where the officers had been deployed, as she sat down and logged on to the computer to see what the job was. The screen loaded at the same time she heard Cain's deep voice over the airwaves.

'Control, we can't get inside. The flat is locked up tight, but I've lifted the letterbox and there's a bad smell. I think we need to put the door through unless anyone from the council is available with a key.'

'Is there any chance the person inside is injured and needs immediate assistance?'

Morgan held her breath waiting for his reply.

'I would have to say in my professional opinion that they are past the point of needing medical assistance, but it's your call, Control.'

She let out a sigh. What Cain was trying to put ever so politely was that whoever was inside that flat was dead, and if the smell was bad, they had been for some time.

She stood up, grabbed her jacket and checked the address on the log. A shiver ran down her spine at the realisation it was Ben's street. At the opposite end of the street to Ben's spacious Victorian house, some of the larger houses had been converted to housing association flats. She tried to remember if she knew anyone who lived there; there was only Kath, who Morgan had been having run-ins with since she'd started, and she hoped it wasn't her.

Waiting for a chance to speak, she pressed the button.

'Control, this is DC Brookes. I'll attend the scene.'

She didn't hear the reply. Stuffing her radio into her coat pocket, she grabbed her bag, hoping that by the time she'd finished, she'd be able to go straight to Ben's for a shower and a change of clothes. It was so strange that she'd been living with him for a month now and still couldn't call it home: it was always going to be Ben and Cindy's house, which was hard to get her head around.

Ben's house was all in darkness. He wasn't home yet. Driving past, she wondered if his radio was still turned on, although if he was listening, he would have shouted up too.

The van was parked outside the entrance to the last house, which was twice the size of Ben's. She had no idea how many flats it had been turned into. There was another car pulling up just in front of her, and she smiled to see Mads getting out of it, cap in hand before he tugged it onto his head. He was from the old-style school of policing and never went anywhere without it.

She walked towards him, and he nodded.

'Evening. What brings you out of that cosy office on a night like this, Brookes?'

'Same thing as you. If there's any suspicious circumstances, it will save you hanging around waiting for CAST, won't it?'

He nodded. 'You're good. Glad to see you're as keen as ever despite everything.'

He walked through the front gate, and she followed him. 'Despite everything' included being abducted and badly injured by a serial killer named The Travelling Man, a cold-blooded murderer who was now locked up thanks to Morgan and the rest of the team.

Cain's voice echoed down the stairs. 'Top flat.'

Mads muttered under his breath, 'Isn't it always?' making Morgan smile because he was right – a lot of jobs included running up and down staircases to top-floor flats, but at least they lived and worked in Rydal Falls not Manchester. A top-floor flat here was lucky if it was on the fourth floor rather than the fourteenth.

There wasn't a lot of room at the top. Cain was standing there along with another officer who had joined not long after

Morgan. She smiled at Amber, who nodded; she was standing as far back from the door as she could.

'Don't mind Amber. She's not partial to the smell of decomp, are you?'

Amber glared at him, and Morgan had to turn away so she couldn't see the smile on her face.

'What's not to love about the smell of a corpse? To be fair, it probably smells better than your aftershave, Cain.'

Mads held up his hand. 'Behave yourselves, children. Do we know there's a body inside?'

Cain lifted a gloved hand. Using two fingers, he pressed against the letterbox, pushing the flap in, and the stench hit them all, making Amber groan. Mads shook his head, and Morgan stepped closer, breathing through her mouth.

'Whammer?' she asked Cain.

'In the van. Do you want me to do the honours or have Control managed to get hold of someone with a key?'

'If you would be so kind, Cain, let's get in there and see what we have.'

He turned, taking the stairs two at a time to go and get the heavy red metal battering ram better known as a whammer or a universal door key. A minute later he was back, panting a little but with the whammer in one hand.

'At least it's a wooden door and not one of those new composite ones. They're a bastard to put through.'

Everyone stepped back, giving him room to swing it at the lock on the door. Three loud bangs and the wood around the door cracked and splintered.

Pushing his shoulder against the wooden door, he managed to get it open a couple of inches, then it stopped. What didn't stop was the ghastly stench that was now filtering through the battered door and filling the narrow hallway. Amber turned and began to run down the stairs; her cheeks had taken on a shade of grey-green that even Morgan hadn't seen before.

Mads lifted his hand to his nose. 'Bloody hell.'

Cain looked over his shoulder at Morgan. 'I'm not getting through that gap.' He patted his stomach, and she realised he wanted her to squeeze through. She stepped closer; he passed her a torch. 'You might want to suit and boot before you go inside, or you're going to have to burn those clothes to get rid of the smell.'

She knew he was right.

'Amber, get Morgan some kit out of the back of the van and bring it up here now. Please.'

Mads gave his order over the radio, and a few moments later, a sheepish Amber appeared with some plastic packets in her hands. She had her nose buried in the crook of her arm.

Morgan took them from her and began to rip them open, tugging on the white paper suit, shoe covers and double gloving for once. Cain reached out, pulling the hood of the suit up over her hair, covering her topknot. She nodded at him, and he smiled.

The entrance to the flat was in darkness. Morgan pushed the torch inside the slim gap, trying to look around, but she couldn't see anything. She sucked her breath in and tried to squeeze through but still wasn't able to fit. 'I need a bit more space.'

Cain leaned his shoulder against the door, managing to push it a couple of inches more, and she dragged herself through the gap and let out a yell as she stumbled over a rolled-up rug that had fallen behind the door, stopping it from opening properly. She felt herself falling and tried her best to stop herself, windmilling her arms to try to propel herself past the carpet, but failed miserably. She landed on all fours near the sofa, where a waxy white hand dangled next to her face, and grimaced whilst screeching at the same time.

Morgan clambered to stand up then leaned against the wall, slowly moving the torch beam down towards the body. Her stomach lurched at the sight of the woman lying on the sofa in a pair of sky-blue silk pyjamas. At first appearance, anyone would have thought she was asleep, but the stench made that impossible.

Morgan shone the torchlight onto the woman's head; she had a pleasant face, some frown lines around her eyes, and she looked to be well in her sixties. Morgan lowered the beam down onto the woman's chest and, bending down, she lifted her top a little in case by some miracle she was still breathing.

'Oh my God,' she shouted.

There was a white mass of writhing maggots.

Mads had his face pressed against the gap in the door.

'Stop messing around in there, Brookes. What have you got?'

'Body, female, been here some time, lots of—' She paused. 'Insect activity – maggots all over her chest. She's on the sofa and there's some kind of rug wedged between here and the door.'

'Suspicious or natural causes?'

Morgan's head shook from side to side. 'I can't call it – too difficult to say. We need fire and rescue to help move the body. The undertakers are going to struggle, but we also need CSI, and someone try and get hold of Ben.'

She shone the torch around the small flat. It was pretty sparsely furnished with the bare minimum: TV, coffee table and a small kitchenette. There was a large frame on the wall opposite which had a towel draped over it; next to that was an old-fashioned clock with a pendulum which wasn't moving.

Morgan reached over to lift the towel and see what was hiding underneath it. She jumped at the dark shadow that moved and realised it was her own reflection: it was a mirror.

She dropped the corner of the towel and moved the beam over the face of the clock; it was stopped at six o'clock. There was a light switch next to the clock, and she pressed it, but nothing happened, and Morgan wondered if there had been a power cut.

She sidestepped around the body on the sofa then pushed herself out through the gap.

'Natural causes then?'

She shook her head. 'Impossible to say but there's something weird going on in there.'

'How weird?'

'The mirror is covered and the clock stopped at six.'

Footsteps on the stairs made everyone turn around to see who it was. Morgan felt a small sigh escape from her lips at the sight of Ben's concerned face.

He took one look at her, wrinkled his nose at the smell emanating from her and nodded.

'What have we got?'

TWO

Ben cleared the area, asking Cain to start door knocking to find out as much information as possible about the person who lived in the top flat, and Amber to stop anyone coming into the property. Mads was keen to get back to the station, and Ben told him to leave but to chase up who was the duty CSI and get them out here. When it was just him and Morgan, he reached out and touched her arm.

'Are you okay with this? If it's too soon, I'll manage – you can go home.'

She smiled at him. 'I'm fine but thank you. Besides I'm not leaving you here on your own. I want to see what you think.'

He had been to the van and was also suited and booted. 'Cheers. Judging by that smell, I'm not sure I want to go inside. You're a lot tougher than you look, but I've always known that.'

Morgan was squeezing back through the gap; she turned her head, putting her hands on her hips in mock annoyance. 'And what is that supposed to mean?'

'I'm not getting into an argument. I just mean that you can handle stuff most seasoned detectives or coppers would rather not; you handle me just right.' He winked.

'What, like Mads?'

Ben grinned. 'I'm not naming names.'

She found herself back in the dark space, and this time she was careful where she put her feet so she didn't fall over the carpet. They couldn't move it out the way until CSI had documented the scene. Ben struggled to get through the gap and was huffing.

'You have to really suck it in – too many beers in The Black Dog aren't helping. You know they sell cocktails now – maybe you should switch to them.'

'Cocktails.' With a loud grunt, he dragged himself inside with a ripping sound as his protective overalls caught on the door, tearing a large hole around his midriff, and Morgan had to stifle a giggle. It was highly inappropriate, and she felt terrible.

Shining the torch down across the room onto the body, Ben let out a gasp.

'Holy shit, that's awful. How long have they been here, and where's the light switch?'

Morgan shrugged. 'No idea, but I wonder if they died at six o'clock.'

He turned to her. 'What? How do you surmise that?'

She turned the torch onto the clock that wasn't ticking, the pendulum frozen in time.

'And look at the mirror. Why is it covered?'

'Maybe she didn't like mirrors? And covered it herself. Or maybe I don't have a clue.'

'There's something weird going on here. Oh and the lights aren't working.'

'You think so? That's your professional opinion?'

'You know what I mean, Ben. Would you lie down to die? Wouldn't you be phoning for an ambulance if you felt ill?'

'Not if it's a suicide or if you died in your sleep, you wouldn't.'

'True.'

'I better call Declan and get him to come take a look, in case it's not a suicide.'

Instead of trying to squeeze back out, Ben walked into the compact living room and rang Declan Donnelly, the forensic pathologist – and one of his good friends – for this part of the county.

There was a knock on the door. 'Can I come inside?'

'Of course you can, Wendy. We would leave but Ben struggled to get inside. It's a bit of a tight squeeze.'

Wendy's arms and legs appeared through the gap. 'Oh Lord, this is tight.' But she managed to get in, leaving her heavy case on the other side.

Morgan pointed the torch down at the body, and Wendy grimaced.

'Bless them.'

'I know, it's sad. How are you, Wendy? You must miss your nan.'

Wendy nodded. 'I'm okay. You have to be, don't you? There's always someone worse off than you.'

'That's true. I'm glad to see you. It's been pretty q—' She stopped herself from completing the rest of the word – speaking the word quiet out loud was like invoking an ancient Egyptian curse. The minute anyone at work stated they were having a quiet shift, all hell would break loose, every time. Morgan felt terrible for Wendy, who had turned up to work the murder scene of one of The Travelling Man's victims only to find it was her much loved nan.

'Sounds about right. It's like the world was waiting for me to come back to work. Anyway, how are you?'

'As good as I can be. Not sure my brain will take any more beatings, but for now it's okay.'

Wendy smiled. 'You're tough, Morgan, and isn't it a good job that you are?'

Morgan shrugged. 'You're the second person to call me that tonight.'

'It's a compliment, not a dig. Right then, let's do this. Do we have any idea who this is?'

'Cain is door knocking to try and find out some more information, and Control were trying to get hold of the out-of-hours team who run the building.'

Ben ended his call and turned around. 'Who rang this in?'

'Neighbour next door said there was a bad smell coming through the air vents; it came in as a concern for welfare for a Shirley Kelly. I read the log before I came here.'

Wendy was shining her torch on the body. 'Her chest is moving?'

'Yeah, lots of maggots under that top.'

Ben shook his head. 'There's not much room in here. I'll squeeze out and let you work.'

Both Morgan and Wendy shuffled into the living room so he could get out.

Wendy whispered in her ear, 'He hates maggots.'

Morgan nodded. 'I know. I'll stay in case you need anything.'

Wendy reached out, her warm fingers squeezing Morgan's arm in way of thanks.

Heavy boots on the wooden stairs leading to the flat signalled the arrival of fire and rescue, and Morgan was glad they were here. After Wendy had documented the scene, they'd be able to help move the body, so they'd have easier access to the flat.

THREE

JANUARY 1989

The house was huge, empty and always cold, although today it was much busier than usual. There had been police knocking at the door this morning; he'd heard them whilst he was hastily getting dressed, teeth chattering and knees knocking with the frigid air that seemed to fill all of the rooms upstairs. Of course, he hadn't known they were the police. He'd thought it was the boy who worked at the grocer's, bringing their weekly delivery of fresh produce that his grandmother insisted they eat.

What first gave it away was the fact that there were two men speaking. Their voices had filtered up from the large hallway through his open bedroom door, and he'd heard words. Not all of the words, but the really important ones like *sorry, terrible accident, nothing could be done*. And then the voices stopped.

Intrigued as to who they were talking about, he pulled up his trousers, slipped on his school jumper and crept barefoot from his bedroom out into the hallway. Leaning over the thick oak banister, he couldn't see anyone – they'd all disappeared. This was the most exciting thing that had happened here since he'd moved in so he ran down the stairs to find which room the visitors had been ushered into.

Emmie, the housekeeper, burst from the drawing room, her eyes streaming with tears and her sleeve pressed against her mouth. She looked at him and pointed to the stairs but didn't stop and carried on to the kitchen, where the cook would be making some of the horrible porridge that his grandmother insisted he ate every day before school. At least he knew where everyone was now. He wouldn't have to waste time listening at the many doors down here that led into the library, dining room, music room or study.

He looked around to see if Emmie was watching him: she wasn't. In her haste to run to the kitchen, she hadn't shut the door properly. Grandmother would be annoyed about that one, but if she was busy, she might let it slip. Shutting doors was her thing, her bug bear that she complained about day and night. At first when he was brought here, he'd forget and would run from room to room leaving them open. Not anymore. She'd shut him in his room for hours and hadn't let him eat or drink anything until she was happy that he'd remember to close the doors.

He crept closer, peering through the crack, and saw two policemen, their caps in their hands, and his grandmother sitting on the chair staring at them.

A sharp pain in his ear tore his gaze away as he felt himself being dragged backwards, and, turning, he saw the cook. He had no idea what her name was because everyone called her Cook, but she was dragging him away by his ear.

He opened his mouth to yell, but she lifted her finger to her lips and shushed him, whispering, 'Don't you dare make a sound. Get yourself upstairs and ready for school now.'

She released his ear, which was still burning, and he rubbed it furiously to ease the pain. She was pointing to the stairs just like Emmie had done, and this time he did as he was told. Cook was an angry, short, ginger-haired woman whose cheeks were permanently red. She scared him almost as much as his grand-mother did.

He ran back up the stairs, his ear burning and a fire in his chest, because he wanted to know what was going on and why no one would let him find out. After splashing cold water on his face in the bathroom, washing away the tears, he pulled his socks and shoes on, and shrugged his school blazer over his shoulders. He would find out when he came home. Maybe someone in the village would be able to tell him; it seemed the children at that school knew a lot more about his life than he did. They took great pleasure in calling him the boy from the crypt. When he'd asked the only kid who ever spoke to him why they called him that, he'd told him it was because he lived in the big scary house on the hill with its own graveyard.

He hadn't chosen to live here: he'd been dumped in the middle of a cold, frosty evening by a social worker who'd told his grandmother that he could no longer live with his mother because she was unfit. That had been three months ago – three long months ago. His mother was a drunk and liked to have lots of different men to the flat, but there was one thing: it was never cold in there. She might have left him alone for hours on end, but the heating was always on, and he could watch the cracked television when the electric was working.

As he made his way out of the front door, he could still hear the voices coming from the drawing room. Now they were mere whispers. He dawdled down the driveway hoping that he'd miss the minibus that picked him up each morning. He didn't want to go to school; he wanted to know what was happening, but as he approached the imposing cast-iron Victorian gates that were wide open, he heard the engine rattling as it did whenever the bus stopped. Turning around, he saw two figures coming out of the front door and getting into the police car parked outside.

'Hurry up, it's bloody freezing,' the bus driver's gruff voice shouted at him, and he did – he ran to the door and got in.

'Morning.' The driver's voice sounded not quite as angry.

He nodded, his attention still on the police car behind him. There were only two other kids on the bus, and they were both staring out of the fogged-up windows, noses pressed to the glass, watching the police car driving slowly towards them.

'What's going on then?'

He looked at the girl with the two tight yellow-gold plaits. They were fastened with two huge red bows on the end and looked stupid. She was speaking directly to him for the first time since he'd started to get picked up two months ago.

He shrugged. 'Don't know.'

She looked at her friend and giggled. 'Yes, you do. Tell us why the police are at your house? Did you kill that old witch who lives there?'

He wished that he knew so he could tell, but he couldn't so he sat down and ignored her. She was only speaking to him to be nosy; she never spoke any other morning.

He felt something hard bounce off the back of his head and heard the two girls laughing, but he never turned around, his small fingers clenched into tight fists by his side. He stared out of the window wondering what was going on and hoping they'd leave him alone, because he wasn't allowed to get angry in public.

FOUR

Wendy worked diligently, photographing the body and not flinching when she lifted the pyjama top to take samples of the maggots, which would be sent off for the entomologist to study, in case this turned into more than a sudden death.

Morgan looked around the flat again – why wasn't the electric working? Everything seemed so much creepier in the dark.

She pushed open the bedroom door and shone the torch around. The bed was made and nothing looked out of place, except for a sheet draped over what she was assuming was a free-standing mirror in the corner. She crossed towards it wondering why Shirley disliked mirrors so much – it was strange. Wouldn't you not buy any or get rid of them if they were in your flat when you moved in?

She stepped closer. Her heart was beating much faster than usual, and she felt as if her whole body was anticipating something awful about to happen. Reaching out, she took hold of the corner of the sheet.

'Right then, Brookes.'

She screeched, letting go of the sheet and turning around to see a bemused Declan standing at the door to the bedroom.

'You gave me a fright.'

'Apparently so. What's the matter with you, Morgan? You're not usually the screeching kind. Do I look that bad?'

Her head shook. 'No, you never look bad. I'm just a bit freaked out by all of this mirror covering and the dark.'

He snorted back a laugh. 'You're too funny at times. I think the reason it's dark is our dearly departed forgot to top up the electric meter. And maybe she was going to decorate? There are probably lots of reasons. Come on – Wendy said we're good to go. I want to take a quick look at the body. I have a life outside of working for you and Ben, you know.'

She realised he was right – there probably were lots of reasons she was freaking herself out.

'Hot date?'

'Hot something, if I get out of here before it's too late and manage to get rid of the awful smell that's going to be clinging to me for hours.'

She followed him out to where Shirley was lying.

'She's been here awhile.'

He bent down, lifting her top then quickly dropping it again. 'Blimey those little blighters are having a great time underneath there.'

'How long do you think?'

'As a rough guide, a blowfly lays its eggs within forty-eight hours of death, then the maggots hatch within two to seven days. A very rough guess would be at a minimum four days, but I'm no expert when it comes to bugs, then there's the heating, which can speed up decomposition, although it's cold in here. I can tell you more at the mortuary where I can see what I'm doing.'

Ben stuck his head through the gap. 'Suspicious?'

Declan looked up at him and shrugged. 'On first appearances, hard to say. The body is quite badly bloated, but I can't see any obvious signs of violence.'

Morgan nodded. 'I just think that the sheets covering the mirrors are weird.'

'It's not enough to indicate murder though. I'm sorry, until I get her to the mortuary, I can't really give you anything. My best advice is to get her moved, and I'll have a proper look tomorrow morning. But I'd treat it as a crime scene just until we know for definite.'

He stood up. 'Is that okay with you guys?'

Ben's head had disappeared. Morgan nodded. 'Yes, that's fine by me. Thanks. Have a good night whatever you're doing.'

Declan whispered, 'I do have a hot date, but now I'm going to have to go home and shower again because you know how much the smell of decomp loves to linger on skin and hair. I don't want to put him off on a first date. I'll save that for second and third.'

She smiled at him, and he pointed to her hair.

'Glad to see you back at work anyway. How's your head?'

'It's good, thanks.'

He squeezed through the gap in the door with a little more ease than Ben had, and she took a final look around.

'We're going to get you moved now, Shirley, and cleaned up, get rid of those nasty bugs and find out what happened. There's some very nice firemen outside waiting to help you.'

With that, she paused then walked into the tiny kitchen. It was clean, spotlessly clean, and there was a big butcher's block on the worktop with some sharp knives sticking out of it. One was missing.

Morgan looked in the sink, lifting the grey plastic washing-up bowl to check underneath it. Nothing.

There were three compact drawers. She pulled them out one at a time, looking for the missing knife. The top one had an assortment of mismatched cutlery; the other two had spatulas, whisks and various other baking utensils but no knife.

She stood back for a moment, her hands on her hips, then

went back to take one last look at the body. There were no obvious signs of a knife being used on her and no pools of congealing, clotting blood either. Perplexed, she shrugged and left the flat.

Ben was waiting outside with the chief fire officer and the undertaker. He looked at her. 'All good?'

'Yeah, I suppose so. You can take it from here. Thanks.'

The undertaker looked through the gap in the door and let out a loud groan. 'Are we okay to move that rug?'

Ben was already on his way down the stairs and he turned and gave him the thumbs up, so Morgan followed him. They would leave it with them to get Shirley out to the waiting private ambulance.

Cain was standing at the bottom of the stairs, his arms crossed.

'Neighbours that were home haven't heard or seen anything, said she was a bit of a recluse and kept to herself. There's the flat next door to her that didn't answer and one down there.' He pointed to a peeling, black-painted wooden door with a sticker on it that read 'No Cold Callers'.

Morgan looked at him. 'Are you going to book her in at the mortuary?'

There was a glint in Cain's eyes when he replied, 'I'm scene guarding – Amber is going to have the pleasure.'

'Does Amber know?'

'Does Amber know what?' The woman in question walked through the front door, her face much paler than before.

'That you're booking our dead lady in at the mortuary.'

'You've got to be kidding me. What, on my own?'

Ben raised an eyebrow at Cain, who nodded. 'That's right. It's something we all have to do so you might as well do this one and get the experience.'

Morgan smiled at her. She almost offered to accompany her,

but Ben must have read her mind. 'Come on, Morgan – let's get cleaned up and back to the station.'

Amber was still glaring at Cain and shaking her head. 'Bloody hate this job.'

They left them to it. They were like a married couple.

As they stripped off their protective clothing at the van, Ben sniffed the sleeve of his shirt. Then he leaned over and sniffed Morgan.

'Urgh, I don't think your Chanel Mademoiselle is supposed to smell that bad. You better go home and get cleaned up.'

'Cheers for that. What are you going to do?'

'Well seeing as how I don't smell as bad as you, I'll go back to the station and finish off.'

'I should think so, seeing as how I took one for the team.'

'And that, Brookes, is why I love you so much – you're such a selfless being.'

'Hey, there was a knife missing from the block in the kitchen. I checked everywhere for it.'

Ben shrugged. 'She didn't look as if she had any knife injuries. Maybe it broke and she threw it away.'

'Yeah, maybe.' But she wasn't so sure.

He walked to his car and got inside, then put the window down. 'I'd walk home if I was you or your car is going to smell even worse than it already does.'

He drove off with a grin etched across his face, and she was tempted to give him the finger, but he was right. It was only a short walk to Ben's house, where she now lived. She had moved in recently, after her latest run-in with a crazed murderer had finally made her realise that she wasn't safe on her own.

As reluctant as she'd been to give up her gorgeous apartment and living the single life, Ben's large house was more than big enough for the both of them. She was thankful, and as much as a part of her still didn't believe that she needed to live with anyone, she loved Ben so completely, and moving in together had felt right. From the start, he had worded it so that she wouldn't feel she'd overcommitted herself to him and that it was an equal partnership, a house share sort of thing. If knights in shining armour actually existed then Ben Matthews was definitely the one who had come into her life to make her feel safe – and more loved than she'd ever been. They made a great team both in and out of work and, thinking of work, he was right: she may as well go and get cleaned up.

As she headed down the street though, Morgan couldn't stop thinking about the covered mirrors and the stopped clock inside Shirley Kelly's flat. A scene from the film *Four Weddings and a Funeral* flashed across her mind – she'd bawled her eyes out when John Hannah read the poem 'Funeral Blues' by W.H. Auden. She tried to remember it, but it was just that first line that had stayed with her.

Was what had happened in Shirley's flat just a coincidence, or was there some deeper meaning to it?

FIVE

The walk to Ben's house took minutes. The ancient sodium vapour gas-discharge, orange street lighting at this end was in the process of being replaced. All the pavements were dug up and it was pitch-black compared to the opposite end, where police and fire vehicles illuminated the inky night sky.

Morgan stopped suddenly, positive she'd heard echoing footsteps behind her, and whipped around to see who was following her. Her breathing was shallow, and her fingers were shaking. She was unable to see anyone, but she was certain she wasn't alone.

Her eyes didn't make out any dark shadows or lurking figures as she stood her ground, slowly scanning the street and houses. Of course, someone could be hiding behind a bush or a tree, but they would have had to clamber over a wall, and she hadn't heard that kind of noise: it had been more of a double tap of a shoe trying to keep pace with hers.

She had nothing on her to protect herself with and felt a deep anger in the pit of her stomach – no radio, torch, cuffs or CS gas if someone should attack her. What the hell had she been thinking? She knew better than anyone how easy it was for someone to come out of nowhere when you were least expecting it. A shudder ran down her spine, leaving her feeling creeped out.

She glanced towards Ben's broken gate. It was literally ten steps away, and Cain wasn't too far if she needed help; she may not have anything to protect herself with, but she had her voice.

She fished the key to the front door from her pocket, clenching it tightly in her fingers so at least she could gouge someone's eyes out if she had to. Her head held high, she was determined not to show anyone who might be watching the fear that had enveloped her entire body as she walked faster to the safety of Ben's house.

When Ben had asked her to move in with him, the first thing he'd done before she'd even agreed was to buy a new bed and turn the second largest bedroom into the master. It was further away from the bathroom, but she'd appreciated his thoughtfulness in realising that she wouldn't want to sleep in the same bed or room he'd once shared with his wife. What he didn't realise was that Morgan was more relieved than he could have ever imagined. She hadn't known Cindy and had nothing but the utmost respect for her, but it troubled her thinking she would be imposing on her space.

Morgan slipped through the gate and opened the door, then stepped into the airy hallway, slamming the door shut behind her a little too hard before turning the lock. She flicked the light switch on so the entire hallway was brightly lit. There were no dark corners in Ben's house. Bless him, when she'd agreed to move in here with him, he'd had an electrician come out and replace all the beautiful cut-glass chandeliers with rows of LED lights so there was nowhere for the bogeyman to hide.

Morgan pressed her back against the door, her legs trembling so badly that she found herself sinking down onto the floor as a big wet tear slid down her cheek.

Tucking her head into her elbows, she wiped it away with

her sleeve and sucked in a deep breath. She could do this – there was no way she was letting The Travelling Man, or anyone else for that matter, get to her this way. She was tough – both Ben and Wendy had told her this, but she was also human and after everything she'd been through, a deep-seated fear had started to grow inside her. No matter how hard she tried to keep it buried, it was always there, lying dormant like some terrible disease. Lingering like the bad smell on her clothes.

She didn't know what had come over her – there was no reason for anyone to be following her. Gary Marks was dead, and despite the terrible things he'd done, at the end he'd been there for her at the moment she'd needed him the most. The Travelling Man was locked up in a high-security prison and would never get out.

Are you sure about that? Gary Marks managed to escape – why wouldn't he?

Morgan forced herself to stand up, shushing the voice inside her mind. For the time being she was safe. It was early days of being back in work and Shirley Kelly's flat had freaked her out. That was all it was. She was having a wobble. It was perfectly natural and normal – no one could go through the trauma she had and not have moments of pure fear.

Nodding to herself, she set the security system that Ben had also installed, that they'd both forgotten to alarm before they left for work today. He'd turned his charming, beautiful Victorian house into a fortress to keep her safe and for that she'd be eternally grateful.

After she'd showered for the longest time, and washed herself and her hair several times, she dried off, spritzed herself in Chanel and pulled on the soft dressing gown Ben had bought her. He was good to her, too good, but she appreciated it and him more than she could ever show him.

Looking at her reflection, she found her complexion was a better colour than before. The steam had left her with rosy cheeks, and she felt more like herself. She was fine; she would be fine even if the sudden death turned into a suspicious one. It wasn't anything she couldn't deal with.

Her phone began to ring in the bathroom, and she retrieved it, glad to hear Ben's voice.

'I hope you smell better.'

'Jesus, Ben, you need to work on your pick-up lines – they're terrible.'

The deep, gruff laughter made her smile, and she felt a warmth inside her chest that was thawing the block of ice lodged there, making her feel human again.

'I don't know what you mean, Brookes – it was a generic question. I'm just checking in.'

'Yes, I smell much better, thank you.'

'Good. I'm calling it a night. There's nothing I can do until the post-mortem tomorrow. I'm not convinced it's suspicious though – look at the amount of fruit loops we deal with. It wouldn't be the first time someone has acted this weird, would it?'

'I'm glad you're coming home, but...'

'But?'

'I don't want to spoil your evening, but I think it's suspicious. Sorry, I have this feeling.'

'Stop it right there, Morgan. You're giving poor Shirley the seal of doom before we know anything or have any evidence. For once, let's just assume it's natural and that Shirley had some issues, at least just for tonight.'

She knew he was right. She wished she could turn off the inbuilt sensor inside her mind that picked up on anything mildly suspicious, but she couldn't figure out how to do it.

'Okay, you're right.'

'Where's Morgan and what have you done with her?' His tone was serious.

She laughed. 'Very funny. I'm here waiting patiently to say

I told you so tomorrow, but for now I'll agree to disagree. Come home, Ben. I don't want to be on my own.'

'Now there's an offer I can't refuse.'

He ended the call, and she smiled at herself in the mirror, wishing the smile would reach her eyes.

But it didn't, and she felt as if it had been quite some time since it had.

SIX

Morgan was curled up in bed. She hadn't been able to get warm after her shower and she couldn't sleep either. She lay there listening to the sound of the large, square Laura Ashley clock on the wall as it ticked away the seconds, waiting to hear Ben open the door and his heavy footsteps in the hall. He'd said he was coming home ages ago, and every second felt like a long, drawn-out hour. She hated that she was relying on him being here to make her feel better, and as she stared at the ceiling, she wondered if she'd be better off living on her own, if they had rushed into this too quickly?

It wasn't that she didn't love him because she did. She had begun to slowly fall in love with him as soon as she'd met him. He had this charismatic appeal that had just broken down her frosty barriers one icicle at a time. Not to mention he was so damn sexy. But – and she didn't like herself for even wondering this – was she too reliant on him? Was it supposed to be this way? She wasn't sure. This house, this living mausoleum where he had lived with Cindy, was never going to feel like her home, not with the ghost of his dead wife hovering around.

She wondered if she'd have got along with Cindy: would

they have been friends if she'd got the chance to meet her before she died? Or would they have taken an instant dislike to each other because they both had feelings for Ben?

It was hard to understand why she felt this way. She was supposed to be happy; they were in the mad throes of passion and the burning excitement that a new relationship brought. Maybe it was her – she was too damaged after everything she'd been through in life to think straight. Was she on a path to self-destruct, pushing away at the only thing she'd wanted because she didn't deserve to be this happy?

Staring up at the ceiling, she whispered: 'Are you okay with this, Cindy? Are you still here somehow or someway? Do you want Ben to be happy or would you rather he spent the rest of his life in pain and misery because of what you did?'

The front door slammed, jolting her from her one-way conversation with Ben's dead wife, and she heard the beep of the security system being reset. She let out a long sigh and thought about going downstairs to see him, but she felt drained and knew that soon enough he'd come up to see her.

The thought of him being with her and sharing the same bed eased the worry inside her chest, releasing the tight knot that had been making it so hard to breathe. She was screwed up beyond anyone's belief. Maybe she needed to see a counsellor. They did have a service at work where you could self-refer. She promised herself she would look into it tomorrow.

Ben was moving around in the kitchen. He must be hungry; it had been a long day and now evening. He'd come up to her when he was ready. At the thought of this, her eyelids began to flutter. She was safe now – she could sleep.

Hours later, Morgan opened her eyes and felt the warmth of Ben's body next to her. She lay there feeling safer than she ever had her entire life and prayed that her screwed-up way of thinking wouldn't ruin everything she'd ever hoped for. She loved Ben, he loved her – why was she so determined to make everything far more complicated than it needed to be? And then a voice whispered *stop all the clocks* inside her mind.

Turning on her side, she picked up her phone, putting her head underneath the covers so she didn't wake Ben with the bright glare from the screen. She googled the poem and the meaning behind it and found it had been written as part of a satirical play. Then she searched why did people stop the clocks when someone died and discovered it was part of a Victorian mourning ritual, to mark the passing of a loved one. They also covered the mirrors. What could this mean? Was whoever killed Shirley Kelly following some old tradition?

Frustrated at not having the answers, she pushed her phone back under her pillow. Turning back to Ben, she snuggled up to him and began to take some deep breaths, trying to make her mind go blank and quit the needless worrying so she could go back to sleep in the arms of the man she loved.

SEVEN

Breakfast was toasted bagels, ground coffee and the usual mindless chatter about what to have for tea before Morgan and Ben drove to work together. She went into the office, leaving Ben downstairs chatting with Mads, and smiled as their laughter filtered up the stairs. The phone on Ben's desk was ringing, so she opened his office door to answer it, but it stopped, and Morgan's desk phone began to ring . There was only one person who would try and ring either of them at this time in the morning. She picked up the receiver.

'Good morning, Declan.'

'How did you know it was me? Have you developed psychic abilities due to all those head injuries and, if so, what are this week's EuroMillions numbers, please?'

She laughed. 'No, sorry, I haven't. You always ring Ben first then me. It was a good guess.'

'Damn, never mind. Good morning. Where is the handsome brute anyway? Has he got a day off?'

'No, he's downstairs. Can I help you?'

'Yes, you can. I'm looking at the X-ray of the woman from last night, Shirley Kelly, and here's an interesting find. Her neck was broken. I'm pretty certain that she was strangled to death, and once we clean her up, there will be some form of ligature marks around her neck. Of course, it's difficult to see because of the decomp, and she is a bigger lady so there is quite a lot of subcutaneous tissue in that area.'

'Bloody hell.'

'Yes, my thoughts exactly. Do you want to break the news to Ben or should I?'

At that minute, Ben pushed through the door with two steaming mugs of coffee in his hands, a grin on his face that was soon wiped clear when he took a look at Morgan's.

'You can tell him – he's just walked in.' She held out the phone towards him. He put the coffee down, taking it from her, and she mouthed, 'Declan.'

'What can I do for you, Declan?'

Morgan picked up the smaller mug of the two and blew the steam away; she wouldn't say it, was determined not to say it, but she knew she'd been right to feel the way she had last night.

Ben's voice was getting louder by the minute. A shiver ran down her back. Who had strangled Shirley Kelly then gone to the effort to cover all the mirrors and stop the clock? What had she done to someone to suffer such a terrible fate? Although Morgan was pretty sure that the majority of murder victims hadn't done anything to deserve being murdered. Apart from the few, rare exceptions.

There were echoes of the Potters' murder with the body left for days, but their killer had been caught and was serving multiple life sentences. He had covered the Potters' faces with white cloths after killing them because he knew them and he hadn't wanted them to see him after he'd done it. Did this mean that Shirley's killer was the same? Had he covered the mirrors because he didn't want to see himself? Or did this weird ritual have a different meaning?

The door opened and a tall black man entered in a cloud of

aftershave. His charcoal suit was expensive and he looked as if he'd just come out of the shower, his hair still damp, and his face was glistening as if he'd recently moisturised. If she had to guess, she'd say he was in his late thirties – younger than Ben but definitely older than her. He pulled out his lanyard from underneath his shirt. She saw Ben turn to look at him, and he smiled at them both.

'Sorry I'm late. We have three bathrooms, two teenage daughters and I still can't get in one of them to make it to work on time. You must be Morgan; I've heard a lot about you.'

He walked towards her, his hand outstretched, and she reached out to take it, subtly trying to see the name on his ID card. But it had flipped back to front and all she could see was the holographic constabulary crest.

'And you must be Ben?'

He let go of her hand and extended his towards Ben, who was looking at him with one arched eyebrow that Morgan knew meant *and who on earth are you?*

'Is this a good time?'

Ben ended his phone call. 'A good time for what? And you are?'

'Sorry, I should have said. I'm Detective Inspector Marcell Howard, but please call me Marc. I'm Tom's replacement; I'll be working with you and your amazing team.'

Morgan stood up, feeling awful that she hadn't done so when he'd first walked in. He'd totally caught them off guard.

'Sorry, sir – I didn't realise.'

He waved his hand at her to sit back down. 'Honestly, I'm good – none of this standing to attention. This isn't a public school; we're all equals here. It's just a rank and number, nothing special – well except maybe for the better pay scale.'

He winked at her, and she laughed, sitting back down. Ben looked a little bemused, and she guessed that he hadn't known about this or expected it.

'I thought you weren't starting until next week, sir?' Ben asked.

'I'm supposed to, but we got back from a week in Scotland yesterday morning and to be honest with you, I've had enough of my family. Don't get me wrong, I love the bones of them, but you know teenage girls aren't the most pleasant of people to be around. So I decided to come back to work and perhaps not take any leave until they're at least twenty.'

Morgan giggled – she liked him immediately. Ben nodded with no hint of a smile, however, and she wondered if there was some kind of alpha male thing going on between them. 'How old are they?'

'Fourteen going on twenty-five. No one warns you about this bit, do they? Still, hopefully they'll grow out of it before I lose all of my hair.'

'They do – some quicker than others. Would you like a drink?'

He shook his head. 'I'm good, thanks. I could do with a tour of the station though. I've never been here before, which is pretty strange considering all the major cases you've had going on here, and you can fill me in on the rest of the team.'

Ben was watching him.

Morgan stood up. 'No problem. I'll give you a quick tour. There's not much to see, to be honest. It won't take you long to find your way around.'

'Good. All I need to know is where the canteen, gents and escape routes are in case I get angry chief supers hunting me down.'

She grinned and led him into the corridor. Holding the door for him, she smiled at Ben. He looked miserable, and she wasn't sure if it was because of their new arrival or the news of the suspicious death that Declan had just broken to him.

She quickly led Marc around, pointing out the various doors and departments. She could see officers watching them both, eager to find out who he was but not bold enough to ask. Apart from Mads, who strolled out of his office and headed straight towards them.

'Morning, I'm Duty Sergeant Paul Madden, although soon to be promoted once there's an opening to inspector.'

He reached out his hand, and Marc shook it. 'Marc Howard – Tom Fell's replacement. Is there much happening at the moment?'

Mads shook his head. 'You'll soon get used to it. It's either dead or mental. There's no in-between, is there, Morgan? Especially when she's on duty.'

He was laughing at his own joke, and she shook her head. 'No comment.'

This set him off laughing even more, and he turned to walk away.

Marc arched an eyebrow at her.

'He has a weird sense of humour. You'll get used to it. I guess he's right though – things have been a bit full-on around here and everyone seems to blame me.'

Marc stared at her; his brown eyes seemed to bury themselves deep into the depths of her soul.

'You're not to blame though, are you? It's just an unfortunate turn of events. With a team as small as yours, when a major investigation comes in when you least expect them, the chance of you being on duty is always going to be fifty-fifty with such a small number of detectives. Don't blame yourself – it's unfair.'

She broke his gaze, which was too intense for her; her cheeks were on fire. Was he being nice or was he trying to get on her good side and make an ally of her because he was new and didn't know anyone?

'Morgan.' Ben's voice echoed down the stairs, and she looked up to see him leaning over the banister. 'We have to go back to the scene and then to the mortuary.'

Marc smiled at her. 'Looks as if your recent lull has been

broken? If you don't mind, I'll come with you both and you can fill me in on the way.'

Morgan nodded, wondering how Ben was going to take this news. Tom had only ever turned up to a scene when it was imperative, and she had a feeling this was going to piss Ben off big time. She took the stairs at a fast pace, hoping to be able to get up there before Marc, to warn him, but he had long legs and kept up with her without even breaking a sweat.

When they reached the top, Ben had his jacket on and was holding hers for her. She moved her eyes in Marc's direction, trying to let him know, but he frowned at her, not realising.

'I'll come along too. I like to be hands-on, and this sounds as if it's something very interesting. You can update me in the car.'

Ben nodded. 'No, that's fine – we're going to need you anyway, although you won't want to come to the post-mortem, so you might be better in your own car.'

Marc paused. 'It's good, I'll come with you two, then if I'm not needed, I'll get a lift back off someone.'

'Actually, I left my car at the scene last night. You could always drive that back.' She glanced at Ben, who was nodding. He didn't seem too perturbed by this, and she hoped there wasn't going to be an awkward silence in the car on the way to the scene.

She needn't have worried. All the way to Shirley's flat, Marc chatted about the weather, the football, where the best places to eat were and, before they knew it, Ben was turning into his street.

He didn't point out his house to Marc, and Morgan, who was sitting in the back seat, kept quiet: that was his choice and his business.

'What exactly is going on here then?'

Ben shrugged. 'Wish I knew. Patrols attended last night

and found the deceased body of a woman inside the flat on the sofa; a rug was blocking the doorway, making it difficult to get inside. Morgan squeezed through and found her badly decomposing body. We called out the forensic pathologist to check out the scene, though to be fair I was pretty certain it was a sudden death. However Declan, the pathologist, rang this morning to say that the X-rays of the victim, a Shirley Kelly, showed that her hyoid bone was broken and it's likely she was strangled.'

'Wow, that's something, isn't it?'

Ben looked at him. 'Welcome to Rydal Falls, Marc.' Then he glanced in the rear-view mirror at Morgan, and she half smiled back at him.

He stopped the car behind the police van, and they all got out.

'We should suit and boot. There's plenty of stuff in the back of the car – I keep it well stocked.'

Marc nodded, getting out of the car.

She couldn't help herself. 'Sir, you might want to leave your jacket in the car – it smells pretty bad inside.'

'Thanks, Morgan, I will.' He shrugged off the suit jacket and she saw how lean and taut his arms were; his biceps were bulging at the seams of the white cotton shirt, and she had to glance away in case he saw her staring like some weirdo.

She let him and Ben get suited up first, going to speak to the officer guarding the scene. In fact, she decided to let them go in full stop. If they needed her, she'd go back and get dressed, but she'd seen it all last night. She had been the one to bring it to Ben's attention and he'd brushed it off, which now she thought about it was incredibly annoying.

She saw Cathy, one of the PCSOs, sitting on the top step to the landing where Shirley's flat was, with the scene guard logbook next to her.

'Hey, how's it going?'

Cathy rolled her eyes. 'It's freezing and it smells. What's happening, Morgan? How long is the scene guard going to last?'

Morgan grimaced. 'Awhile, sorry – the pathologist thinks it's suspicious.'

'Flipping heck, there's three days of my life I'm never going to get back.'

'Sorry, I have something that might just make it up to you though.'

'What? I seriously doubt that.'

'Just you wait and see.'

Moments later, Ben came through the door followed by Marc, and Cathy stood up, stepping to one side to let them past. She fixed her gaze on Marc, and Morgan had to hide the smile on her face; she'd known Cathy would highly approve.

Ben nodded at her. 'Morning, Cathy.'

'Morning, boss.'

Marc reached the top stair and reached out his hand towards her. 'Morning, Cathy. I'm Marc, the new DI. Pleased to meet you.'

She grasped his hand tight and shook it. 'Not as pleased as I am to meet you, sir.'

Ben glared at her, and Morgan shrugged. Marc laughed. 'Well, that's very nice to know. Thank you for this. I know scene guards aren't the easiest of jobs.'

'Oh, it's nothing, all part and parcel of the job.'

Morgan was stifling the laughter because moments ago Cathy had been ready to jump down the stairs at the thought of the coming hours she may have to spend here. Ben was signing the logbook and passing it back to Cathy.

He pushed open the flat door and the awful smell of rotting meat filtered out into the hallway. Marc looked at Morgan with a bemused expression but followed Ben inside.

Cathy turned to her and whispered, 'Be still my beating heart – I've finally found the man of my dreams.'

'He's married with two teenage daughters, sorry.'

'Bloody hell, Morgan, why did you have to burst my bubble that fast? You could have let me have my little fantasies to keep me going whilst I'm sat here counting the bits of wood chip on the walls.'

Laughter erupted from Morgan. It was too loud and echoed around the small hallway they were standing in. Panicking, she cupped her hand over her mouth, to try and quieten the noise.

Cathy was grinning at her. 'A girl's got to dream though. I mean he looks like some male model or a movie star.'

'He's pretty impressive, yes.'

'You better watch out; Ben might feel a bit put out by him. I mean I thought Ben was fit and the station catch, but he's something else.'

'Ben has nothing to worry about. Besides, he has me – what more could he ask for?' She winked at Cathy, who giggled.

'Private health care, in case you kill him off with your antics maybe, good life insurance.'

'Cathy.'

'Sorry, Morgan, but you know what you're like. Anyway, it's not fair. How do you get to work with all the gorgeous blokes in the station? You're just greedy – you should share them round a bit.'

Ben stuck his head out of the door. 'When you two have finished can you come in here, Morgan?'

Cathy pulled a face, and Morgan nodded. 'Sorry, I'll go get suited. I didn't think you needed me.'

She ran down the stairs and out to the car to get dressed and go back into the scene once more.

EIGHT

The small flat didn't smell any better now that the body had been moved, but at least the carpet had been pulled back and the door opened wider, so she could step through with ease. Ben and Marc were in the bedroom, but Morgan stopped to look down at the sofa, where a dark outline left by Shirley Kelly's body fluids had leaked from her decaying corpse and stained it – the source of the terrible smell. Careful not to touch it, she edged her way around it and looked over at the clock stopped at six. Had the killer done that? What was the meaning behind it?

Ben's voice broke her trance. 'You know, it might have been stopped like that for weeks?'

She nodded. 'Maybe.' She couldn't argue with that, but there was a small voice in the back of her mind that didn't think so. She was pretty sure the killer had stopped it, for the same reason she was sure he'd covered the mirrors.

'What's your take on the scene, Morgan?'

Marc was watching her, waiting for her reply.

'I think all of this was done by the killer, for some reason. We just need to figure out why. What it signifies for him.'

Ben looked pained. 'Or the victim was a bit strange? We

have no proof that she didn't cover the mirrors. Maybe she didn't like to look at herself.'

'I'll speak to her doctor and see if she was diagnosed with anything that could result in this kind of behaviour. Maybe she has friends who can tell us what she was like. The guy in the flat below said she was very quiet when she hadn't had a drink, according to the house-to-house reports, and kept to herself. I'll also speak to the housing association and see if they have any record of her or problems.'

'There's someone from the housing association wants to speak to someone in charge,' Cathy's voice called through the gap.

Ben nodded. 'As if by magic. Would you do the honours, Morgan?'

She turned and walked out of the flat, glad to be out of it. There was something creepy and unsettling about all of this.

The woman standing there took one look at Morgan and wrinkled her nose, her face paling at the same time.

'I smell bad. Should we go outside in the fresh air?'

The woman was already making her way downstairs, and Cathy rolled her eyes. Morgan followed her outside but remained standing a safe distance from her.

'I'm Detective Constable Morgan Brookes.'

'Vanessa White. I'm the housing manager of the private association housing in and around this area. Can I ask you what's happened?'

'A call came in last night – the tenant in the flat next door was concerned about a bad smell and hadn't seen the occupant for some time. I'm sorry but we had to put the door through and we found who we are assuming is Shirley Kelly, deceased, in the living room. We haven't had a formal ID yet; I think we're struggling to locate a next of kin for her.'

'Blimey, that's awful. What happens if you can't find anyone?'

'Then we might have to ask a friend or neighbour. Did you know Shirley, and have you got any next-of-kin details for her?'

Vanessa nodded and then realised what she'd just let herself in for. 'Well, I know her, but not very well. I only met her a couple of times.'

'That's good enough. I'm sorry to ask you this but I'm going to need you to identify her. If you could make your way to the mortuary at Lancaster Infirmary, I'll let them know you're on the way. But before you go, could you answer a few questions for me, please? What was she like? Did she have any under-lying health conditions, illnesses, struggle with her mental health?'

'Oh God, I don't know if I can, but I'll do it. I don't think she was so good on her feet; she had a bad knee she complained about and had asked for a bottom-floor flat. She is or was on the list for a move as soon as one became available, but you know what the housing is like around here. It's very hard to get into the flats in the first place, and once people are in, they don't tend to leave unless they have to, or die...'

'Was Shirley paranoid at all? Did she give you the impression that she didn't like to see her reflection?'

'What has that got to do with anything?'

'Just wondering what state her mental health was in?'

'Not that I'm aware of. She was a quiet lady, kept to herself, but she was also a bit of a drinker. The neighbours said she would grumble at them from time to time, if they were too noisy or didn't put the rubbish out.'

'Did she have any major issues with anyone else in the flats? Any animosity between them?'

'Not that I'm aware of. It would be brought up at the monthly tenants' meetings if there were any problems of that nature.'

'Do you know who her GP is?'

Vanessa shook her head. 'Not at the moment, but we probably have it on file at the office. I can phone and ask for you. I'll get them to check her next-of-kin details too.'

'Thanks, that would be great, but if you could still go and ID her that would mean we can get on with the post-mortem quicker.'

Vanessa went back to her car, sliding into the driver's seat and shutting the door. Morgan got the impression she couldn't wait to get away.

Ben came out of the front door followed by Marc. They ducked under the crime-scene tape that Cathy had put across the gate to the property.

'Anything?'

'She's phoning the office for next-of-kin and GP details.'

'Good, I'll get CSI to come back and document the scene outside, but it's a busy communal area. I'm not holding out much chance of finding anything evidential. Did she say if there was any CCTV on the property? Sometimes they have tiny door cameras.'

'I'll ask her.' Morgan walked across to the car and waited for Vanessa to finish her phone call.

The window was finally rolled down and Vanessa passed a yellow Post-it note to her. 'That's her ex-husband's phone number. He lives in Wales. He might be able to help, and her GP is Doctor Waites.'

'Thank you, that's great. We'll be in touch if we need anything.'

Vanessa pulled a face that resembled the expression someone would make if they'd stepped in a pile of steaming vomit. 'Hopefully not. Will you let us know when we can clean the flat and get the door fixed?'

'Yes, of course.'

The window was rolled up before Morgan asked her next question, and she tapped on the glass. This time when it opened, it was only the smallest sliver of a gap.

'Does the building have any CCTV?'

'No, sorry, we've had no issues here. Everything has been fine, no reports of criminal damage or break-ins, therefore not much point in installing cameras.'

'Thanks.'

Morgan turned and walked away, heading back to Ben to pass on the good and not so good news.

'What did she say?'

'No known issues. I have her GP details so I'll go pay them a visit. It's always easier in person than on the phone.'

'Morgan, that's great, but we need to get to the mortuary first. Declan is waiting for us. Sir, what do you want to do? Are you coming to the mortuary?'

She wondered if he would, if Marc would break the general pattern that Tom had taken in leaving them to get on with their investigations. She had liked that about Tom; he had always been happy to run the investigations from the office, which made their life out on the streets much easier. She wondered how he was finding retirement, whether Christine had him working even harder than ever now.

'Actually, I'm going to be a pain and go back to the station, if that's okay with you, Ben. I have a meeting in thirty minutes with the chief super, Melanie, and I don't want to be late on my first day. I take it you two can cope with everything else. Actually that sounds so pretentious, I take that back. I know you two can cope. You've managed without my input before I appeared.'

Morgan was sure she saw Ben's shoulders relax a little, the tension he'd been holding inside easing off the tiniest bit. She laughed. 'Erm, no disrespect to you, sir, but yes, we've managed just fine without you.'

Marc smiled at her. 'Should I take your car back then?'

Morgan nodded. 'You certainly can.' She passed him the keys and watched him walk towards her battered Golf.

There was something about him that was appealing on a

level so deep down. Ben coughed. Breaking her gaze, she turned to him.

'He's got it all, hasn't he?'

She shrugged. 'He's got something. I'm not sure what it is but—' She stopped because Ben's lips were turned down and his eyes were downcast. 'But whatever it is, he's not you.'

She reached across and grabbed hold of his hand, reluctant to bend over and kiss his cheek in full view of everyone, because there was always someone around. Even though everyone knew they were an item, there were some things you kept private.

'Thanks. He seems like a decent boss. Let's hope he is and not just being an arse kisser because it's his first day.'

Morgan laughed. 'Yeah, I kind of hope that too. Imagine if he turned into some kind of control-freak boss — wouldn't that be something?'

'What are you trying to say?'

She shrugged. 'Nothing. I like that you try and control me. It gives me even more reason to ignore you.'

Ben laughed, but his eyes still looked kind of sad, and she felt bad for him. Her fingers reached out and squeezed his knee, then moved slightly higher, making him groan.

'You're a bad influence on me, Brookes. Come on — let's get to the mortuary.'

'And you suck at romantic gestures, Matthews. I mean really, "let's get to the mortuary" is the best you can do?'

He began to laugh. 'I'll make it up to you later, I promise.'

'Yeah, you better.' She glanced at him. His cheeks were tinged pink, but he had a grin on his face, which was far better than the downcast look of defeat he'd worn like a mask all morning.

NINE

The door to the mortuary was opened by the effervescent mortuary assistant, Susie, whose hair today was a combination of neon orange, yellow and red. She grinned to see them, and Morgan spoke first, giving Ben time to adjust to the shock. 'Nice hair.'

'Do you like it? It's a bit bright this time. I'm not sure if it's too much.'

'I love it – it's very you, isn't it, Ben?'

Ben nodded. There wasn't much that left him speechless but Susie's choice of hair colour could usually achieve it. He turned to Morgan and mouthed, 'How?' She elbowed him to shut up.

They followed Susie down to the changing rooms, where she chattered nonstop about her latest tattoo, the music she was loving and the current book she was reading.

'Have you read any Grady Hendrix? He's amazing. I think you'd love him, Morgan; this one is about a book club who turn vampire hunters.'

Morgan stole a glance at Ben, who looked as if his mind had just short-circuited trying to keep up with Susie.

'I haven't but I'll be sure to take a look. I love a good vampire story. *Dracula* is my all-time favourite novel. How about you, Ben, do you like a vampire or two?'

'No, can't say that I do, or that I've ever read anything of that nature.'

Susie turned to him. 'What do you read then?'

A look of blind panic crossed his face. 'Erm, the newspaper, incident reports at work mainly.'

'Come on – surely you read books?'

Susie was staring intently into his eyes, and Morgan wondered what his reply was going to be. His house was relatively book free, but she'd assumed he'd put them away with Cindy's stuff.

'Actually, I read *Salem's Lot* by Stephen King years ago – that had vampires in it.' A triumphant grin spread across his face. 'Yeah, it did. Good story but not my thing really.'

Susie nodded. 'Bloody loved that book too.'

Declan poked his head out of the door. 'What is this, book club? Come on – get yourselves inside and we can get cracking. I'm a busy man you know.'

Susie headed straight for the double doors that led into the mortuary; Ben took the door with the stick man on it and Morgan the ladies to get changed.

TEN

Declan was leaning against the bank of steel fridges that contained the bodies with his arms crossed as Morgan and Ben both walked in within seconds of each other. He eyed them up and down, then nodded. 'How's life treating you both?'

Morgan shrugged. Ben answered, 'Pretty good until you phoned this morning.'

'Ah, I am sorry about that – I hate to be the bearer of bad news. Unfortunately though, the evidence doesn't lie – or at least the X-rays don't.'

He crossed the room to the lightbox where there were a couple of radiographs lit up, showing a clear image of what Morgan assumed was Shirley Kelley's neck. The door slammed open and in rushed Wendy, her cheeks tinged red, her breath a little fast.

'Sorry, sorry, the traffic was crazy on the one-way system; there was a broken-down car.'

Declan smiled at her. 'No need to apologise, Wendy, we haven't got started yet. These two have only just arrived and they didn't even have a decent excuse.'

He continued. 'You can see the damage to the hyoid bone, which is consistent with hanging and strangulation. Given the position the body was found in however, she was most certainly not hanged. Let's crack on, shall we, and see what other evidence is present. Wendy, if you photograph the body as we take off those pyjamas, then, Susie, do you want to wash her down and get rid of those pesky maggots still feeding on her upper body?'

Morgan looked at Ben, whose tanned face had turned a deathly shade of pale. He hated maggots. She had known something was wrong the moment she'd squeezed through the gap into the flat last night, but she wasn't gloating. This wasn't anything to be happy about. The poor woman was dead, and it looked as if it was a homicide. All she wanted was to find out who had killed her and why.

The painstaking work of documenting the body began, Declan, Susie and Wendy working diligently together as each item of clothing was removed. They were photographed then passed to Morgan to bag up because there was no second CSI in attendance like there normally was. Their department was as short-staffed as everyone else, leaving Wendy running it with help from Claire when needed.

Morgan looked up from the evidence bag she'd been writing on to see Shirley Kelley's fully naked, maggot-infested body ready to be examined and felt a crushing wave of sadness. No one deserved this. To suffer the indignity of being scrutinised – every square inch of your body – after being killed was so unfair. The thought filled Morgan with dread. How many brushes with death had she had the past two years? Imagine if this had been her and all her friends having to do this examination? A cold shiver ran down the full length of her spine, making her shudder. Ben's hand pressed against the small of her back, a small, discreet gesture, but she was grateful to him for reaching out to her and letting her know he was there.

Declan pointed to the area of Shirley's neck. The whole of her body was turning purple with green splotches of decomposition. Marbling, that was the correct term for it. Morgan felt as if she knew far too much about post-mortems than she ever should for a twenty-four-year-old.

'It's a mess, isn't it, and I mean that with no disrespect to you, Shirley. I'm sorry that you were left for so long after your death. That shouldn't have happened.'

He was talking to her at the same time as gently lifting her head back to look under the folds of flesh around her neck.

'Ah, look there. Completely hidden by the bloating and extra flesh around her neck area. Well, I never saw that – it looks like a piece of a silk scarf.'

He picked up a pair of scissors, cutting the fabric that had embedded itself into the folds of her neck away from the knot then holding it up in the air for Wendy to photograph then bag up. 'That's a clearly defined, well-grooved ligature mark that even the decomp hasn't affected, even more prominent at the sides of the neck. I'd say it looks as if the killer used this scarf to strangle the life from her. Not easy at all with such a silky material.'

Morgan was staring at the piece of material. 'Whoever did that must have had a real issue with her. That's not the kind of thing you would expect to be used as a murder weapon. We need to see if it belonged to Shirley or whether they brought it with them.'

'You're good, Morgan – I hope he appreciates you.'

Declan winked at her, and she smiled.

Ben shook his head. 'I was going to say that – she beat me to it.'

'Yeah, is that right?'

Morgan knew he was teasing Ben, trying to lift the oppressive atmosphere a little.

'Well, it's a violent form of death that's for sure. Whoever did this had to have some strength in them. It's not easy to strangle a person of this size. Her face appears puffy, and her eyes are bulging, suffused with scleral haemorrhages.'

He lifted an eyelid with one gloved finger. 'Lots of petechial haemorrhages present too, which we all know are indicative of death by strangulation.'

His fingers began to palpate the head, working from right to left, feeling for fractures or pockets of swelling that would indicate a head injury. He stopped, turning her head slightly. 'Would you look at this?'

Both Ben and Morgan leaned forward, and Wendy began photographing the patch of scalp he was pointing at.

'Our boy has taken himself a chunk of Shirley Kelly's hair. See where there's a significant piece missing? Now, why on earth would he do that? No disrespect to you, Shirley, but your hair isn't a thing of natural beauty.'

Morgan nodded. Shirley's red hair had been chopped into an unflattering short cut that was too long on top and almost shaved at the back.

'Maybe she cut it herself,' Ben commented.

Declan was bent down examining the inside of her ear. 'Ah, there you go. Look in here – you can see tiny pieces of hair where it was cut. You know, the ones that get everywhere when you go to the barbers.' He checked her other ear. 'This one is hair free. I'm going to put a twenty-five-pound bet that you have a collector on your hands.'

Ben actually let out a groan loud enough to make Wendy, who was busy photographing, jump.

Declan smiled. 'Sorry to be the bearer of bad news. Of course there's always a small chance that I'm wrong. Let's get on with the rest of the examination, but I'm fairly confident this is a homicide from what I've seen so far.'

Morgan had called it; she'd had an uneasy feeling from the

minute she'd stepped inside that small flat with the covered mirrors and stopped clock and now this. She had to figure out what it all meant in order to catch this killer, because if there was one thing she did know thanks to her love of true crime, it was that killers who collected trophies didn't stop at just one.

ELEVEN

Morgan drove Ben's car back to Rydal Falls station. He was unusually quiet, and she kept stealing glances at him. He turned from staring out of the window to catch her peeking and asked, 'What do you keep looking at?'

'You. Sorry, I'm just worried. Are you okay?'

There was a long pause before he let out a sigh. 'I guess so. It's just not what I was expecting or hoping for. I feel as if I've had my fill of murders and you certainly have. Why do they keep on happening?'

'Isn't that the nature of life? Some people are born killers, and I can't say they're my favourite thing. It's too sad all these people being killed way before they should be. But it's our job, isn't it? We're supposed to be the ones eager to catch the bad guys and girls, to put a stop to it.'

'True – that's very true. So what's your take on this: why has someone decided to kill Shirley Kelly? What is their motive?'

'It doesn't look as if money is the motive, although until we check her bank accounts who can say? She could be a secret millionaire. It happens.'

'Trust me she's not – she wouldn't be living in housing-association property if she had money in the bank; they would have means-tested her.'

'It was just a thought, so if we don't think money was the motive, jealous lover? Ex-husband, angry neighbour maybe. I get the impression she wasn't very well liked by her neighbours. Whoever it was, this killing seems pretty personal. To strangle someone with a scarf means you have to get up close to them, and Declan said it would take some doing. The flat wasn't trashed; in fact there was no mess at all – it was quite the opposite – so I don't think this was a robbery. And then there's the missing hair, stopped clock and the covered mirrors – where do they come in? Could the killer have some kind of a hair fetish? Or are they obsessed with the Victorian times? I did a bit of research that explained how the Victorians stopped clocks and covered mirrors when a loved one died.'

'I hope not – that's really creepy, Morgan. Well right now we need to find out who her friends, acquaintances are. At the moment we know very little about her. Let's get started with the usual searches and see what comes up. If Amy still isn't in, can you check Shirley's social-media accounts? And we need to speak to her next of kin.'

'I'll check, but I don't think she would have been on social media. I didn't see a laptop and she only had a basic pay-as-you-go phone; it wasn't a smartphone.'

Morgan parked the car but before getting out, she took hold of Ben's hand. 'Are you okay with Marc? His arrival was a bit of a shock; I know you weren't expecting anyone to take over from Tom until next week.'

He nodded. 'That's the job for you – we really are just a name and number. Thirty years of service and you're lucky if anyone remembers your collar number let alone your name twenty-four hours after you walk out of the door for the last time.'

'We won't forget Tom – he's one of us. And maybe the new boss will earn our trust and become one of us.'

'And maybe he won't. Let's just see. He seems okay for now, but you never know if they have a hidden agenda. Some of them use these postings as a step on the career ladder and don't care about who they crush on the way up. Which is why you should try and take your sergeants exams if you get the chance. You don't want to be stuck here forever, Morgan. You're far too good for that, and it would be a waste.'

Morgan clenched his hand tight. 'I'm not stuck, I'm here doing what I love with a team that I am very lucky to work with, except maybe for Des. And I love being with you, Ben. Why would I want to leave any of this behind?'

A darkness filled his eyes for the briefest of seconds, then it was gone, and she wondered if he was thinking of Cindy leaving him out of the blue, choosing death over living and making him suffer day in, day out with the what ifs. She would never do that to him.

He squeezed her hand. 'Because you're far too stubborn for your own good, Brookes. I just don't want you to ever feel that you can't move on, that you're tied here to me and the department.'

'Bloody hell, Ben, a new boss walks into the nick and you're suddenly all full of woe and telling me I'm not tied to you and the department.'

He laughed. 'All right, all right, maybe I'm a bit thrown by the new boss – and having another death on our hands. So you do like him?'

She shrugged. 'I don't know him; he looks good and smells even better, but that doesn't mean he's a good person inside. Ted Bundy was a handsome, charismatic guy and look how that ended.'

She exited the car and began to walk towards the back door, Ben following behind.

'Well, that makes me feel a whole lot better. You have a way with words that just soothes my soul.'

She chuckled to herself, pressing her warrant card against the fob. The door clicked, and she pushed it open, holding it for Ben.

As they walked up the stairs to their office, Morgan pushed Ben in the back to urge him to walk faster, laughing at his complaints.

Neither realised they were being watched from the corner of the atrium by Marc.

TWELVE

1989

School dragged on even worse than usual. He'd sat at the small desk and chair at the far back of the room, tucked into a corner. That way no one could sit behind him and whisper about him. The whispering drove him mad on some deep level he couldn't control. It filled his ears and whooshed around in his brain like some kind of tornado, gathering speed, picking and choosing the words that were the most hurtful; *ugly, weird, freak* – they would spin around and around inside his mind at such a force he'd have to squeeze his eyes shut to stop the pain.

Yesterday had been awful.

'Am I keeping you awake? Did you not get enough beauty sleep last night?'

The classroom had been silent, except for the teacher's voice, which pierced the air in his direction. He'd opened his eyes to see every kid staring his way, then they'd all begun to snigger at him.

So today he wasn't taking any chances. He would sit and keep his eyes on the board, on the teacher if he had to, anything to not draw attention to himself. Although it didn't last long.

The snotty little cow with the blonde pigtails, Tamara, was whispering to the girl next to her and kept glancing back at him.

He felt the familiar blackness rising inside his chest. It began in the bottom of his stomach and then rose up, coating his insides in a sticky dark cloud of fury that would explode from either his mouth or his fists. Usually his fists, because he struggled to get the words out of his mouth in coherent sentences at the best of times. He wasn't sure what that meant, but his grandmother was fond of describing him this way to anyone who asked why he was so quiet.

Tucking his fists under his thighs so he was sitting on them, he tried to take a large gulping breath of fresh air into his lungs. Pure, white, clear air to try and smother the blackness, but it still kept on bubbling up inside of him. He was breathing fast now, almost panting at the struggle to keep the anger inside of him.

He looked around the room, out of the window onto the playground, but it still kept on moving upwards until it was at the base of his throat and it was all he could feel. He was choking on it, trying to push it back down.

Frantic now, he held up his hand: if he could be excused to go to the toilet, he might be able to stop it; if he could just get out of this stuffy classroom... but the teacher ignored him.

He waved his curled fist in the air to catch her attention. She looked at him the same time as the blackness reached his mouth, her face contorted into something that might have been classed as concern, but it was too late. He couldn't control it and he pushed himself out of his chair, the legs scraping hard against the parquet flooring then crashing to the floor as he ran towards Tamara. He couldn't stop if he wanted to, and before he knew it, he had a pigtail in each hand and was dragging her out of her chair, ripping the stupid bows out.

He could hear the teacher shouting at him now, the other kids all screaming, but it didn't matter – he wanted to destroy the rude girl. He would stomp all over her until she was nothing but crushed flesh and bone.

Then he felt two rough arms grab hold of him and it was him who was being dragged. He had to let go of the girl's hair as he was wrestled to the ground. He did, but not without clinging on to a handful of blonde hairs that he'd ripped out of her head. Clenching his fingers around them, he kept them safe in his hand as he stopped fighting.

Mr Atkinson, the burly maths teacher that also taught rugby, was dragging him out of the class as if he was a sack of coal, and he let him. It was over – the blackness had gone back to wherever it lived inside of him, and he knew he was in big trouble this time.

THIRTEEN

Amy was sitting behind her desk when Morgan and Ben entered the office. The tip of her nose was chapped, her eyes were watery and puffy, and a box of tissues and a packet of honey-and-lemon Strepsils lay on the desk in front of her.

'What are you doing here?'

'Passing my germs on to you lot – I'm not suffering on my own.' She grabbed a tissue just in time to catch the loud sneeze that echoed around the room.

Ben grimaced. 'Well, gee, thanks, kid, we all want a bit of what you've got. Honestly, you might be better off working from home if you're that desperate to do something.'

Amy nodded. 'That's the plan. I came to get my laptop but thought I'd see what was going on first. Is it true that the sudden death is a murder?'

Ben sighed. 'It certainly is. How do you know?'

'The new boss was in your office when I came in. You never told me that we were getting Luther to take over from Tom. I'm torn between dying at my desk whilst drooling over him or going home to die on the sofa dreaming about him.'

Ben frowned. 'What was he doing in my office?'

Amy shrugged. 'No idea. He came out pretty sharpish when I walked in, did a quick introduction and disappeared. I haven't seen him since, which is a real shame.'

Morgan grinned at her from behind Ben, who was clearly annoyed that Marc had been snooping around.

'Anyway, when he said it was a murder, I thought I'd hang on and see if you needed me to do anything. I didn't want to leave you stuck, although you could always call Des back early from his rest days if you're desperate.'

'I'm not that desperate, Amy, that I need Des back before he needs to be, or for you to be sitting here sharing your germs. If you could go home and do some searches on the victim, I'll email you what I need. That would be amazing.'

She stood up and gave him a little salute. 'Yes, boss.' Then she grabbed her Strepsils, pushed them into her coat pocket and picked up her laptop bag, before passing Ben a sheaf of papers.

'I've already done the initial intelligence checks for you and printed out some of her associates. She was a bit of a drinker and got into a few drunken arguments down The Dirty Duck. Nothing major – a couple of fines, nights in the cell, a caution and one restorative justice. You know that you're my favourite boss and always will be, don't you, boss?'

Ben laughed. 'Nice try, Smith. Thank you, I really appreciate these. Now get out of here and let me know what you find.'

She grinned at him, then screwed her face up as she tried to hold back another sneeze, failing miserably. 'Ah, I really hate snotty noses.'

And with that she was gone and it was just Morgan and Ben again. He turned to her. 'What do you think Marc was doing in my office? I don't like that – it's sneaky.'

She shrugged. 'Ask him – call him out on it.'

Ben shook his head. 'Not yet. I'll see how he goes, but I

don't like it. There's nothing in there worth checking on. What was he looking for I wonder?'

'Maybe he's trying to get a handle on you, see what you're like, that kind of thing.'

'What, by that mess? There's nothing in there except work papers, files and empty coffee mugs. I have nothing personal in there. It's my workspace; I don't have framed photos or quirky gifts.'

Morgan was smiling. 'What, don't you have my photo in a frame on your desk as a declaration of your love for me? No, you're a miserable git at times, Ben, but that makes me love you even more. I see it as my sole purpose in life to cheer you up and make you happy as well as catching killers.'

He stepped close to her, pulling her towards him, his lips brushing hers. 'You definitely make me happy.'

She enjoyed the brief moment then stepped away from him, wondering where this sudden show of affection was coming from. 'Good – I try my best.'

'You also make me a nervous wreck when you almost get yourself killed, but you can't have everything I suppose – you have to take the rough with the smooth.'

She lightly slapped his arm. 'Cheeky.'

He smiled at her, then looked around. 'Right then, we need to figure out what the hell happened to Shirley Kelly, don't we? Let's go and see if we can find someone who can tell us more about her. If Amy is doing the rest of the intel checks, we can do some mooching around with what she's already given us and find out what Shirley did her entire life to end up living a sad, solitary existence.'

'Hey, it's not that long ago the both of us were living sad, solitary existences. There's nothing wrong with being alone. Partnerships aren't for everyone – you should know that, Ben.'

'Sorry, you're right – that was a bit harsh. I didn't mean it in a horrible way. I just meant let's find out why she was living her life the way she was, what kind of woman she was.'

'Good because we all go through shit times, and we both know that more than anyone.'

She wondered where this had all come from, her defence of the dead woman she'd only briefly met. Shirley might have been lovely, she might have been a monster, but it wasn't their place to judge. It was their responsibility to find out the facts, get all the pieces of the jigsaw and slot them together until they had the full picture of what happened to end in the tragedy of Shirley Kelly's murder.

FOURTEEN

Morgan squeezed Ben's car into the small parking space available nearest to her favourite café, The Coffee Pot, which brewed the best coffee this side of the Lake District.

'I need coffee and a sandwich – anything will do.'

'I take it I'm going in then?'

'Obviously. I'm driving – the least you can do is run in.'

Ben tutted but got out of the car, his head down against the sudden flurry of raindrops that were bouncing off the pavement.

Morgan stared into the distance. The hills and fells were shrouded in dirty grey rainclouds, making them look like they'd had the tips cut off. She wondered if anyone was up there walking at the moment – unlucky if they were. The weather around here was so changeable: one minute the sun was burning, the next there could be fog, torrential rain or hailstones pounding against the pavement.

She loved living here though. Sometimes she wished that she spent more time exploring the fells and enjoying the beautiful scenery. Instead, she'd go for a half-hearted run or more like a brisk walk a couple of times a week, to try and keep herself fit enough so that she could outrun the bad guys who seemed drawn to her like moths to a flame. What was it about her that made her such a target for the most depraved members of society, and was there some way she could turn down the glow that attracted them?

A loud thud on the glass made her screech and almost jump out of her seat. She looked to see the mucky face of one of the local characters, Kath Mutton, pressed almost to the glass, her motorised scooter so close to the driver's door Morgan couldn't open it if she tried. Instead, she rolled down the window and smiled in greeting.

'Afternoon, Kath. How are you?'

Kath shrugged. 'Did you hear about the woman next door?'

Of course, Kath lived in the same flats as Shirley Kelly. Morgan sometimes had to dodge her as she whizzed past on her scooter when she was leaving Ben's house.

'The lady who died?'

'Yeah, Shirley, I can't believe it.'

'Did you know her well?'

'She lived next door to me; we'd both go to The Duck for a drink now and again. Was she murdered?'

Morgan had wondered how long it would take for the news to get out. She looked at Kath's face, black smudges of cigarette ash streaked all over it. She had a soft spot for Kath. She hadn't had the best of lives and was often seen chasing people through the main street on her scooter, shouting and swearing at them. She'd lost count of the number of times she'd had to pay a visit to her at home with Taylor when she'd been a student officer. He'd always make her go alone into the run-down, messy flat where the air was so thick with cigarette smoke it was like walking into a steam room. She hadn't minded. She would sit on the arm of the sofa and remind her not to go chasing the tourists away, and every time Kath would promise to be on her best behaviour – at least until the next time anyway.

'I think so. Did you see anyone go into her flat a couple of days ago?'

Kath shook her head. 'No, but there was a bit of noise a couple of nights ago.'

'What did you do?' Morgan knew there was a good chance that Kath had given her a load of verbal abuse through the wall.

'Used my stick to bang on the wall and told her I was ringing the council.'

'Then what happened?'

'It stopped. No idea what she was doing but I've never heard a racket like it, and Shirley isn't like that really – she knows I can't stand loud noises.'

Morgan wondered if she had unwittingly told the killer to shut up, and what she'd heard was Shirley's last living, breathing moments before her life was cruelly taken away from her.

'Kath, do you know what day this was? It's very important.'

The woman nodded. 'Last week. Pretty sure it was Tuesday night, early hours, definitely after midnight, but it stopped before I went to bed at one.'

'Did you go outside your flat or see anyone leaving?'

'No, I was watching TV. Once I climb those steps, I don't go out of my flat again until I have to. It takes me all night to recover.'

'Thank you.'

Kath grinned at her, stuck up a thumb and then whizzed away as fast as she'd arrived on her scooter.

Morgan looked over to see Ben standing in the café doorway holding a small brown paper bag and two coffee cups. The rain had stopped as abruptly as it had started, but she knew he'd been waiting for Kath to leave.

He walked back towards the car, and she leaned over and opened the door for him. He passed her the cups and she put them into the drinks' holders.

'What did she want?'

'I think she might just be the closest thing to a star witness that we have up to now.'

Ben let out a groan. 'You're kidding me? Not Kath?'

'Stop being so judgemental – that's the second time today. What's up with you? And I'm not sure. Last Tuesday night she heard banging around midnight coming from Shirley's flat. She gave her some abuse through the wall, and it stopped. I'd say there's a good chance that was her being killed.'

'Did she see anyone leaving or going in?'

'No, unfortunately not.'

Ben was sipping his coffee. 'With her eyesight that's probably not a bad thing. She'd probably point her finger at the wrong person and waste countless hours of our time following up on it.'

Morgan smiled; Kath did have bad eyes even with her glasses on. 'Well, at least we have a timeframe to narrow it down to now. That's much better than nothing.'

Ben grunted, and she took the paper bag from him, peering inside.

'What did you get?'

'Two chicken mayo baguettes, no salad.'

'Good choice. Do you want me to drive to your house and we can eat there then walk down to the flats?'

'I'd rather not. I just don't want to be in and out of my house and the flats in case anyone notices. I know they probably wouldn't, but I don't want anyone knocking on my door all hours thinking I'm a copper that's never off duty – or even worse, knocking when you're there on your own.'

'Are you not? I thought that was the whole idea of the job. We get to live, breathe and eat it twenty-four hours a day, seven days a week.'

'Not this one. I've been doing it far too long to have to be available when it's my day off.'

He unwrapped his baguette and took a large bite, signalling the conversation was over.

She didn't push him: she supposed he had a point. She did the same, and they both ate in silence, although Morgan couldn't stop thinking about who had got into Shirley Kelley's flat and just what it was that Kath had heard.

FIFTEEN

In the last hour, the whole street had been sealed off. Ben had requested a full search team to look for any evidence. There had been no signs of stab wounds on Shirley's body, but Morgan was sure that the missing knife may be evidence, and she had convinced Ben to take her hunch seriously. Even if the killer had handled it and left prints for them, it would be worth the time and effort to track it down. There was also the rest of the missing scarf that had been used to strangle Shirley. It could have been discarded anywhere. There was a sea of black uniforms searching in bins, drains, under cars, poking under bushes with long sticks – you name it, there was a task force officer, who was highly trained to search, looking in or underneath it.

Morgan parked in front of the blue-and-white police tape.

'Impressive. I didn't realise there were so many task force officers on duty today.'

'Al called down some extra support from Carlisle and Workington.'

They got out of the car. What had started off as a sudden death was now in the full throes of a murder investigation.

Sergeant Al McNulty came walking down towards them, a smile on his face.

'Morning. That flat is a bit grim, isn't it?'

Morgan nodded. 'It is. It's going to take a while to get rid of that smell.'

Ben ducked under the tape. 'How are you getting on?'

'Not wonderful. The dog did a walk-through earlier but didn't find anything. I'm under the impression it's been quite a few days since she was murdered going by the smell in the flat, and it's rained quite a lot so we're struggling to pick anything up.'

Morgan interrupted. 'We have a possible witness who makes us think it could have been last Tuesday night/early hours of Wednesday morning.'

'Yeah, that's a decent length of time elapsed between the murder and her being found. Like I said, not much to go on at the moment, especially with it being a communal entrance. There are at least eight people who go in and out of it on a daily basis, without including the post or delivery guys that go in and out, not to mention visitors. CCTV is a no go; there's a couple of residents with those Ring doorbells, but nothing on them that's any use.'

'It might be worth asking them again now that we can narrow the timeframe down – and, Ben, did you check yours?' Morgan asked him.

Two tiny circles of red appeared on his cheeks.

'It's okay, I'll take a look when I get a minute, see if there's anyone of interest passing by early hours.'

He nodded. 'Thanks. So what's the plan, Al?'

'Once the search has been conducted, we can revisit the flats, do a more intense house to house, see if anyone remembers anything from last Tuesday night. I think there's a good chance if your guy took the knife or the scarf, he kept hold of them. He seems to have covered his tracks pretty well up to now. Can't see why he'd discard either under a rose bush, but I'm not giving in yet. We'll keep on searching and make sure everything is covered.'

'Yeah, I think maybe you're right, although I keep remembering that he covered all the mirrors and stopped the clock, so he's definitely acting very strange. Have we done background checks on the other residents in the flats, in case there's anyone there with a history of this kind of behaviour?'

Al smiled. 'That's your area of expertise, Ben; mine is searching for the clues and evidence. I'll leave you the pleasure of dealing with people. By the way, Kath has been zooming up and down on her scooter looking for you, Morgan. We've had to chase her away a couple of times.'

Morgan laughed. 'She found me, thanks. She's my star witness.'

Al groaned. 'Oh God, she can't see a thing even with her glasses on – good luck with that.'

'And we'll also take the statements.'

He gave her a thumbs up then walked away, and she turned to Ben. 'We could also do with going to The Dirty Duck; Shirley Kelly drank in there.'

'Let's get this over with first, then we'll make our way there. I don't know what's worse, that pub or the thought of having to go into Kath's flat for a statement.'

'I'll deal with Kath; you can take the others.'

'Well, that's an offer I can't refuse.'

SIXTEEN

No one except for Kath had noticed anything strange or unusual. They managed to speak to every person in the flats except for one, and the woman next door to him on the ground floor thought that he'd been taken into hospital last week.

'Ralph's a real dormouse, and never had a falling out with Shirley. Bless him, he suffers quite badly with his nerves though, and occasionally needs to go into the Dover Unit to get his meds adjusted. So you think someone murdered Shirley then?' The woman seemed to want to settle down for a gossip, so Morgan ended the conversation quickly and went to join Ben outside.

As they walked down the street back towards the car, Morgan glanced up towards Ben's house.

'Do you think it's possible the killer would have walked, or driven, past your house? I would have thought they'd come in at the end where the flats are. It's a long way to walk past.'

'Probably not, but I'll check the doorbell footage just to make sure, whilst you drive to the pub.'

Morgan nodded, wishing instead that she was driving to The Black Dog for a glass of ice-cold rosé or even a cocktail or two. The Black Dog was a much better establishment than The Dirty Duck, which was as rough as a pub could be situated in the Lake District. It was on the outskirts of Rydal Falls, tucked away down a small alley away from the tourists. This one was for the locals, and they liked to keep it that way. Everyone knew if you wanted a fight, to score some weed or to get your leg over, it was the regulars at The Duck who would provide all of the above and more without any trouble.

She parked the car at the end of the street; there was no point trying to park in the tiny car park at the rear of the pub, where no doubt someone would be outside smoking and run in to tell them to lock the doors because the cops were here. Better to catch them off guard and hopefully find someone drunk enough to speak to them.

She got out of the car and walked around to the passenger side, where Ben was so busy staring down at the Ring app and the footage on his phone, he hadn't even noticed she'd parked up. She tapped on his window, and he jumped and stared at her in amazement, putting down the window.

'How the hell did you get out there so fast?'

Morgan grinned. 'I'm super-fast, that's why. Anything?' She pointed to the phone screen.

He shook his head. 'Not that I can see; except do you know how many times a day Kath rides past on that scooter? She's up and down all day and all hours of the night.'

'Bless her, it's a shame she wasn't out that night; she would probably have ridden straight past the guy.'

'Yeah, and scared the shit out of whoever it was. Have you seen how fast she goes?' Ben got out of the car. 'Jesus, we get to go to all the best places. Why is Des off and Amy ill? I would have sent them here.'

'Ha-ha, I know you would. Come on – let's get it over with. Try not to start any fights whilst we're here.'

'Who me?' Ben's voice was high-pitched; he sounded offended.

They walked towards the pub, looking like extras off *The Matrix*: she was dressed all in black with a long black coat and her trusty Doc Martens; Ben had on black trousers, a navy jumper and a black coat. They stood out like sore thumbs, and to top it off, they had their Cumbria Constabulary lanyards dangling on top of their clothes, but they both reached up to tuck them underneath before they entered. Morgan knew it was best to figure out the lay of the regulars before they revealed who they were, although they would figure it out the moment they stepped inside the doorway.

'We practically radiate copper vibes without opening our mouths – you know that, don't you?'

Ben nodded. 'Have you got your pepper spray and cuffs in case all hell breaks loose?'

'I have my radio and some cuffs in my back pocket. Let's hope they want to play nice.'

'Don't count on it. That way you won't be surprised when the shit hits the fan.'

As they walked into the small walled garden at the front of the pub, an image of Stan, her late dad, drinking a pint of lager at the bar entered her mind so clearly that she had to blink back the tears that pricked at the corner of her eyes. He had liked this pub, had spent a lot of time here after her mum had died, drowning his sorrows and ignoring his life's responsibilities, including Morgan.

The door opened and out walked the biggest guy that she had ever seen, snapping her out of the memory and filling her veins with fear. She wasn't scared of much, but this bloke was a giant. As he stumbled towards them, they both sidestepped out of his way, not wanting to get caught up with him.

He laughed then said in a slurred voice, 'Look who it is – the men in black. You've come to the right place if you're looking for signs of alien life – that place is full of freaks.'

He carried on stumbling towards the cars in the car park, and Ben whispered, 'Oh shit, please don't let him be about to get in a car. I don't think I have the strength to wrestle him for his keys.'

They both watched in horror, wondering if he was that stupid, but he reached a faded yellow van and pulled open the passenger door.

A woman's voice filled the air. 'Look at the state of you. What the hell? I've only been gone forty minutes and you're a drunken mess.'

Their relief that he wasn't drink-driving was short-lived as Morgan wondered if this was the start of a domestic. But the big guy never said a word as he closed the door and the engine started.

'Phew, thank God for that.'

'Yes. Come on then – let's get this over with. It might not be much better inside mind.'

Morgan knew Ben was right, but they needed to do it for Shirley, and hopefully they'd make it out with some information and without having to fight or arrest anyone.

Ben went first, pushing open the door and stepping into the gloomy pub. It smelled of burned cooking oil and stale lager. There were two older guys in the corner of the room watching the television, and no one else.

She whispered, 'So far, so good.'

There wasn't even anyone behind the bar. The two men turned from the television to look them up and down then turned back to the programme. Ben leaned across the bar to peer through the doorway to the back room. 'Hello.'

He turned to Morgan who shrugged, then whispered, 'I'd rather not spend longer in here than we need to.'

A bleached-blonde woman came tottering through the door on heels that were impressively high, wearing a low-cut red top that showed off her impressive cleavage. She gave them an almost identical look up and down as the guys in the corner.

'Look what the cat dragged in. What do you want?'

'A half of Stella and a small rosé over ice, please,' Ben asked.

'Piss off – I'm not serving you two when you're clearly on duty. What do you really want?'

'Ah come on, Lisa, what's a little drink between friends?'

'You are no friend of mine. What do you want?'

'That hurts, you know – I thought we were mates.'

Morgan had no idea how these two knew each other and decided it was time to interrupt the catch-up. 'Have you heard about Shirley Kelly?'

Lisa nodded. 'Yep, I'd say it was a shame, but she wasn't the nicest of customers. Always arguing with anyone and everyone, over nothing sometimes.'

'Did she have a lot of enemies? Any particular people she upset in here?'

'Not really – everyone took her with a pinch of salt. She probably argued with Kath the most. Two peas in a pod, both loud and a bit psychotic. She'd even argue with the bar staff, and I'd have to tell her to apologise, or she wasn't allowed back in. She always did. She knew I'd throw her out and not let her back. What happened?'

'It's looking like she was murdered, Lisa. Would you like to reconsider what you just told us and have a think if she really upset anyone enough that they'd do something so bad?' Ben asked.

Lisa was glaring at him. 'I hate you lot and your questions, but I wouldn't not tell you something that important. Have you spoken to Kath? She didn't run her over with that scooter, did she, or bash her brains in?'

'Yes, and it's nothing to do with Kath.'

'Have you spoken with her ex? He hated her more than anyone.'

'Is that the ex who moved to Wales?'

She nodded.

'Did she have any relationships with other people? Was there a boyfriend or a lover on the scene?'

'Not that I know of – like I said, she'd come in, get drunk then fall out with anyone for no reason at all. Everyone was used to her though; I don't think they'd get that upset with her that they'd go round and kill her. I mean that's serious stuff – it's not some drunken shouting match.'

Morgan smiled at Lisa. 'Was there anyone she drank with? Was particular friends with?'

'Kath, I guess – they argued but they were also close. Sometimes Mick would join them but if she started getting argumentative, he'd leave her to it.'

'Can you give us Mick's surname? Where does he live?'

'Christ, am I doing your job for you or what?' She glared at Ben.

'It would be a massive help if you could point us in the right directions, Lisa, then we can get out of your way.'

Lisa turned to Morgan. 'You're a bit too nice to be a copper. What are you doing hanging around with him?'

Morgan didn't even glance in Ben's direction. She had never heard anyone speak to him or about him with such animosity. She thought it might not be the best move to admit they were now living together.

'He's my boss; I have to hang around with him – I get paid to.'

Lisa laughed. 'Yeah, poor you but at least you're getting paid. Mick Oswald – he lives on Ullswater Road, in one of those terraced houses. You'll know his; it's got a broken boat outside.'

Ben leaned closer to her. 'Thanks, Lisa, you're a star.'

She growled at him. 'I'm not doing it for you; I'm doing it for Shirley and her.' She pointed a finger towards Morgan. 'Now get out before someone comes in who really doesn't like coppers.'

She turned away.

Ben shrugged and walked back towards the door, Morgan close on his heels.

Morgan didn't ask him what was going on until they reached the unmarked car at the end of the street, but the words were choking her, she was that desperate to know.

'I guess Lisa has never fallen for your charms like the rest of us.'

Ben didn't answer at first. He got into the car, and she hurried around to the driver's door. When she got in, he was staring straight ahead. 'It's a long story.'

'We have plenty of time – you can tell me on the way to find Mick's house.' Morgan was wondering if she didn't know Ben at all, and maybe he'd treated Lisa terribly – what would that say about his and Cindy's relationship if he had?

He nodded. 'It's ridiculous – she holds a grudge forever. It's not even worth talking about; it's her problem not mine.'

'But I want to know.'

Ben sighed. 'A few years ago, there was a spate of burglaries around the rural properties and we had plain-clothes officers at some of the farms. Lisa's partner, Andrew, was our prime suspect; he's been a petty burglar all of his life. Well, I caught him sneaking through the back fields of one of the farms. When we searched his house, we found a treasure trove of stolen items, and he got sent away for a long stretch. She wasn't happy about it so gives me grief whenever she sees me. That's it, nothing more to it.'

This statement – and it was a statement because he gave

her the distinct impression the conversation was over – unsettled her more than she wanted to admit. She didn't answer him; instead she drove to Ullswater Road and slowed the car to a crawl, looking for a house with a broken boat in front of it.

On the grass verge in front of the row of tired-looking terraced houses there was a battered wooden rowing boat missing one side.

'Blimey, she wasn't lying when she said he had a broken boat outside. What the heck can he do with that? It's knackered. I'm surprised no one has set it on fire.'

A man came out of the house behind the boat, wearing a woven fleece-lined checked shirt, dirty grey combat trousers, and a big woollen hat pulled low down over his ears.

She stopped the car, and Ben jumped out.

'Excuse me, are you Mick?'

He turned to look Ben up and down, then shook his head. 'Depends on who wants to know – could be me or he could be my brother.'

'Lisa told us where to find you. Can we have a word, please? It's important.'

Mick looked at Morgan, giving her the same once-over. 'If it's about Shirley, I know nothing. I had nothing to do with it, and I haven't got nothing to tell you.'

'That's a whole lot of nothings, Mick. You can either speak to us now or we can go to the station for a chat – it's your choice.'

Mick held out his hands, lowering his voice. 'You better take me to the station because you're not coming in my house unless you have one of those search warrants they talk about on the TV all the time. I'm not looking like a grass in front of my neighbours. I'd never live it down.'

Morgan opened the rear door of the car for him and pointed to the back seat. 'Get in and mind your head.'

He did, grunting at the effort and swearing as he hit the top of his head on the door frame.

Ben glanced at Morgan; she shrugged then closed the door.

'We may as well take him to the station. I don't want to go inside his house anyway. He doesn't smell as if he uses a lot of Zoflora around the place.'

Ben finally broke a smile and laughed. 'Had enough of substandard-smelling premises for one day, eh?'

She nodded. 'Absolutely, one hundred per cent.'

'And you were calling me out for looking down on people earlier.'

'I'm not looking down on him. I just don't want to smell like that the rest of the day.'

After getting back inside the car, they drove back towards Rydal Falls police station.

As soon as they left Ullswater Road, his reputation safe, Mick began to talk and he never stopped until they reached the rear yard.

'Look, she wasn't a bad woman. She had a few anger issues, that's all; don't think she ever got over her husband buggering off and leaving her like he did.'

'Was she seeing anyone? Did you and her ever have a romantic relationship?'

He shook his head. 'Christ no, she terrified me, but she was good-hearted if you know what I mean. A bit like Kath – she has a bad reputation around town, but when you sit and talk to her, she's okay; she's funny and a lot cleverer than anyone expects. It's sad really how misunderstood she is.'

'I know, I like Kath. I didn't know Shirley though.'

'No, she was quiet as a mouse without a drink down her, used to be a cook in a big fancy house years ago. I worked there now and again helping in the gardens, that kind of thing. Then the drink got the better of her and she was sacked. Not long after that, the woman who owned it had a stroke and it all went to ruin.'

'How long ago and where was it?'

'Not a hundred per cent sure but I'd say it was in the nineties. Armboth Hall – such a grand house that sat looking onto the banks of Thirlmere. It's on the other side though, nearer to Keswick.'

'Has she worked since then?'

'I think she helped out at the Salvation Army in the kitchens when the mood took her, but nothing recent.'

'Can you think of anyone who would want her dead?'

'No, I mean her and Kath argued as much as they were buddies, but that's just how they were. Kath wouldn't do anything like that. There's no point – she hasn't got many friends. I don't think Shirley fell out with anyone in the pub either since the last time she got arrested. Lisa told her if she did anything like that ever again, she'd be barred for life.'

'What about Lisa – how did she get on with Shirley?' asked Ben, taking over the questioning.

'Same as the rest of us, I suppose. She puts up with us because we drink in there and she's got to pay the bills. I don't think there was any love lost between them, but she'd have no reason to kill her. She doesn't have enough regulars as it is, so she isn't going to start bumping us all off or she'd go bankrupt.'

Mick started laughing at his own joke then took a pouch out of his trouser pocket, unzipping it. The air inside the car filled with the sour, earthy smell of tobacco.

'You can't smoke in here, Mick.'

'I know, just rolling one for when you decide you've had enough of me and let me out.'

'Did Shirley have money – any savings stashed away? Had she come into a windfall, inheritance, anything like that?'

'Not that I know of. She hated that flat – always said if she had enough money, she'd be out of there in a flash. If she had the kind of money you're thinking about, I promise you she wouldn't have been living there.'

Morgan glanced at Ben, who nodded. 'Thanks, Mick, you've been very helpful. Would you like a lift home?'

'What, that's it? You're not taking me in for questioning?'

Ben turned to look at him. 'Do we need to? Is there something you want to confess?'

'No, I just thought—'

'We only wanted a quick word – we told you that.'

Mick was slowly nodding his head up and down. 'Fine, that's great then. Can you drop me at The Duck? Can't go home yet. I'm going to have to pretend you arrested me if I don't want to get a brick through my window.'

Ben got out of the car. 'Morgan will drive you there.'

He slammed the door and walked off, leaving her staring after him.

'Is he normally this much of a grump? I'd go home if I was you, love. Don't put up with him bossing you around and being an arsehole.'

Morgan laughed. 'He's my boss and not having the best of days. I kind of have to do what he wants.'

She didn't tell him that he was also her partner and she lived in his house because that wasn't Mick's business.

SEVENTEEN

Emma Dixon's teeth were chattering. She could see her breath plume out in big, foggy clouds every time she exhaled. She slammed the front door shut. It was colder inside this house than it was outside. She checked the dial on the central heating to make sure it was on full, but it wouldn't turn any further, and she couldn't see the markings because they'd rubbed off long ago.

Pressing her hand against the radiator, she sighed – it wasn't even hot, just lukewarm. If she lay against it, she still wouldn't feel the heat. She was sick of this, sick of living in a council house that seemed to be last on the list for repairs. She had no kids, no elderly parents or anyone that classed as vulnerable, so she was bottom of the list.

When she went to work in the bakery, she was thankful for the warmth; it was never cold in there, and it always smelled so good – of meat and potato pies, shortbread and freshly baked bread. Jan, the owner, always let her bring home anything that hadn't sold. Today she had two chicken and mushroom pies that were a little burned around the edges. It didn't matter though; she could smother them in sauce or gravy.

She opened the fridge and stared at the contents. Her eyes widened as a creeping sensation made the hairs on the back of her neck bristle, and she was scared to turn around in case someone stood behind, watching her.

She closed her eyes and opened them again, but it was still there: on the second shelf where she never kept it, ever, was the remains of a block of red Leicester cheese. Cheese was always kept on the top shelf. She couldn't help that everything had to be in its place, and she knew she hadn't put the cheese there.

Forcing herself to turn slowly around, she looked behind her at the doorway. Empty.

Emma closed the fridge door, slid the cutlery drawer open and took out the biggest knife she owned. Clutching the black plastic handle tightly, she turned around and hid it behind her back.

She lived alone, had done since her boyfriend had walked out to go back to his ex-wife – not that she'd even wanted him back. That meant someone she didn't know had been inside her house, looked in her fridge and touched the things inside it. The house was a two-up two-down with a bathroom upstairs and a living room down. She looked for her pay-as-you-go phone, grabbing it off the table. There was no credit on it, but she could still ring 999 if she had to – at least that was free.

She moved silently into the living room and checked behind the worn leather sofa, to make sure no one was hiding there. Her heart was racing, and it was making it hard to breathe quietly because the air was too cold for her lungs. She was torn between shouting out or keeping quiet.

The space behind the sofa was empty; the kitchen was empty. Putting her fingers around the narrow door in the hall-way, Emma pulled the door open and was greeted by her battered old Henry hoover, two coats, and a pair of bright green wellies she'd got at the charity shop.

A creak on the floor above her made her stifle a cry into the palm of her hand. Someone was in her bedroom, and she had two choices. She could go upstairs and see who it was, or she could run out of the front door as fast as possible and ring the police.

Not stupid or brave enough to do the first, Emma turned, opened the door and ran across the road to her friend Paula's house whilst pressing 999 on her phone keypad.

She hammered on the door, the whole time watching her house. A dark shadow moved across the bedroom window, and she let out a scream. At the same time Paula opened the door, a voice on the other end of the phone asked her what her emergency was. She fell into Paula's entrance, which was bright and warm, slamming the door shut behind her.

'Police. It's an emergency – there's someone in my house.'

Paula ran to the front-room window to look over at Emma's house, whilst Emma begged them to send someone quick. The voice on the end of the line told her to stay inside her friend's house and keep on the line until patrols arrived.

Minutes later, the sirens turned into the small street, lighting up the late afternoon sky with a royal-blue haze. Emma still didn't go out of the house, waiting until she saw a large man and a much smaller female officer get out of the car. She opened Paula's door then and ran over to them.

'I don't know who it is or what they're doing but there's someone upstairs in my bedroom.'

The tall officer nodded. 'You go back inside your friend's house until we've done a search. We'll come and speak to you shortly, okay.'

He smiled at her, and she instantly felt better. He had a warm smile, a kind smile. She turned around and went back inside to join Paula and her teenage daughter at the front window. They all watched intently as the officers went inside her house.

'Who is it? What do they want?' asked Paula.

Emma's voice trembled as she replied, 'Well, whoever it is is going to be severely disappointed they chose my house to burgle because there's fuck all worth stealing.'

She looked at Paula and they both started laughing. It was a high-pitched, nervous laughter, but it felt better than the fear she'd felt moments ago.

'Did you see the size of that copper? He was huge. I wouldn't mind him checking my bedroom out.'

Emma poked her friend in the ribs. 'Trust you – you're awful, you know.'

'Hey, when it's been as long as it has, you'll take anything.'

'God, Mum, shut up, that's disgusting.'

They stopped talking as the landing light turned on, followed by the bedroom lights. A few minutes later the woman was crossing the road towards Paula's house, and Emma opened the door.

'There's no one there you'll be pleased to know. They must have left before we arrived. But can you come inside with us and check if anything has been taken?'

She nodded. 'Thank God, yes, of course.'

'I'm Amber and my colleague who's inside is Cain. Are you okay?'

Emma shook her head. 'I've never felt so scared in my life.'

And then they were back inside her cold, miserable house. Even with all the lights on, it wasn't homely like Paula's was. There were no mirrored furnishings or sparkly signs on these walls that said 'Live, Laugh, Love'. Suddenly she felt ashamed that she'd never even tried to turn this into a home.

The policeman came down the stairs and smiled at her. 'No one was up there, and we can't see any signs of a break-in, but could you have a look and tell us if anything is missing?'

Emma's heart was still beating too fast, but she nodded and followed him upstairs, suddenly mortified that this man had been inside her bedroom, and she prayed she hadn't left any dirty washing piled on the floor.

She stepped inside, relieved that it wasn't messy and that she'd thrown the duvet over before she left for work. She looked around; it all seemed okay.

'Do you want to check inside the drawers, where you keep your valuables – iPad, laptop, jewellery – and make sure it's all there?'

She laughed. 'Oh, it won't be missing.'

'Why? Those are very easy, accessible things for a burglar to take.'

'I don't own any of them. Well, I have some cheap costume jewellery and my crappy pay-as-you-go phone, but that's about it.'

Her cheeks turning pink, she walked towards the drawers and pulled them out just to check that some freak hadn't been in and stolen her last few pairs of M&S full briefs that her gran had sent her the money to buy. The packet was still there, along with the three washed-out cotton bras. She shut it quick, not wanting the most handsome man she'd ever had in her bedroom seeing the state of her underwear. 'Everything is there.'

He nodded. 'Let's check the other rooms just to be sure.'

She did; he followed behind as she pushed open the spare bedroom door to reveal the empty boxes and a suitcase. The bathroom hadn't been touched: she opened the cabinet with her only bottle of expensive perfume that was almost empty – another gift from her gran. Then she went downstairs and checked the kitchen, living room and small closet once more.

Amber and Cain were standing in the living room.

'Nothing's gone.'

'Well, at least that's good,' replied Amber. 'What made you think there was an intruder?'

Emma thought about the creaky floorboard and the cheese on the wrong shelf, and felt her cheeks turn pink.

'I, erm, I just got in from work and opened the fridge and things have been moved around.'

Cain frowned. 'What things were moved?'

Now her cheeks weren't just pink, they were fully burning as if they were on fire.

'I'm sorry to have wasted your time.'

'You didn't. You heard something, and you called us; you did the right thing.'

Amber didn't look as concerned as he did and asked, 'What was moved in the fridge?'

Emma exhaled. 'The cheese was on the wrong shelf.'

Amber glanced at Cain as if to say *WTF?*; she could tell by the look on her face that she thought Emma was crazy. Cain didn't acknowledge it.

'How could you know that?'

'I always keep it on the top shelf, along with the other dairy products – not that I have any in right now. I need to go shopping. But I have never in my life put the cheese on the middle shelf with the raw meat.' She also knew there was no raw meat either; literally all she had was that block of cheese, two eggs, and just enough milk for a cup of tea when all this was over with.

'There's no way you were rushing and put it on the wrong shelf? It's easily done,' Amber asked.

She shrugged, questioning herself now, because she had been running late this morning and could have moved it. 'I'm sorry, I suppose it's possible.'

'What about the noise you heard upstairs? Do you think it could have been the floorboard settling? It's cold outside and these things can happen.'

Cain was smiling at her but not in a way that told her he thought she was nuts; he seemed to genuinely want to make her feel better. She looked around the small room and realised that she wanted them to leave her alone. She felt stupid and was ashamed that she'd freaked out, dragging them there when they had far more important stuff to do.

'Thank you, yes, it probably was, and I panicked. I'm so sorry to have wasted your time.'

Amber smiled at her and walked towards the door. 'You're welcome – take care.' She was already getting back inside the police van. Cain was still hovering in the living room.

'Keep your phone charged, lock the doors and close the curtains. If you think anyone is outside or hanging around, you phone 999 again, okay. It's what we're here for. It's our job to keep you safe.'

She nodded, her eyes filling with tears at this total stranger's kindness towards her, and whispered, 'Thank you, I will.' She didn't lift her head to look at him because she thought she might start bawling like a baby.

He walked past and patted her shoulder then was suddenly outside, and she closed the door behind him, locking it.

She waited for them to drive away before she rushed around turning off the surplus lights. She had no idea how much was left on the electricity meter and no money until tomorrow to top it up.

Her phone began to ring, and she looked down to see Paula's name flashing across the screen.

'Everything okay? Come over here and tell me what they said.'

'Yes, they didn't find anyone, and there's nothing missing. Thanks, but I think I'm going to get a shower. I don't want to leave the house again tonight. Not now that it's been searched, and I know there's no one here.'

'You could have sent that copper over to search my house. He could have strip-searched me and I've had said yes please.' Paula began to laugh, and Emma smiled.

'What are you like?'

'Desperate – I told you it's been a long time. Ring me if you need me – you know where I am.'

The line went dead, and Emma looked at her phone. She couldn't ring her if she wanted to, not until she topped up the phone credit at the post office tomorrow.

She wasn't cold anymore, at least there was that, but as she walked into the kitchen, she couldn't shake the nagging doubt that someone had moved her cheese. She knew for sure that not once had she ever put the cheese on that shelf, whether she was in a rush or not. So someone had to have moved it, but who? No one except the council had a spare key for this place. Though she did keep a spare under the neon pink-garden gnome Paula had bought her for her birthday, around the back of the house.

Suddenly, cold fear lodged inside her throat, making it hard to breathe. She needed to check if someone had found the key and moved it, but suddenly she was too scared to go out and check.

EIGHTEEN

For the second time in an hour, Morgan found herself back at The Dirty Duck. She stopped the car to let Mick out and wondered if she should go in and speak to Lisa, to see exactly what her problem with Ben was, or was that going too far? It would be like spying on him and she didn't want to turn into some paranoid girlfriend.

'Thanks for the lift, kid. You want to come in for a drink? I'm buying – you can let that miserable sod of a boss sulk for a bit.'

She turned around and smiled at the scruffy man in the back of the car.

'Are you flirting with me, Mick?'

Mick laughed. 'I'm too old for that, and you're too young and pretty for me, but you can't blame a guy for trying. My motto is to never stop trying, otherwise you might as well roll over and die.'

She laughed. 'I guess you're right; we should never stop trying. Thank you, that's a very kind offer, but it's been a long day and we still haven't got any closer to finding a viable suspect, so I have to get back to work, for Shirley.'

He got out of the car. 'Well, that's very good of you. I'm pretty sure Shirley would thank you for it if she was here. Take care, Morgan – I like you. If you ever get fed up with working for the right side of the law, come find me and I'll help you find something better.'

She nodded, holding in the laughter that was threatening to escape from her mouth. Bless him, he meant well, but what the hell was he going to offer her?

He walked towards the pub, stopped, turned around and waved once, then he darted through the door as the rain began to hammer against the pavement once more. She let out a loud yawn – she was tired and ready to call it a day, but that wasn't going to be happening any time soon.

Reversing the car, Morgan waited for a break in the traffic and then made her way back to the station.

The sky was a bank of dirty grey rainclouds, and she knew they were set in for the rest of the evening. It was cold and miserable; October was usually much warmer than this. Either that or she was turning into a wimp.

Morgan was glad to get inside the station. Their office wasn't much, but it was dry and warm. She headed upstairs, pausing to switch the kettle on to make a coffee for her and Ben, then pushed open the door to see Marc, Ben and Al deep in conversation. For a moment she felt as if she was intruding because all three of them stopped talking and stared at her.

'Coffee?'

All three heads nodded, so she turned around and went back to brew up. This time as she walked back in with three mugs, they didn't stop their conversation, which was better. She passed the coffees around and sat down.

'What's happening?'

Ben smiled at her. 'Not much – we were trying to decide

where to search next. To be honest, we're not doing so well with
finding anything helpful. Al's team didn't find anything; our
house to house wasn't very revealing. We could bring in Kath
and Mick for further questioning, but they have no motive –
and how on earth is Kath going to have got in and out of that flat
when she struggles on her feet? I don't think Mick would have
fared much better. They would have definitely left some trace
evidence behind.'

Al nodded. 'It's baffling me, it really is. Did anyone speak to
her ex-husband?'

Ben stood up and passed Morgan a piece of paper. 'Would
you do the honours? Amy emailed his records through too. It's
the same as Shirley – a couple of drunken arguments where she
was the instigator. He has no violent crimes, no arrests and,
according to this, he's been living in Hawarden, north Wales for
eight years. No domestic assaults on his records; he's pretty
clean.'

Morgan took the Post-it note from Ben and pointed to his
office. He nodded.

Taking her mug of coffee, she slipped inside and closed the
door. It was untidy in here, which was always strange to her
since Ben's house was the complete opposite. Now that he'd
cleared it of all Cindy's belongings, it was always kept immaculate, with nothing out of place.

She sat at his desk and looked around, wondering what
Marc had been snooping around for earlier. What had he
expected to find in amongst the chaos?

She dialled the number off the slip of paper and waited for
the phone to connect. There was a short delay: all the work
phones were internet ones and not as fast or as good as the old
landlines.

A woman's voice answered; Morgan hadn't been expecting
that.

'*Hello.*'

'Good afternoon, I'm Detective Constable Morgan Brookes. I'm calling from Rydal Falls police station. Is it possible to speak to William Kelly?'

'Lord, what has she done now? I'm sick of telling you lot to stop bothering us every time that woman gets herself in trouble. He's been divorced for eight years. I'm not sure what you expect him to do about her. She's not his problem.'

Morgan closed her eyes and tried to inhale deeply as she realised no one had bothered to pass on a death message. Rubbing the bridge of her nose, she carried on. 'This isn't about an arrest. Is William there?'

'William! William!'

The voice was so loud in her ear she had to hold the phone away so her eardrum didn't burst.

'Christ, he's deaf as a post. Hang on – I'll have to go get him.'

The receiver was banged loudly at the other end, and Morgan heard heavy footsteps walking away. A few moments later, a man's voice came on the line.

'This is William Kelly; how can I help you?'

'Mr Kelly, I'm afraid I have some bad news for you. I'm very sorry to tell you that your ex-wife, Shirley Kelly, was found deceased in her flat yesterday.'

'What? You'll have to speak up – I didn't quite catch that.'

Morgan repeated herself, louder.

'Oh shit. She's really dead? Mary, this policewoman said Shirley is dead.'

He shouted to Mary, who must have been hovering around because she heard the woman say: *'Thank Christ for small mercies.'* Morgan guessed there was no love lost between the pair of them.

'Yes, I'm afraid she is, and we think it's a homicide.'

'A what?'

'Jesus, William, give me the phone. It's like having a three-way conversation with a bloody monkey.'

'Sorry, you're better off speaking to me; his hearing aid isn't working properly, if he's even put it in.'

'I'm afraid we think it's a homicide.'

'Murder? You think she was murdered? By who?'

'That's what I'm trying to find out. Did you have much contact with Shirley?'

'Only every other week when she'd phone up drunk and asking for money, or calling us both names.'

Morgan sat up straight. Could these two have had enough of her harassing them and decided to put a stop to it? 'What did you do when she phoned?'

'Unplug the damn thing. That woman was a nuisance, and I don't like to speak ill of the dead, but she just wouldn't let William get on with his life. He never did a thing wrong to her, but enough was enough and he had to leave for his own safety. She was getting violent, and I used to tell him to smack her back, and he wouldn't; he never lifted a finger towards her. He's never lifted a hand towards anyone – too soft for his own good.'

Mary spoke darkly, as if she'd be happier if William had been a wife beater. Morgan decided not to engage.

'Did you not change your phone number or report her to the police?'

Mary laughed. 'I begged him to, but he wouldn't – he said he felt bad for walking out on her, the least he could do was leave her with a contact number.'

'When was the last time either of you saw her?'

'Not since the day before we packed my car and drove out of Rydal Falls, to come here and stay with my elderly mum. That was eight years ago.'

'You've never come back here? Don't you have family or friends here?'

'William is from there; his parents are dead though and he's an only child. I'm from Hawarden – all my family are here. I only came through for work and to get away for a little bit, fell in *love with the soppy old goat and we ran away together like a pair of lovesick teenagers. The pair of us have nothing to go back for, and William struggles to walk more than a few metres now. My knees are knackered – I couldn't cope with the hills. No, Rydal Falls is a distant memory and nothing more.'*

The tiny surge of excitement she'd felt at the prospect of having a potential suspect had been pushed back down as disappointment washed over her. She would still need to confirm this, but either she or Amy could do that.

'Do you know if Shirley had any enemies, or anyone who would want her dead?'

'To be honest with you, no. It seemed she'd mellowed a lot the last couple of years and calmed herself down, so unless she was driving someone mad then no, not really.'

'Can I ask you where you and William were last Tuesday?'

Mary began to laugh. *'Oh Lord, are you thinking that we knocked her off? Sweetie, we're too old, too knackered and too bloody lazy to think about something so strenuous. I mean I'm assuming you saw her body if she's dead and you're investigating it. She wasn't a little woman; she was a big, strong woman who could stand up for herself. Hell, I bet she'd give that boxer, what's his name? Tyson Fury, that's it. I bet she'd give him a good fight in the ring.'*

Morgan smiled; she knew that it wasn't a foolproof alibi – for all she knew they could be the fittest, oldest pair of assassins in the country – but her gut told her that Mary was telling the truth: that Shirley's murder was nothing to do with them.

'Thank you for your time. Please accept my condolences.'

'That's it? You don't need William to come and identify her body?'

'No, the housing officer was able to confirm her identity. If there's anything else, I'll be in touch. If you have any questions, you can phone 101 and ask for DC Morgan Brookes. Take care.'

She hung up the phone and opened the door back into the main office. The others had left and Ben was now alone.

'What's going on?'

'Not a lot. We're at a bit of a standstill, unless you're going to tell me that her ex has admitted to killing her?'

'Nope, sorry – he's in bad health and can't walk far. He hasn't been back here for eight years.'

'Bollocks. I guess we're going to have to rely on the CCTV enquiries then. I'm going to get the PCSOs to canvass the whole area for cameras, dash cams, doorbells. Not sure what else we can do. How about we go home and pick up a couple of pizzas on the way?'

Morgan smiled; pizza was her favourite. 'Sounds good to me.'

He seemed a bit calmer than he had all day, more like the Ben she knew. She didn't like this uptight, stressed version. Not that he didn't have a very good reason to be uptight and stressed, because a murder investigation was never going to be easy, especially when they had as little to go on as they did.

She turned the lights off and followed him down the back stairs, feeling as if they were playing hooky and were going to get caught any minute, but there was literally nothing else to do.

NINETEEN

Cain felt bad for the woman who'd phoned up earlier; he couldn't stop thinking about her. She had been so scared, and it had been freezing inside that house. When he'd opened the cupboards and fridge without thinking, it had made him feel sad that she barely had any milk or life's essentials. No one should be living that way. He guessed she was a few years older than him, in her forties, and wondered if he should go back and offer her one of the vouchers for the foodbank that he always carried around with him. Or would that offend her? Everyone went through tough times. He'd hit rock bottom himself when his wife had walked out on him, but he'd managed to drag himself back up.

He stopped the van outside the Co-op on the main street.

'Do you want anything, Amber?'

'Bag of those giant chocolate buttons, please.'

He nodded and jumped out. Inside, he grabbed a basket and put milk, bread, biscuits, butter and a small jar of coffee in it. He added the chocolate Amber had asked for and took it all to the till, where the assistant bagged it up for him.

He paid and got back inside the van.

'Christ, I thought you were doing a weekly shop. What's up? Needed to stock up?'

He shook his head and took the buttons out of the bag, passing them to her.

'Thanks.'

'You're welcome.'

They'd been aimlessly driving around for over an hour. No further calls had come in so he began to head in the direction of Emma Dixon's house.

Amber paused in the act of stuffing handfuls of chocolate buttons into her mouth. 'Where are you going?'

'I just want to do an area search of Fell Close, make sure everything's in order.'

She stared at him. 'You're such a big softie, Cain. What's up? Are you feeling sorry for that nut job who rang in before?'

His fingers gripped the steering wheel tight; Amber was like an annoying little sister, and she was pissing him off tonight even more than she usually did with her attitude.

'That's out of order. You're so rude about everyone, Amber, you want to listen to yourself. I don't know where you get off thinking that you're better than everyone else, because quite frankly you're not. You're like a spoiled teenager and it's not a nice trait. What did you sign up to the job for, remind me?' He glared at her for a second before turning his attention back to the road.

'I am not. How dare you!'

'Yes, you are. You don't know her story, you don't know what she's been through or why she was so scared. It doesn't make her a nut job, and you should know better than to be so judgemental. It makes her a vulnerable, scared woman living on her own, who needed our help and called us out. That's what we do – we help people who need it; we don't look down on anyone because that's not our job. We're there to lift people up, make them feel safe and protect them. So if that's not your thing, maybe you'd be better suited looking for another job; a debt collector would suit you fine.'

Amber was staring at him with her mouth open, and he felt bad that he'd just spoken to her like that, but she was rude and he wouldn't let her keep thinking that the people in the community they were supposed to be serving were beneath her.

Amber carried on glaring at him, but he ignored her. She could stare all she liked. He was fed up with her attitude.

After parking the van outside the front of Emma Dixon's house, Cain got out, grabbed the green plastic Co-op bag and walked up the path. He knocked gently on the door, not his usual loud police rat-a-tat-tat. There was only one light on, and it was coming from the back of the house.

He figured Emma must be in the kitchen, so he tried the narrow wooden gate that led to the rear of the house. It was unlocked. He frowned, wondering why she'd leave it unlocked when she'd been scared to death an hour earlier.

It was dark in the narrow passageway, but it only took him ten steps until he was at the gate to the tiny back garden. He pushed it open and glanced into the kitchen window, his hand lifted to wave at her because he didn't want to scare her to death. His hand stopped mid-air as he wondered what the red liquid was that was all over the inside of the window.

Pushing his face nearer, he dropped the bag onto the cracked paving stones and let out a loud yell. There on the floor was a still, blood-soaked Emma.

Cain pressed the red button on his radio – 'Urgent assistance, ambulance now to Fell Close, the house we were at earlier.'

Adrenalin surging through him, he barged the back door with his shoulder and it flew open, hitting the wall with such force the plaster cracked and fell off. Tugging a pair of gloves out of his pocket and onto his hands, Cain dropped to his knees.

There was so much blood; it was pooling around her neck on the floor in a large puddle.

Emma's eyes were wide open in terror.

'It's okay, I'm here. You're going to be okay, Emma. Stay with me.'

He looked around for something to stem the bleeding and cover the gash which ran from one side of her throat to the other. He grabbed a small cream hand towel and pressed it to her neck, terrified of hurting her but needing to put the pressure on. She let out a small gurgle, and a trail of blood escaped from her lips, running down her chin.

'Stay with me, Emma – the ambulance is going to be here any minute.'

He stared into her eyes and thought he saw the faintest flicker of recognition in them. Cain's heart was racing from fear for the small woman he knew was dying. Her blood continued to run from the neck wound like a red river. He sat on the floor and scooped her into his arms, gently resting her head on his lap as Amber ran into the room, a look of horror etched across her face.

Cain held the towel against Emma's neck wound and gently stroked her hair with his other hand. Faint sirens in the distance signalled the arrival of the paramedics, but he felt her body go limp as a small sigh escaped her lips, and he knew she was dead.

They were too late; they could have saved her if they'd come just five minutes earlier. Maybe if he hadn't wasted time shouting at Amber.

He blinked tears back; Amber was busy on the radio giving an update of the scene. He would not cry in front of her. But he knew that when he got home, he would bawl like a baby, because they could have prevented this. He was going to wear this guilt like a lead cloak for the rest of his life. He could feel the warm stickiness of Emma's cloying blood all over his trousers and hands, as he'd felt the life bleed from her.

Amber had stopped talking into the radio and was now bent over double, her head as near to her knees as she could get with the tight, rigid body armour that was strapped to her torso. She was a ghostly shade of white, and he remembered that she didn't like dead bodies or blood.

'Deep breaths, in through your nose and out through your mouth, and if you think you're going to pass out, go back outside.'

She was sucking in air. All he could hear was her panting, as if it was her who was struggling to breathe. 'Is she...?'

He didn't answer her as two more officers and paramedics arrived at the scene. He couldn't tear his gaze away from Emma's face and the terror that was forever etched deep into the depths of her eyes.

TWENTY

Morgan and Ben were sitting waiting for their pizzas at Gino's pizzeria when both of their phones began to ring simultaneously. Ben sighed while Morgan answered hers. The girl behind the counter shouted Morgan's name, and he stood up to collect for her. The two large boxes of steaming hot pizza in his hands smelled like the finest thing on earth. Morgan had stepped out of the door whispering on the phone, and Ben knew that whatever it was about, it meant that they weren't going to be eating this pizza any time soon. She was already in the car, still on the phone, when he opened the passenger door and slid the boxes onto the back seat.

'What's up?'

'There's been a murder at Fell Close, after Cain had attended a job there. Emma Dixon reported an intruder in her house. He did a search, secured the property and found no evidence of an intruder, so he gave her the usual crime prevention advice and left her to it. He called back an hour later to check on her and found her with her throat slashed, bleeding to death on the kitchen floor.'

Ben stared at Morgan. 'What the hell? Oh shit!'

'Paramedics have just called it.'

She began to drive his BMW a lot faster than she normally would, to get to Fell Close, which was only a few minutes away. Ben's mind was racing: what had happened for a routine call to end up so spectacularly wrong?

Morgan abandoned Ben's car in the middle of the street, hastily pulled on a set of the protective clothing that he kept in a box in the boot of his car, and rushed around to the back of the house. She liked Cain a lot – he was always there for her when she needed him, so she wanted to repay the favour.

The front of the house was in darkness while the rear was lit up like a beacon. Amber was standing by the back gate not moving, and Cain was next to her. He was trembling, a large slick of dark red blood covering his body armour and hands.

He looked at Morgan in disbelief. 'There was no one here. I searched the entire house.'

She crossed towards him, placing her hand on his arm. 'I know you did, Cain. You did everything right; this isn't your fault.'

'Isn't it?'

'No, it's not. You know what the job is like – you attended a call, you found no evidence of an intruder, you checked the house, and you came back to check on her an hour later. Most officers wouldn't have even given her a second thought – they'd have carried on with their shift. But not you – you came back. The only person to blame here is the sick bastard that did this.'

Ben squeezed past them to take a look at the bloodbath that had once been a clean if sparse magnolia-painted kitchen. 'Jesus, so much blood.'

Morgan was standing next to him, and her breath caught in the back of her throat when she looked down to see the body lying soaked in a sea of its own blood, a discarded, saturated towel next to her. The air was thickly scented with the metallic, cloying, earthy smell, and she sucked in a tiny gulp of air. There were smudges in the pooling blood where Cain must have been sitting as he'd held the dying woman.

'I'm sorry, Benno, I messed up the scene. I couldn't let her die alone. I tried to stop the bleeding, but it was too late, so I did the next best thing and held her.'

Morgan couldn't stop herself and a loud sob escaped her lips, for this poor woman who had been brutally killed and for Cain who had given her what little comfort he could. She turned away, walking into the tiny rear garden, sucking in gulping breaths of clean air that wasn't tainted by the smell of death.

Amber hadn't moved – she was still standing like a statue by the gate. There was a green carrier bag dropped on the ground, the contents spilling onto the grass.

'What's that?'

Amber looked down then back to Morgan and whispered, 'That's why we came back. Cain felt sorry for her: she had no food in the fridge. He went to the Co-op to buy her some essentials and wanted to check on her to make sure she was okay, the big softie.'

She left them, heading towards the van parked out front to grab a scene guard booklet.

If Morgan's heart wasn't already aching for the poor woman on the floor, then it was breaking in two now at Cain's kindness.

She walked back to Cain, wrapped her arms around him and whispered into his ear, 'You need a hug. You're one in a million, Cain – I hope you know that.'

He patted her back, and she knew he was trying not to get blood all over her. He whispered back, 'Thanks, kid. I was too late though, wasn't I?'

There was a lot of shouting around the front of the house,

and Amber's voice could be heard telling whoever it was to back off, this was a crime scene.

Cain whispered, 'Her friend lives across the street.'

He began to walk around to see what was going on, but Morgan stopped him. 'I don't think it's a good idea – you're covered in blood.'

'Oh shit. Yeah, it's instinct, you know.'

Nodding, she walked around just in time to hear the woman who was shouting at Amber draw back her hand and slap her across the face. The sound of her open palm connecting with Amber's cheek filled the air, ringing out, and Morgan ran over to the two women, stepping in-between them. Amber was clutching her cheek with one hand and had pulled out her taser with the other and was now trying to red-dot her attacker.

'Step back, you crazy bitch. She hit me – did you see it?'

Morgan whispered, 'Are you okay? Get yourself back to Cain and wait there.'

'But she hit me.'

Morgan didn't condone violence, but there was something about Amber that made her want to slap her too.

'Go on, you snotty little cow – taser me and see what you get. This is my best friend's house. What's happening? I have the right to know. Is she okay?'

Pushing Amber in the direction of the small alley, Morgan whispered, 'Go on – we'll sort this out later.'

Amber walked around the back where Cain was standing there grinning at her.

'Did you just get bitch-slapped, Amber?'

'Piss off, it's not funny. That's police assault, we should be arresting her.'

'You need to work on those people skills. I've told you this before. They're not doing you any favours.'

Morgan turned to the other woman. 'Could we go over to

your house? This is a crime scene and I'm sorry, but you can't go in there. You wouldn't want to, lovely – it's not nice.'

The woman's bleached-blonde head nodded slowly, but she turned around and click-clacked her way back to her own front door in a pair of neon orange slippers that were far too big for her.

Morgan followed her inside the brightly lit house. It looked like someone had spent an entire month blinging up every surface with crystals and mirrored tiles. There were large vases of artificial flowers on almost every surface, which made the sparse apartment she'd owned on Singleton Park Road look like a sterile hospital room. It was lovely and cosy, not Morgan's thing, but she liked it; this house gave off good vibes, unlike the cold, unforgiving building across the road.

She followed the woman, who introduced herself as Paula, into the kitchen, which had a silver glittery kettle, toaster and microwave; she didn't even know you could buy kitchen appliances that glittered.

Paula pointed to the small table and chairs. She sat down at one and Morgan sat opposite her.

'It's not good news I'm afraid.'

Paula nodded, her eyes filling with tears, but she didn't speak. It was as if she'd used up every ounce of her energy arguing with Amber.

'What's not good news, and why did you just smack a copper, Mum? I saw you out of my window. Are you crazy?'

Morgan turned around to see a teenage girl standing behind her, leaning against the door frame. Her make-up was immaculate; she looked like a model from a magazine, her eyeshadow was so sleek and her face so contoured.

'Go upstairs, Ashley.'

'No. What's going on? Where is Emma?'

'Just go and I'll tell you as soon as I know.'

Ashley looked about to put up a fight, but Paula began to cry, and suddenly she turned and ran up the stairs – heavy, thudding footsteps. A door slammed above them, rattling the whole house with the ferocity of it.

'Sorry, she's thirteen going on bloody thirty – you know what they're like.'

Morgan had to stop her jaw from dropping open. Thirteen? Ashley would have passed for early twenties.

'I haven't got any kids, but I remember being thirteen. It's a tough age.'

Paula nodded. 'I'm not looking forward to when she discovers boys, that's for sure. So why isn't Emma over here telling me why the police are all over her house and back garden?'

'I'm afraid she's dead.'

'What? How? I don't understand. She was here not that long ago, and then that big copper came and took her back home. He said there was no one in her house. How can she be dead?'

Morgan inhaled deeply, letting the breath go slowly.

'I can't tell you an awful lot because we don't know ourselves. And what I can tell you is confidential because we have to find whoever did this.'

Paula nodded. 'I can't believe it. How can she be dead? How did she die?'

'Cain, the officer who attended the original call and checked the house, was worried about her. He wanted to check on her and called at the shop to get her a few essentials because she didn't have much in.'

'That big guy did that?'

'He's a very nice person; yes, he did. From what I can gather, there was no answer at the front door, so he went around the back and found Emma in the kitchen. He called for an ambulance, but it was too late – she died in his arms.'

Paula let out a loud sob, then lifted her arm to wipe her eyes with her sleeve. 'How did she die?'

Morgan was torn. She didn't want to release the details and get in trouble, but this was Emma's friend – she had a right to know but not the full-blown, gory details that would give her nightmares for the rest of her life.

'From a knife wound.'

'What, are you telling me some sick bastard broke into her house and stabbed her then left her bleeding to death on the floor?'

Morgan nodded. 'I know this is a lot to ask but are you up to telling me about Emma, her life, her relationships?'

Paula stood up. 'I need a drink; do you want one?'

She walked over to the fridge and pulled out a bottle of rosé and took a glass from the cupboard.

At this moment in time Morgan would have loved a glass of wine. She shook her head. 'No, thanks, I'm driving.' She took her notebook out, placing it on the table, and uncapped the black pen ready to write.

Paula sat back down and unscrewed the cap on the bottle, filling the glass full. She smiled. 'I prefer white wine, but this is Emma's favourite. I always buy a bottle so she can have a glass when we're bitching about life.'

She paused, her eyes filling with tears. She lifted the glass and drank half of it down in one mouthful, then topped it back up.

'She's a good woman – works in the bakery on the main street. She's single, never married and the last guy she dated was a bit of an arsehole. He drank too much and spent all his time in The Dirty Duck.'

Morgan's senses kicked in at the mention of the pub: that's two victims who were connected to that bloody pub. 'Did

Emma go to The Duck?' She wrote 'Dirty Duck' and under-lined it twice on the blank page.

'A couple of times, but she didn't like it. She said she might be skint and having a run of bad luck at the moment, but it still didn't mean she had to stoop that low and drink in there. She wasn't too keen on the regulars. I told her he was a waste of space and to drop him.'

'Did she?'

Paula nodded. 'Yes, she did, thank God. He spends all his money on weed and drink, and he was too old for her anyway – not the kind of guy you'd take home to meet your parents. He wasn't exactly the perfect son-in-law material; in fact he was probably as old as they are.'

'What was he called?' But Morgan had a feeling she already knew exactly who she was going to say.

'Mick – Mick... what was his second name? I know it – I can't remember it. Bloody hell, it's on the tip of my tongue.'

'Oswald?'

'Yes, that's it. How do you know him?'

'I just do. Was there any violence in their relationship? Any domestic assaults? How was the break-up? Was he angry about it?'

'Nah, I don't think he had the energy to hit anyone. He's super laid-back, probably too laid-back. He was fine, told her he loved her, that he wouldn't forget her and that if she ever changed her mind, he'd be there for her, and then he went skulking back to his ex-wife, who didn't want him either. It was all pretty nice, no complications.'

'Did Emma ever tell you that she was scared? Did she have a reason to think that someone was watching her?'

'No, not until tonight.'

'Can you tell me what happened tonight, Paula?'

'About two hours ago, she came hammering on my door. She was terrified and said that someone was inside her house.

She was on the phone to the police. I brought her inside and we watched out of the window for the coppers to arrive.'

'Why did she think there was someone inside her house?'

'This sounds daft really, but Emma is a bit of a... well I wouldn't call her full-on OCD or anything, but she did like everything to be in the right place in the kitchen. Top shelf in the fridge, life's essentials, cheese and wine. She always keeps her cheese on the top shelf, but she said when she got home it was on the middle shelf, and it freaked her out because she knew it wasn't on there when she went to work this morning. Then she heard a noise upstairs and it terrified her big time – came running over here on the phone to the police.'

Morgan was about to ask if she could have made a mistake and put it on the wrong shelf but stopped herself in time. Obviously, Emma was right: someone had been inside her house, and whoever that person was had either found an excellent hiding place that Cain missed or they came back. Either way, they'd meant business. They'd killed her violently and brutally, but for what reason?

'Do you have any details of her parents – names, address?'

'No, sorry. She didn't see them a lot. They live in Barrow, moved there a long time ago.'

'That's fine, we'll find that out and let them know. Thank you for being so honest. I'm so sorry for your loss, Paula.'

Paula's eyes began to water as if she'd just remembered why Morgan was sitting at her kitchen table. She lifted the wine glass to her lips and gulped the rest of it down, nodding. 'Christ, I wish I had a bottle of vodka, you know, something a bit stronger than this. What does it mean, if some psycho has broken in and killed Emma? What's to say he won't do it again? He might come back and kill the rest of us.'

'There is going to be a lot of police activity for the next few days, Paula, then after that, we'll have routine patrols keeping an extra eye on the area; PCSOs will foot patrol.'

'Poor buggers, what's to stop him killing one of them if you send them out on their own, unarmed?'

Morgan realised she was right: there was no way they could risk their PCSOs coming into contact with a knife-wielding, murderous bastard. They were far too valuable.

'I'm confident we'll catch whoever did this. There must be lots of trace evidence. Try not to worry – we're doing our best to find him.'

She stood up and walked to the front door.

Paula followed her.

Morgan stepped outside into the damp, night air.

'I'm sorry about slapping that copper. What's going to happen? Will I get arrested? I don't know what came over me. I've never done anything like that in my life, but she was horrible.'

'Don't worry about it. I'll speak to Amber and tell her you've apologised. Shock can make us act out of sorts and not ourselves.'

'Thank you.' She whispered the words and closed her door.

Morgan heard the key turn in the lock and the sound of something heavy being dragged in front of the door.

Her head down, she jogged across the street, back to the bloody crime scene.

TWENTY-ONE

The flash from Wendy's camera illuminated the garden, and Morgan paused. Cain was standing being photographed in situ.

'I'm going to need those clothes, bud. If I get you a set of overalls, can you take them off for me and drop them into that brown paper sack?'

Cain nodded, and Morgan wondered if he was in shock. The paramedics were still hanging around out the front of the house. Both Morgan and Wendy turned away to give him a little privacy. She wondered where Amber was and hoped she'd been sent back to the station out of everyone's way.

Ben came out of the kitchen door.

'When you're finished, Cain, I want the whole area cleared. The dog handler is on the way. We're all to hold back until it's been and had a good sniff around to see if our suspect has left us a nice trail to follow.'

Morgan thought she saw movement from the upstairs window, just the flicker of a shadow. Every sense went on high alert.

'Has the house been searched, to make sure he's not still inside?'

Ben shook his head. 'I don't know. Cain, did you manage to search the house a second time?'

'No, I was a bit busy with the victim, and Amber was busy freaking out.'

Morgan whispered, 'I think he may still be upstairs.'

Ben turned to look at her. 'What?'

'Movement at the upstairs window.'

'Oh shit. Who's got a taser?'

'Amber, but she's more likely to taser you than anyone else. She's a bit trigger happy.'

'Where is she?'

'In the van.'

Ben lifted his radio to his lips and whispered, 'Amber, I need you around the back now. Make sure a patrol is by the front door so no one can escape that way or out of any windows.'

She didn't answer but they heard the loud slam of a van door. Moments later, she was standing looking at them.

'What?'

Ben pointed to the upstairs window. 'I'm going to need you to draw that taser and follow me inside the house.'

'What about protective clothing? And I thought the dog was on its way?'

Morgan nodded. 'Why don't we cover all the possible exits and wait for the dog?'

Ben looked back at the open kitchen door then the upstairs window. He shrugged, and she knew he wanted to go inside, taser ready, to fry the bastard who had done this – but he'd managed to hide from them once only to sneak back and kill Emma. What was to say he wouldn't slip away again from them? The dog would be able to corner him quicker than they would. He nodded in agreement.

Cain returned, now dressed in a white paper suit that was straining at the seams.

'I'm more than happy to go in, boss.'

'I know you are; so am I, but Morgan's right – we might mess up the trail for the dog, and if he's still up there then the dog will find him quicker than us, and hopefully bite his arse whilst he's at it.

'Let's block exits anyway. Amber, stay here with Cain; Morgan, you go around the side and make sure there's no possible way he could get out of a window that way. I'll go check the front.'

They all split off, Morgan following Ben to the side passage. There was the narrowest window on the second floor with an extractor fan placed in the middle of the glass.

'I can't see him fitting through that unless he's a stick man.'

'I know but I'm not taking any chances. Just wait here and make sure he doesn't try.'

Ben went to the front of the house, and Morgan tried to hide a smile. She knew what he was doing, and it was sweet. He was keeping her out of the way, making sure she wasn't at a point where confrontation could be possible, so she was safe; and after seeing the blood bath and poor Emma's body, she wasn't in the mood to argue. Although she did wonder if put in a dangerous situation, if Amber would have the balls to actually pull the trigger on the taser. She hoped so for all of their sakes.

Ben's voice whispered over the airwaves. '*Control, we think the suspect may still be inside the house. Have we got an ETA for the dog handler? I need her to travel immediate response, please, if she's not already travelling that speed.*'

It wasn't the control-room operator that answered – it was Cassie.

'*I'm almost there, Ben. Hang tight and don't go inside. Leave that pleasure to Caesar – he's itching to go.*'

'*Sirens off, Cassie. I want a silent approach. He already knows he's surrounded by coppers but I don't want him to know the dog's on its way in.*'

Morgan smiled and prayed to God that Caesar was ready to take the bastard out. She'd met the dog before and knew he was capable.

She heard the van arrive. For a crime scene that was full of officers, paramedics, CSIs, you could have heard a pin drop. Morgan felt as if time had stood still; there was no sound of traffic from the streets surrounding Fell Close, no dogs barking, no teenagers kicking footballs. She kept her eyes on that narrow window, not taking any chances that this guy was a contortionist and could squeeze himself into the smallest of places, if he was that good at hiding.

The rear doors of the van opened, and she heard the loud thump as the dog – a black Italian mastiff who was almost as big as a Shetland pony – jumped down onto the pavement. Then Cassie was there in the alley with the huge dog; he glanced at Morgan with the biggest brown eyes she'd ever seen on a dog and was then straining at his leash to get on with it.

'He's ready. Is it bad?'

Morgan nodded. 'Very.'

And then they were gone.

Morgan walked to the corner so she could see in the side window and what was happening. Amber and Cain had stepped back to let them inside the kitchen, and she heard Cassie mutter, 'Dear God.' Then there was the sound of pounding up the stairs.

A few minutes later, Cassie shouted, *'All clear,'* over the radio.

Then: *'Actually, Ben, I need you upstairs.'*

Ben came rushing around, Morgan following him. They sidestepped Emma's body and the pool of blood and went into the living room and upstairs, to where Caesar was sitting growling in the corner of the spare bedroom.

'What's up?'

Cassie pointed to a narrow loft hatch above the dog. They

both nodded. There was no ladder, but there was a tall chest of drawers close by which could have been used if the killer was tall enough. Somehow, he had managed to climb up.

She let go of the long lead and whispered, 'On guard,' to the dog; he was sitting there, his ears cocked, ready and waiting for whoever it was that had gone up there to come back down.

She left the room and went downstairs. Ben and Morgan followed her.

'He's not getting out underneath that hatch whilst Caesar is guarding it. We need to send someone up there to check it. You need some ladders. Who's going up? It's not very big.'

Morgan spoke before Ben could. 'I will.'

He shook his head. 'Over my dead body are you going up there. He could be waiting ready to stab anyone who goes up there.'

'Well, you're not going to fit, Cain definitely won't, and Amber probably won't do it, so that leaves me.'

Cassie nodded. 'Makes sense, Ben. You can be behind her.'

His head was shaking violently from side to side.

'I'll borrow Amber's body armour. We haven't got time to mess around.'

He squeezed his eyes closed momentarily, and she knew she was giving him a headache worthy of a decent hangover. But he was letting his personal feelings get in the way of his professional judgement, and besides, she hadn't been attacked for over a month now, so she should be okay – or at least she hoped so. He nodded reluctantly.

She went outside to where Amber was standing.

'I need to use your body armour, please, and your CS gas so I can at least pepper spray anyone hiding up there. Cain, I need you to give me a leg up.'

Amber frowned at her but began to unzip it. Shrugging the heavy armour off, she passed it to Morgan, who fastened the Velcro around her waist as tight as it would go, then zipped it up. It was too big for her but better than no protection at all. Although if he tried to slice her neck open, there was no way to protect it other than with her hands.

She pushed that thought away, telling herself to think positive. There was a good chance she'd find him cowering in the corner, shaking like a scared animal.

She ran back into the house, almost sliding in congealing blood, and managed to save herself. Cain was behind her. He was the tallest person here; they didn't have the time to wait around for someone to locate them a pair of stepladders.

She was back in the small box room. Ben looked as if he was about to cry when he saw her, so she smiled at him. 'I'm good, Ben – I can do this.'

He nodded. 'That's what I'm afraid of.'

Cain stepped in, and Cassie grabbed Caesar's leash, pulling him away and whispering, 'Good boy.' He was watching Morgan intently, never taking his eyes off her, and she couldn't resist. She bent down and gave him a quick hug.

'I need you to have my back, okay, Caesar? If I push the bad guy out, you corner him – deal?'

The dog pushed his nose against her arm, leaving a big trail of slobber, and she grinned. 'It's a deal.'

She looked at Cain, pointing to the hatch, and he nodded before bracing himself and cupping his hands for her to step into. Without hesitation, she put her boot into them and felt him push her entire body upwards towards the hatch.

She lifted her hands and pushed it off with the palms, then grabbed the side of the opening and pulled herself up. Unclipping the torch from the body armour, she shone it around the empty space. There was no sign of anyone, and she called down, 'It looks clear.'

She straightened up as best as she could and moved forward. When she shone the torch down, she saw a footprint on the dust-covered floorboard, and her breath caught in the back of her throat. Over the radio, she whispered, 'Someone has been in here though – there's footprints on the boards.'

'Morgan, be careful. Come down – let's get someone from task force to do a thorough search,' Ben whispered.

She ignored him. Where did these footprints lead to?

Careful not to step on them so Wendy could document them, she sidestepped around them. There was a noise from behind her and she jumped. Turning, she aimed the light in that direction and saw Ben's head appear through the hatch. He was squeezing himself to push through.

'You're gonna get wedged and then we've had it.'

'Well, if you did as you were bloody told I wouldn't have to. Get back down here now, Morgan – that's an order.'

She smiled. He was panicking, and she felt bad for making him worry so much.

'Look at those – they look recent, so where are they leading? What is he, Harry Houdini? He can't have just disappeared.'

She called out into the dark space, 'If you're hiding up here, you should know that I have a taser and there is a very big dog waiting to say hello to you. So come out now and we can do this painlessly.'

Her voice echoed around the empty space. She waited, listening for heavy breathing or any sign of movement. But there was nothing, only Ben letting out a grunt as he forced himself through the opening, a loud ripping sound filling the air as his paper suit tore across the middle again.

'You're going to have to use bigger overalls if you keep ripping them, boss.'

He scrambled to his feet. 'Honestly, I am raging, Morgan, and I don't know if it's with you, the arsehole who's up here or these crap bloody suits.'

She stifled the laughter that was threatening to explode from her mouth because it wasn't remotely funny, but it was.

They were in a dangerous situation that could turn worse in a split second. She shone the light onto the footprints.

'Look – they lead across the attic to that side.'

'Shame we can't get the dog up here.'

Cain's voice filtered through the hatch. 'Are you trying to kill me, Benno? You were heavy enough. I can't lift that man beast – he'll probably bite me.'

Morgan passed Ben the cannister of CS gas, and they both cautiously stepped forward until they reached the point where the footsteps stopped by a small wooden doorway. It was square and didn't look much bigger than one of those old coal-bunker doors that some of the older houses in Rydal Falls had from the days when central heating was a pipe dream.

She reached out with a gloved hand and pulled it open. Her heart was racing as she expected to see a face peering back at her. But it was a black space.

She turned to Ben and whispered, 'What do you think it is?'

'Something from my worst bloody nightmares is what I think that is.'

Crouching down, she shone the torch inside and let out a small gasp. 'Oh crap, it's a doorway into next door's attic.'

Moving the light around this one was the opposite: it was full of boxes. The beam fell onto the doorway at the other end: it was identical to this one.

'We have a major problem. There's another door like this in the next attic. They must go on, giving access to each attic. He could be anywhere, in someone else's house.'

'Oh Christ. We need to evacuate this row of houses. Now.'

Blind panic filled Morgan's chest; the killer could be in any one of these houses. Everyone on the row was in danger.

She slipped through the hatch into Cain's waiting arms. Ben squeezed himself back through next, Cain doing his best to catch him.

Once he was on the ground, Ben spoke to Cassie. 'He has

access to the entire side of this street; I need every house searching.'

All of them rushed downstairs, out of the front door and began to hammer on front doors.

Ushering shocked residents out onto the street, Morgan pointed to the police van and shouted, 'I need you to all to wait by the van – we'll sort someplace out for you all to go.'

It was utter chaos. There were dogs, kids, parents, older people all ushered out towards the van. She called the control room on the radio.

'We need somewhere to go until their houses have been searched. Can you get hold of the keyholder for the community centre and ask them to open up, please?'

Ben added, 'I need task force ASAP. Are they on their way? The suspect has access to every attic in the street. He's armed and dangerous – there's no knowing which house he's hiding out in.'

With all the chaos and people out in the street, no one noticed the door of an empty house, which had a FOR SALE sign outside, ten doors down, as it opened, and a shadowy figure stepped outside. They headed towards the gathering group of neighbours who were chattering loudly about what was happening, mingling with them, and, once they were sure the police weren't paying attention, veered off to the opposite side of the nearest police van.

A quiet voice asked, 'Where are you going? We need to stay here?'

He looked at the blonde kid, who was dressed in a pair of Fortnite pyjamas with a matching dressing gown, and lifted a finger to his lips. 'It's a secret. Can you keep a secret?'

The kid beamed at him, nodding.

'Good. Don't tell anyone you saw me.'

'Why, who are you?'

He looked around to see if anyone was paying them any attention but no one was – they were all too busy gossiping with each other, so he leaned in closer. 'The bogeyman, and if you tell, I'll come back and take you away to a dark place where no one will find you.'

And then he was gone, into the shadows. He didn't try to get out of the street because it was full of police and too many people.

The kid was staring after the man who smelled really bad, like he'd been playing with a rusty tin can, who was dressed in dark clothes with a black baseball cap pulled low down on to his forehead. He looked to see where his mum was. She was busy talking to Ann, the old woman from next door. He didn't know what was going on or why everyone was outside, but he did know that the man he'd seen was scary. He thought about telling his mum, but he'd told him he was good at keeping secrets and he'd come back for him if he told.

He walked back to his mum. Reaching out for her hand, he slipped his small one into hers and held tight. She had told him the bogeyman wasn't real, so who was that man and why had he said that's what his name was?

She didn't notice how much his hand was trembling, but he had never felt so scared in his life.

TWENTY-TWO

Every available patrol from Kendal and the south Lakes had been sent over, and a task force was on their way from Barrow. A PCSO arrived with a key for the community centre a couple of streets away, and every resident was ushered there, to be taken care of by a couple of PCSOs until someone volunteered to take over. As the last people left the street, the noise returned to silence once more. Morgan breathed a sigh of relief; her head was pounding. Ben had asked for every man, woman and child to be signed in and accounted for on their arrival at the community centre, so they could cross-reference the names they gave with the voters registered.

Morgan crossed to Ben, who was talking to Wendy.

'What about the opposite side of the street – are we leaving them at home?'

'We'll have to. It's bloody madness without adding another hundred people to the mix. Our guy hasn't got access to their homes. I reckon he's hiding out either in one of the attics or in one of the houses. Are there any empty ones?'

She pointed to the one all in darkness with a For Sale sign

attached to the upstairs window. 'What about that one? Should we start with the obvious and then work our way through the rest of them?'

Ben nodded. 'Yes, good idea. If you were trying to escape, where would you hide out or where would you gain access to if you were hiding out?' He looked around to see if there were any other empty properties. On the other side, there were three all with signs outside. 'Christ, he could be in any of those. Let's see if Caesar can pick up his scent.'

He went to find Cassie, who was still in the back garden of Emma's house with the dog.

'Do you think he could have a sniff around the street and see if he can pick up anything?'

'We'll try, won't we, boy?' She bent down and gave his ears a good scratch. The dog tilted his head back and stared at her. 'But I can't promise anything. How many people have just walked all over this crime scene? Fifty, a hundred, all with their own scents. Caesar's good, but he's not a miracle worker.'

'There's an empty house – maybe if you try around that part of the street, he might pick something up there?'

She nodded. 'Come on, Caesar – let's do this and find the bad guy.'

She led the way out the front, and he began sniffing around. He pulled her in the direction of the empty house, and she gave Ben the thumbs up.

Stopping outside, Caesar sat down on the ground, and she shouted, 'Bingo.'

'How do you want to play this? Are you going in with him or sending him in on his own?'

'Do you not want to wait for task force? The force incident

manager has given them the go ahead to arm up. I'd rather officers with guns go in to search than put him at risk.'

Ben shrugged. 'Yes, I suppose you're right.'

Cassie began to walk the dog back to the van, passing
Morgan, who reached Ben and asked, 'Have you upset her and
the dog?'

'No, she thinks armed officers would be better.'

Morgan nodded. 'There was no knife with Emma's body, so
it's likely he's still got it, and we know he's not afraid to use it.'

'God, this has all gone tits up in a spectacular way. I'm not
going to lie; I don't know whether I'm coming or going.'

A car turned into the street, and their new DI jumped out
wearing a stab vest over the top of his crisp white shirt.

Ben leaned towards Morgan's ear and whispered, 'I feel
safer already now the DI is here and ready for action.'

She nudged him with her elbow. 'He is ready for action.'

'He's ready for something, I just have no idea what.'

Marc waved and came jogging towards them. 'How are you
both holding up? I heard it all going off and had to come and see
if there was anything I could do, be of any assistance?'

Ben inhaled. 'Thanks, we're at a bit of a standstill until task
force arrive, but there's a possibility the suspect is inside there.'
He pointed to the dark, unloved terraced house.

'Send the dog in?'

'Cassie doesn't want to risk it.'

'What? Isn't that why we have dogs?'

Ben shrugged. 'I guess she loves the dog.'

'Ridiculous.' He began walking towards the dog van when a
large riot van turned into the street, blue lights flashing but no
sirens blaring.

'Phew, that dog has just had its arse saved by the boys in
black,' Ben muttered to Morgan, who replied, 'Good, he's such a
gorgeous dog.'

'I didn't know you liked dogs.'

'Yeah, I love them but it's not practical when you live on your own and work as much as we do.' She realised her mistake. 'When I used to live on my own; now I don't need a dog because I have you.'

She smiled sweetly at him, and he shook his head, walking off towards the riot van.

TWENTY-THREE

Al came walking over towards Morgan with Ben.

'Morgan, all right, chuck?'

She smiled at him – even amongst the total chaos he was still down to earth.

'Your plan of action is...?' He looked at Ben and Marc. 'I take it we're taking over the search for the suspect. Are you bronze commander?'

Marc nodded. 'I am indeed.'

Ben nodded. 'Yes, please. The killer is likely to be still carrying the knife and very dangerous.' He pointed to the house shrouded in darkness. 'He's possibly hiding in there.'

Al nodded. 'Leave it with us.'

He jogged back to the assembled officers, two of them armed with guns. Morgan watched, fascinated – it was like a rugby scrum as they all bowed their heads forward and decided on their entry plan.

She turned to Ben. 'If this wasn't so horrific it would be quite exciting.'

Both men looked at her and she decided to go and stand with Wendy, who was hovering at the side of Emma's house.

Wendy would appreciate the sea of men armed and ready to go into battle more than a couple of blokes.

'This is unbelievable, Morgan. How did it all come to this?'

Morgan shrugged. 'Nothing to do with me, I swear.'

Wendy bowed her head, but she caught the grin. 'I don't know what to do – carry on processing the scene or watch *Law and Order* storm that house.'

'I suppose everything is on hold until we know where the suspect is. We can't have you working away in there on your own, in case he doubles back and tries to get back in the house.'

A tall officer who neither of them recognised walked towards them. 'I'm going to guard the attic and make sure he doesn't try and double back. Is this the way in?'

Morgan glanced at Wendy and arched an eyebrow. 'It is. I'll show you the way.'

She led him to the kitchen. He looked at the bloodied body on the floor and visibly flinched. 'Dear God, what a shame.'

'Tragic, bless her.'

'I hope to God that prick walks into the attic whilst I'm waiting up there.'

Morgan looked at him and nodded; she hoped he would too. Karma was a real thing – look at what had happened to Gary Marks. Even though he'd died saving her, he'd done terrible things to innocent people and ruined so many lives, but it had caught up with him eventually. Whoever had killed Emma needed stopping now, before anyone else got hurt – or worse, killed. Morgan would be more than happy to deliver some karma his way.

Wendy was standing at the kitchen door. 'My poor crime scene has had more traffic than Aldi on payday.'

'I know, but it's one of those situations where you're damned if you do and damned if you don't. I suppose you'll be able to get cracking when they've secured the area.'

'Do you think he's really still hanging around here waiting to be caught though, Morgan?'

'I don't know. Possibly.'

Morgan looked down at Emma's lifeless body, her glazed eyes staring in horror, and wondered what she'd seen in those last seconds. They looked as if they were looking at the clock on the wall. The clock that read six o'clock. But it had been almost seven when she and Ben had gone for pizza on the way home, and that had been well over an hour ago. Morgan felt an icy-cold fear reach inside and grab hold of her heart.

'What time is it?'

'Eight thirteen.'

'Fuck.'

Morgan rushed out of the back garden and across the road to Paula's house and hammered on the front door. The door was opened a tiny sliver and she saw one of Paula's eyes staring at her.

'Did Emma's clock in the kitchen work? Had it stopped and needed a new battery?'

Paula opened the front door wider and stared at Morgan.

'What? Why do you want to know that?'

'It's important.'

She shrugged. 'It was working this morning when I popped over for a coffee before she went to work.'

'You're sure? What time did it say?'

'I don't know, I wasn't really paying it much attention.' The words came out slurred, and Morgan wondered if she'd finished the bottle of wine she'd opened earlier.

'It was, yes it was, I remember glancing at it to see if it was time for me to go to the hairdressers. It said 10:35. Is that what you want to hear?'

'Yes, but only if it's true.'

'Of course it's bloody true. What's with the stupid questions and why are the Keystone Cops running all over the place and what's in his hand? Oh my God, is that a gun?'

Paula stared at the officers about to enter the empty house. 'Christ, you think he's in there, don't you? Oh my God, he could do it again.' She slammed the door shut in Morgan's face.

'Don't open the door again to anyone, Paula.'

'Stop bloody knocking then.'

Morgan smiled as she jogged back over to where Ben was standing with Marc.

'I think it's the same killer as Shirley Kelley.'

Both men turned to look at her; Ben looked genuinely puzzled. 'How do you come up with that, Morgan? They are nothing alike. The crime scenes are the complete opposite of each other, like polar opposites.'

'I know, but Emma's clock has stopped at six o'clock, and Paula said it was working this morning.'

'So? It could have just run out of battery.'

'I don't think so. We need to take them both in and dust them for prints. We might get lucky and get a DNA sample from them. Did we even seize Shirley Kelly's clock?'

She turned and began walking back to Wendy, leaving them staring after her.

'Wendy, did you check the clock for prints in Shirley Kelly's flat?'

'No, sorry. I photographed everything but there wasn't anything obvious on the front of it. Why are you asking?'

'Her clock was stopped at six o'clock, but we think her time of death was somewhere in the early hours, so whoever messed with her clock took the battery out and moved the hands. But why? What does this mean? What's significant about the number six?'

Wendy shrugged. 'Christ, it's not some religious nut, is it?'

'What?'

'Six-six-six, the number of the beast, the mark of the devil and all that jazz.'

A cold, creeping horror filled Morgan with fear. 'Oh God. What, do you think he's summoning a demon? Do people really do that stuff, or is that just in the movies? There must be some other explanation. Or he's just crazy as a box of frogs.'

'Now you're creeping me out, girl. Enough of that talk, and I need to stop watching horror films. Surely not – that's like next-level scary stuff. I don't think we're prepared for someone like this. I don't think I'm ever going to sleep again thinking about it.'

A loud bang from upstairs made them both screech as heavy footsteps came pounding down the stairs. Morgan pushed Wendy behind her and looked around for something to protect them with. The only thing to hand was a sweeping brush and she grabbed it, clutching it in her hand.

The task force officer came running towards them, took one look at them and spoke.

'Sorry, I slammed the loft hatch too hard. Did I scare you? The house is empty. We're about to search the other houses. Cain is going to come back and guard the loft.'

Wendy let out a breath as he rushed past them. 'What a bloody idiot – I nearly died on the spot.'

Morgan nodded. So had she.

Cain's voice filled the air. 'What are you doing with that brush, Morgan? Are you going to sweep him to death if he appears?' He chuckled to himself.

'Where were you?'

'Had to speak to the boss and fill him in.'

'I didn't see you.'

'I also went for a pee and to wash my hands at the community centre. Is that okay with you, super boss?'

Wendy shook her head. 'Good job I took samples from

under your nails before you did, isn't it? You should have asked before you did that, Cain.'

'I thought you'd finished with me. I was worried I'd put my fingers in my mouth. I wanted to get rid of the smell of blood that was lingering on them. Besides, I had nothing to do with this. Ask the people's person, Amber – I was with her the whole time, boss.' He emphasised the *boss* to Wendy, who tutted.

'I know, sorry. It's just: look at the state of my crime scene – it's ruined.'

Cain reached out, patting a hand on her shoulder. 'You'll find something – you always do. Stop giving me a hard time, and I won't tell anyone you two screamed louder than a group of teenagers on the Wonder Waltzers when action man came running down the stairs.'

They smiled at him, nodding.

Morgan pointed to the clock. 'I think it's the same guy. The clock is stopped like Shirley Kelly's.'

Cain blew out a breath. 'Jeez, that's all we need. You'd better get your thinking cap on, Morgan, and use those crime-solving superpowers of yours before anyone else is killed.'

'If only I was that good – or psychic.'

Wendy opened her case and took out a large plastic evidence bag. 'Come on, big guy – get a pair of gloves on and take that clock off the wall for me.' She passed Cain the gloves and stepped inside, beckoning him to follow her.

Morgan didn't miss the pained look of sadness that washed over his face as he glanced down at the body on the floor.

She felt bad for him. He had come back with the intention of doing a good deed and had ended up being the only person there to give comfort to Emma as she'd lain dying in his arms.

TWENTY-FOUR

Every house that could be was searched; two armed officers made their way from one attic to the next, making sure the suspect wasn't hiding out in any of them. The loft hatch in the empty house was slid to the side and fresh footsteps were found in the layers of dust leading to it. There was also an old wooden ladder.

'Ben, we've found his exit route. He did escape through the empty house, but he's not here now.'

Ben looked at Marc. 'We need a joiner ASAP.'

'To secure the empty house?'

'Yes, that and to secure all those small access doors that lead into each other's attics. If he puts a bolt across them on both sides that should be enough. Why the hell would they build houses that you can just wander around into next door's attic and help yourself?'

'These are old houses. Back in the good old days, people never had to lock their doors, and they probably didn't worry about anyone stealing what little they did have from the attic.'

'We need the dog to do an area search again. He must have escaped when we evacuated everyone. He probably walked right past us all running around like headless chickens with a grin on his face.'

Ben spoke into his radio. 'Any PCSO at the community centre?'

Cathy's voice answered. *'Yes, boss?'*

'Is there anyone inside that isn't accounted for, or has anyone given you details that seem a little bit dodgy? I'm assuming this is a man. Are there any single men in there with you?'

In the community centre, Cathy rolled her eyes and looked over at Tina, who was crouched on the floor talking to a little girl about Peppa Pig, and mouthed *we should be so lucky*. Tina pointed to a guy on his own, sitting in a corner, on his phone. Cathy turned away, walking into the kitchen area away from the crowd.

'Actually, there is a guy on his own. Do you want me to get his details?'

'No. Don't go near him. I'm coming down with Al. Keep an eye on him but don't make it too obvious.'

A mild look of panic crossed Cathy's face, and Tina whispered, 'What's up? I didn't catch that last bit.'

She leaned towards Tina and whispered, 'They're coming down to speak to the guy on his own. Which house did he say he was from?'

Tina picked up the clipboard from the side and began scanning the pages of hastily scribbled names, looking for one that was on its own.

Ben's voice filtered over the radio: *'I need you to tell everyone to form a queue and then let them out a household at a time. Tell them they can go home now. Then I want you to tick them off your list as they leave. When it's the guy's turn, don't act any different and let him out. We can't come inside if it's him and he kicks off. There's a room full of potential victims or hostages.'*

They both looked at each other, realising the seriousness of the situation they were all in. 'Yes, boss.'

Tina took the clipboard and stood by the main doorway.

Cathy walked into the room where everyone was talking in hushed whispers about what had happened in the street to cause this.

'Can I have your attention, please?'

Everyone looked at her except the guy, but she quickly focused on the little girl with a head full of brown curls who had been telling her about Peppa.

'Thank you for your patience. You are able to go home now. I'm sorry I can't tell you much at the moment, but you will all be visited at home and spoken to individually.'

A guy with a shaved head and long grey beard stood up. 'This is ridiculous. You chase us out of our homes then tell us we can go back and none of us have a clue what's going on. What is happening? We have a right to know.'

Ben walked in on his own and stood next to Cathy. 'I'm sorry, you're right, but all I can say at the moment is there has been a serious incident and this has all been for your own safety.'

'Well, that's not good enough.'

The woman next to him grabbed his sleeve and hissed, 'Shut up, Alan – they're doing their best.'

'As my colleague explained, we will come and speak to you all individually. There are certain things we can't talk about in front of your children. I'm sure you would agree it's best to do this when they're not around. Now if all the residents with children would line up first, let's get you all back into your homes, then we'll take it in order – the older people like me, and so on.

All you youngsters with no kids can go last. Thank you for your help and cooperation.'

Ben turned, leaving them to it, getting back outside to where Al was standing waiting for him.

As Tina and Cathy ticked the people off their lists, they all began filtering back out into the night. Parents and children walked hand in hand the short distance back to their houses, not all of them aware they were surrounded by armed officers watching their every move. It took some time but finally they were down to the last few.

Cathy looked over to see the guy was still busy on his phone. He hadn't even bothered to stand up.

Ben's voice whispered into their ears, *'As soon as everyone is out, get out and move away from the door quick. No hanging around. Is he in the line?'*

Tina answered. 'Not yet.'

'Good, get the rest of them out and then yourselves. I'll go in and deal with him.'

Eventually, after what seemed like forever, both Tina and Cathy appeared, coming out of the entrance of the community centre.

Al rushed forward and ushered them away out of the sight of the doorway. 'Where is he?'

'Still on his phone.'

'Still?'

Cathy shrugged. 'I think he's playing a game or watching a film. He must be – he hasn't paid any attention to what's been going on at all.'

Al headed through the doors, followed by Ben. They looked into the large room, which was empty.

'Shit, he's got out somehow.'

Ben checked the kitchen, and Al began to check the row of cupboards at the back of the hall. From the opposite end came the sound of a toilet flushing, then the loud sound of a hand drier filtered through the door. Al stood there with his taser aimed at the door, the red dots moving in minute circles. Ben was next to him with his CS gas.

The door opened and a guy in his early twenties walked out, took one look at the red dots now on his chest area and screeched, 'Jesus Christ, I only went for a pee.'

'Hands in the air and step away from the door.'

A look of pure panic stretched across the guy's face as he raised his arms up and slowly stepped forward. 'I haven't done anything, I swear.'

'Why weren't you lining up with the others?'

'What? I didn't know they were. I was watching Netflix.' He pointed to his ears and slowly pulled an AirPod out of each ear. 'I didn't hear anything. Look I don't even know what any of this is about. I got in from work, put my microwave chicken tikka in and was rudely told to leave my house and come here with no explanation. Has there been a gas leak or something?'

Al glanced at Ben, then stepped forward. 'Sorry, pal, but I need to do a quick search then we'll escort you home, okay? Do you have anything in your pockets that is sharp, any needles, weapons, anything I should know about?'

The guy shook his head rapidly. 'No, I've got my phone, AirPod case and that's it.'

'What's your name?'

'Daniel Walker.'

Al began patting him down whilst Ben requested a PNC check on him by the control room.

'You're right, Daniel. Let's get you home and we'll talk about what's happened tonight. Is that okay?'

He nodded. 'Should I go first? You're not going to take me out with that taser, are you?'

'Not if you don't make me I won't.'

Al laughed but the guy looked horrified.

They followed him back to the street.

He led them to the last house on the row.

'Look, it's a bit of a shithole inside. I'm not the best at cleaning. Do you want to talk out here?'

Al shook his head. 'Sorry, bud, we need to come inside and have a quick chat.'

Daniel pushed open his front door and immediately the smell of chicken tikka filled their nostrils, reminding Ben of just how hungry he was. The house was untidy but they'd both seen a lot worse.

'Are you going to tell me what this is about?'

'There's been a murder a few doors up. We think the suspect escaped through the attic.'

'Oh God, that's awful. Who's been murdered?'

He asked with such sincerity that Ben instinctively knew that the only crime Daniel had committed was failing to hoover and pick up his dirty clothes.

'Do you know Emma Dixon?'

He shook his head. 'I don't think so; I don't really know anyone.'

'She works in the bakery on Main Street. Do you ever go in there?'

His hand flew to his mouth. 'Oh God, not the nice one who gives everyone the good stuff half price near to closing time? She lives up the street somewhere, but I only know her to say hello to. That's awful. How can someone escape through an attic? Did she have one of those skylights?'

'No. Have you ever been in the attic?'

'No, I don't own a ladder and, to be honest, I haven't got enough crap to fill the house, never mind the attic. Why?'

'For some strange reason they all have connecting doors;

obviously whoever did this we think is a single male on his own, which is why you came to our attention.'

Daniel collapsed down on the worn leather-look sofa and looked up at them.

'I never – I wouldn't.'

Ben held up his hand. 'No, we know that now, but we had to check. You understand that, don't you?'

He nodded his head. 'Of course. Yeah, you do. I hope you find him.'

'We will. Thanks for your time.'

As they headed towards the front door, Ben turned around. 'There's going to be a joiner coming shortly to put bolts on both sides of the attic doors. He'll need to get access to your loft. I suggest you let him in. You don't want to risk anyone using yours as an escape route.'

Daniel shivered. 'I will. God this is so creepy, dude. Like something off a horror film creepy.'

'I know. Take care, and if you see anything ring 999. There's going to be police outside for the next few days at least, so you can always speak to one of the officers if you're worried about anything.'

'Thanks.'

They left him to it, closing his door behind them.

Al looked at Ben. 'Well, what do you think?'

'He's nothing to do with it. How could he have got cleaned up so fast? And your lads checked all the houses – nothing obvious with regards to forensics, and we know that the suspect was in the empty house next door.'

'Yeah, I think so too. I think we just scared the shit out of him though. We might have to perfect our questioning to a better standard for the families and older people, otherwise they're all going to be scared to stay in their houses and scared to go outside.'

Ben smiled. 'This is a complete mess. It's turned into a

carnival. Do you think he knew it would and did this on purpose to mess up the crime scene, or is it just a lucky break for him that he managed to avoid being captured in a street surrounded by armed officers?'

'I have no idea. He's either a lucky bastard or he planned the whole thing. Either way it doesn't matter because he's managed to evade being captured and left us with this circus to deal with.'

Ben headed back to the house where Emma's body lay. He needed to concentrate on that crime scene and leave the searching to Al and his team.

He turned around to see the officers regrouping and nodded in appreciation. He was grateful for their assistance. It was pure bad luck that the evil bastard had managed to slip through the net. He may have escaped, but they would find him. It was just a matter of time.

TWENTY-FIVE

1989

He waited for Mr Atkinson to take his eyes off him. He knew he'd get bored of babysitting him, and it didn't take long before he began chatting to the school secretary, Miss Benson. She wasn't very old, at least not as old as the rest of the teachers, and she always wore tops that were so low cut you could see the outline of her very full boobs. Mr Atkinson was talking to her, but his head kept bobbing down in the direction of the bare flesh on her chest. He rolled his eyes at the conversation they were having. As if the fat old bastard was trying to chat her up when he was sitting behind them. Miss Benson lowered her voice and was whispering so low that he had to lean across the desk even closer to her. Neither of them paying attention to him, he didn't wait another second.

He stood up and made a run for it. He was as quick as a cheetah and as silent as a panther about to pounce on its prey. He pushed the glass doors open and ran like never before. He pumped his legs hard as he ran down the steps and onto the gravel drive. The door slammed shut behind him, only to be thrown open again.

'Stop there, boy. I'm warning you, if you don't turn around, you're going to be very, very sorry,' the teacher was bellowing after him. He could feel the anger in the words, and he knew right now if he caught up with him, he would make him pay.

He didn't turn around to look in case he was a fast runner and about to take him out with a rugby tackle. Instead, he began to laugh and ran even faster. The school was surrounded by woodland, and he ran, boy did he run, straight into the trees. Zigzagging through them, he didn't care that his arms and legs were getting scratched on the bushes. All he knew was that he was going back to his grandmother's house to find out what was going on. He could hide out in the big mansion for days if he had to and no one would know where he was. He'd spent hours exploring and knew every nook, cranny and hiding place. As long as he managed to get inside without any of the staff who worked there seeing him.

Convinced that there was no way Atkinson was still following him, he began to slow down. Breathing heavy, he clutched his side, where a stitch had formed, making it hard to suck in enough air. Figuring it was safe to take a minute, he stopped and leaned against the nearest tree, resting his forehead against the rough bark. He sucked in gulping breaths of the pine-scented air. He didn't know if he was heading in the right direction to the house. He didn't know where he was, but he wasn't scared. He knew that he'd find his way back; he was in no rush.

Eventually, the pain in his side dissolved, leaving him feeling as if he could get moving again. This time he walked – there was no need to run, not unless the dickhead had phoned the police, but even then he was sure he'd hear them crashing through the woodland to come and find him. The big house was on the shore of a lake, set back on the fell, so if he walked towards the water, he would be able to follow it around back home. He listened for the sound of lapping water and closed his eyes. When he opened them, he realised that these woods were unusually quiet. No chirping birds or small creatures going about their daily business, and he wondered where they all were.

He walked in the direction that he thought the lake was and after ten minutes was greeted by the reflection of the sun as it glinted off the water through a narrow break in the trees. He stood on the shore of the lake and grinned. He could see the outline of the big house in the distance, almost on the opposite side of the lake. It was going to take him some time to walk there but it didn't matter. He had nowhere to be and no one to give two shits about him.

His grandmother was doing her best, but she wasn't the most caring of people. He missed his mum. Even though according to his grandmother she had been a junkie whore, she had still made sure she hugged and told him how much she loved him, when she remembered. He wished that she could want him more than she did her next fix or the men who gave her the money for it, but she didn't – she liked her crack much more.

He picked up a large stone and threw it at a bird out on the lake. It missed, and the bird took off, flapping and squawking. Picking up a handful more, he pelted them into the water as hard as he could, tears rolling down his cheeks all the while. He tasted their salty wetness as they ran down his lips, and he let out a roar that was as fierce as a mighty lion at the unfairness of his life. Home, he thought, was now that cold, empty crypt where he'd be trapped for the rest of his life.

As he wiped the snot and tears from his face with the sleeve of his school jumper, his stomach let out a loud growl and he realised he was hungry. He may as well go back to the house and see if that miserable cow the cook would give him something to eat. Anyone would think she paid for the food she was so mean with it.

Following the lake, he trudged along the shore, passing a

couple of guys about to launch a canoe. They both looked at him. He carried on walking, wondering if he'd ever have friends when he was older to do fun stuff with.

'Hey, kid.'

He lifted his head, turning slightly to look at the ginger-haired guy who had just shouted him.

'Are you okay? Have you lost your way, mate?'

He shook his head.

'Where's your school friends? Are you on a field trip?'

'I'm going home – I'm not on a trip.'

The two guys looked at him.

'Where do you live?'

'Can't tell you that – you're a stranger.'

They laughed. 'Okay, but if you need a lift or any help...'

He shook his head again. 'Thanks, but I only live over there.'

He didn't point to the house, but it was the only one in view. He wondered if they would grass him up, phone the police, but they shrugged and turned away from him, focusing their attention back on the red canoe as they began to push it into the water. He was glad; he didn't need the help of two strangers. It was strange though, that they had shown him more kindness in the briefest conversation than anyone had the last three months.

He reached the drystone wall that separated the grounds of the house from the rest of the area and scrabbled over it. The jetty was his favourite place to sit even on the coldest of days. The guys in the canoe were paddling at some speed and as they sped past him, he lifted a hand and waved. The ginger guy waved back.

He decided to go in the side door.

There was a big black van outside the front of the house. Squatting down, he saw two men all dressed in black get out of the front of the car and walk around to the rear doors. One of them walked up to the front door and rang the bell. This was his chance – he could sneak in whilst they were being spoken to.

He ran, keeping himself bent low through the bushes and shrubs to the side door that the staff used to come in and out of. Grabbing the handle, he breathed a sigh of relief when it turned and then he was inside the dark, gloomy house.

He could hear hushed voices by the front door. Why was everyone talking so quiet today? He sneaked out of the pantry door and ran down to the servants' stairs at the end of the corridor.

It took him seconds and then he was inside his bedroom on the top floor. He tugged his school jumper over his head, loosened the tie, and got dressed in the camouflage trousers that he lived in and a black hooded sweatshirt. He remembered how hungry he was, and after swapping his stiff leather brogues that he hated for a pair of Nikes, he went out and peered over the banister. He could hear voices, but he couldn't see where they were coming from. They didn't sound as if they were coming from the kitchen. He might be lucky; that miserable bitch might have gone into the town to get some groceries.

He made it to the second floor when Emmie's voice screeched.

'Oh Jesus, what are you doing creeping around? Why aren't you at school? They're all out looking for you, you stupid little arsehole.'

He glared at her. 'Who's looking for me?'

'Mick has gone out on his pushbike, and your grandmother has taken the car and gone to speak to the teachers at the school, as if she needs this today of all days. What did you do now?'

Her tone was sharp, accusatory, and he looked at her standing at the top of the second-floor stairs and wondered what kind of noise she might make if he ran at her and pushed her down them. Would she scream and bounce down them or would she land at a funny angle and snap her neck?

'What are you staring at, you little creep? Cat got your tongue?'

He stepped closer to her, too close for her liking, and she backed away.

Turning around, she walked down the stairs, putting distance between them. He followed her as she scurried off towards the drawing room.

He went to the kitchen and was glad to see there was no sign of the cook. Opening the fridge, he took out some cooked chicken drumsticks, a block of cheese and some fresh tomatoes, then took out a plate, carved himself two thick doorsteps of fresh bread and took it all into the dining room, where he sat and ate in silence.

Two men had been knocking on the front door when he arrived, and everyone was now busy with them. Good – they could stay that way. He just hoped that his grandmother didn't come back until he'd finished eating because he was hungry. He hated them all. They were all horrible, except for maybe his grandmother. She was sometimes nice to him, and he could tell that she wasn't the kind of woman who was used to being nice to too many people.

The door opened and in walked the cook. Her mouth dropped open so wide he could see her thick pink tongue.

'What on God's earth do you think you're doing?'

He carried on gnawing the almost bare chicken drumstick, ignoring her.

'As if you have the nerve to cause trouble in school, run away, then come here as bold as brass and help yourself to the food in the fridge without a bloody care in the world. Whilst today of all days your poor grandmother is out chasing her own tail looking for you.'

'And what has it got to do with you?'

'What?'

She stepped closer, her face turning a deep shade of crimson that he didn't think he'd ever seen on a person before.

'I said what has it got to do with you? Do you pay for this food? Is this your kitchen? Do you own this house?'

She took another step towards him, her pudgy fingers clenched into fists, and he knew that she wanted to hit him. If he was honest, he wanted her to because then he would draw back his fist and smash the angry little cow in the nose and watch it explode everywhere. As if sensing this, she didn't come any closer – instead she hovered where she was.

'You wait until I tell your grandmother what an insolent, rude little boy you are. You'll get what's coming to you.'

He stood up, walked to the bin and scraped the gnawed-bare chicken bones into it, then he put his plate on the side and turned back to look at her.

'And let me tell you that if you do, one day you'll get what's coming to you. It's only fair, isn't it?'

He walked past her, out of the kitchen and back upstairs to his room, ready for his grandmother to come home and dish out whatever punishment she thought was appropriate. He would take it from her: she was his flesh and blood, she was family, but he wasn't going to be talked to like that by that horrible woman who wasn't even that good at cooking.

TWENTY-SIX

Morgan stifled a yawn – she was beyond exhausted. So far she and Ben had worked a thirteen-hour shift, and she hadn't eaten since those chicken mayo baguettes they'd had that afternoon. Her stomach growled to remind her it needed feeding. She couldn't wait to reheat the pizza currently sitting in the back of Ben's car, although it wasn't going to taste as good as it would have piping hot and fresh from Gino's oven. Declan's car turned into the street, and she walked down to meet him. He got out looking dishevelled; his hair was tousled at the back and his shirt was buttoned up wrong.

'Were you asleep?'

He laughed. 'No, I was having the time of my life for the first time in forever.' He went to the boot of his car and began the process of suiting and booting.

'Oh, sorry.'

'I'm going to say it's not your fault, Morgan, because it usually is, but it's okay. He's a surgeon – he understands the lifestyle.'

'That's good then – at least you're on the same level.'

'Yeah, it is pretty good, or I should say it was pretty good until the moody incident manager rang me and rudely interrupted.'

She stifled a giggle. 'If it's any consolation, we had just picked up fresh pizzas from Gino's.'

Declan paused from fastening the shoe covers around his feet. 'Nah, none at all. Hot pizza and hot sex are not comparable.'

'I don't know, have you tasted a meat feast from Gino's?'

He laughed. 'Morgan Brookes, you're incorrigible. So, what have we got here?'

All small talk was over with, the light-hearted banter switched off as he turned on his full forensic pathologist mode.

'It's horrible – really bad.'

'I hate to say this but whenever you're involved, I can guarantee they usually are.' He arched an eyebrow, and she nodded.

'Yes, I know but this one is really creepy.'

'How so?'

'We think he hid in her attic waiting for her to come home, killed her then escaped back through that attic. All these houses have these strange, half-sized doorways in them adjoining each other. It's really weird.'

'How did he know about them? Does he live on this street?'

A cold shiver ran down the full length of her spine. Did he? They had checked every property on Emma's side, but if he lived on the opposite, that would explain how he'd managed to slip away unseen when there were so many officers looking for him.

'Maybe. Search teams have been through every house and attic on this side of the street. Oh crap, I need to speak to Ben.'

'Where is the golden boy?'

'Waiting for you at the crime scene.'

'Then you lead, and I'll follow.'

They shuffled together in silence, Morgan leading the way around the back of Emma's house.

Ben was standing with Wendy, who smiled at Declan.

'How are you, Wendy?'

'I'm okay, Declan. You?'

'I'll let Morgan fill you in on my updates. Am I good to go in?'

'Yes, practically the whole of Fell Close has been in and out of the cordon anyway – knock yourself out.'

He reached out his left hand, squeezing her shoulder gently, a sign of commiseration and understanding. Then he stepped into the kitchen and whispered, 'Dear God, what the heck happened here?'

Ben was about to follow him when Morgan whispered, 'We need to search and check the houses on the opposite side of the street. Declan made a fair point; how did he know about the adjoining attics? He must live here or know someone who does.'

If Morgan didn't know any better, she would have said that Ben looked as if he was going to burst into tears, but she knew it was exhaustion and frustration with how this crime scene was turning into a logistical nightmare.

'Will you stay with Declan? I need to speak to Al.'

He didn't wait for her reply. He left them to it.

TWENTY-SEVEN

Morgan opened the curtain in Emma's living room to see what was happening outside and saw Ben. He was watching from the compact square of grass that doubled as the front garden of Emma's house as armed officers began knocking on doors opposite. She wanted to join in and help search – the more hands the better – and she guessed Ben probably did too. He would be feeling helpless watching. Declan was busy taking the samples he needed from the body to send off for testing, so she found herself walking up the stairs to take a look in Emma's bedroom.

Her room was tidy, a bit sparse, and all painted white with blush pink and copper tones. It was nice, very shabby chic.

Stepping inside, Morgan felt momentarily bad for invading Emma's personal space, but it was necessary even though it was unpleasant, and if she was dead and Emma was having to search through her things, she'd much rather it be like that than task force, who would come in like bulls in a china shop and tear the place apart.

There was a double bed, two small stools either side which had been painted a chalky pink, with a lamp on each as well as books on them both. She walked over and picked up a well-worn copy of *You are a Badass* by Jen Sincero and flicked through the pages that had multiple parts highlighted in fluorescent yellow. Morgan sighed; Emma obviously had found some connection deep inside this book.

On the other table was a copy of *The Book of Magic* by Alice Hoffman. Morgan had read this in two sittings on her last days off and had cried inconsolably at the beautiful story, glad that Ben hadn't been home to see her in such a sorry state. There was a bookmark tucked between the pages near to the end, and a sharp pain filled Morgan's chest at the sadness and injustice. Emma never got to read the ending – she would never know what happened to the Owens girls or if Aunt Frances survived losing her dear sister Jet.

She felt her legs wobble from underneath her and found herself perched on the end of the bed feeling all sorts of overwhelmed. She flicked through this book in case there was a note inside. Then tucked the bookmark back where it belonged and put the book back.

What happened, Emma? Who did this to you? Did you keep a diary I wonder?

After giving herself a minute to think, she pushed herself off the bed, crossed to the tall chest of drawers and began searching through them carefully. There was nothing but underwear and T-shirts; lots of black leggings too. Just like her own drawers at Ben's house. She lived in black T-shirts and leggings on her days off, if she had nowhere to go and get dressed up for.

She glanced in the mirror at her reflection. Her copper hair had all but fallen out of the bun she'd wrapped it in before setting off for work this morning, her green eyes were a little bloodshot, and her winged eyeliner was smudged from her repeated eye watering over this crime scene.

Movement behind her made her entire body freeze. It was a fleeting dark shadow. She spun round to see what it was, her heart racing – she was here with nothing to protect herself and couldn't even move fast in these bloody awful paper overalls.

He's come back. We missed him somehow; he must have been hiding. How the bloody hell did we miss him?

Picking up the nearest thing to hand, which was a large, flat paddle brush, she whispered into her radio, 'Cain, can you come back inside the house, please. I'm upstairs.'

She couldn't see anyone on the narrow landing behind her, but someone or something had passed by the doorway.

'Morgan?' Cain's deep voice filled the air from the bottom of the stairs.

'Up here.' Had her voice just quivered then? She hoped not as she heard the heavy footsteps making their way up.

She stood at the entrance to Emma's bedroom, facing Cain, who was standing on the top step.

'What's up?'

She pointed to the spare room, whispering, 'I saw something.'

He pulled out his baton, which was tucked into his pocket, all he had on him, and extended it to full length with an expert flick of the wrist. He motioned for her to stay where she was as he walked towards the room with the door ajar. But she followed, unable to stand back and watch as he pushed the door open with the metal tip of the baton.

The room looked empty. There was only a built-in cupboard and some small boxes – nothing to hide behind. The ladder she was sure had been removed from the loft hatch and propped against the wall earlier was now underneath it again.

Cain pointed to the cupboard. Stepping closer, he glanced at Morgan, who was brandishing the hairbrush, and shook his head. Then he turned his full attention on the cupboard door, grabbed the handle and, with a twist, pulled it open so fast it fell off one hinge and yelled, 'Jesus Christ,' at the guy dressed in black, cowering against the clothes.

Morgan let out a small screech, not expecting anyone to be in there. Then she pressed the red emergency button on the top of her radio and shouted, 'Backup now, suspect on premises.'

Cain, who had recovered his composure enough to speak, lifted his baton. 'Step out of there now – put your hands in the air and move slowly.'

The guy looked up, staring at Morgan, and she felt a cold shiver at just how young he was. Too young to be some messed-up murderer. He took a step towards Cain, who towered over him.

'I'm sorry. I didn't do it; I didn't do anything. I just wanted to come and check on Emma to see if she was okay.'

Morgan glanced at the ladders then back at him. 'Then why didn't you knock on her door like any normal person would?'

Al, Ben and two armed officers ran into the already cramped room. Ben took one look at the man who was holding his hands out for Cain to cuff him.

'Read him his rights and get him taken to the station, please, Cain. I'll come and deal with him. His name is Daniel Walker, and he lives a few doors down.'

'Please – I didn't do this. It's just a misunderstanding.'

Morgan glared at him. 'A misunderstanding? You are sneaking around in a murder victim's house that is still a crime scene and out of bounds to anyone except police staff. How is it a misunderstanding?'

Daniel's eyes looked at Ben, fear and something else in them. Morgan couldn't decide if he was guilty of the murder or an absolute moron. She watched as Cain cuffed him, read his rights, and then marched him down the stairs right out of the front door, the rest of them following.

'I want to see Emma, please. I need to see her.'

Cain pushed him in the back, making him move forward.

'The only thing you're going to see, pal, is the inside of the cage in the back of my van and then the four walls of a police holding cell.'

Daniel craned his neck around as far as it would go, trying to see through into the kitchen, but Morgan stepped in front of him, blocking his view.

'No way – keep moving.'

And then he was out into the street, snivelling and shaking as he was marched to the van by Cain and an armed officer.

Morgan stood next to Ben on the doorstep and watched as he was first searched and then manhandled inside it, the sound of the heavy doors being slammed shut echoing around the street.

Ben leaned close to Morgan. 'That could have turned out a lot different.'

'What do you mean?' But she knew exactly what he meant; he was insinuating that she could have ended up hurt or worse.

'I was searching Emma's bedroom and saw movement. I was good: I called for Cain. I didn't go in alone.'

Ben pointed to the hairbrush. 'Just as well – I'm not sure how effective that would have been against a homicidal maniac. Well done – you may have just saved us a lot of hard work. Let's follow them to the station and get him interviewed.'

'What the bejesus just happened here? There I am in a world of my own, collecting samples, when all hell breaks loose. I'm not going to lie, I didn't know whether to run back to my car and lock the doors or stay put and pitch in.'

Morgan grinned at Declan. 'Sorry about that. Are you okay?'

'Me, I'm fan-bloody-tastic. How about you, flower? I mean it's like you have this criminal radar built into your DNA that keeps on searching until you find them out. I've never known anything like it. If you were a Marvel superhero, you'd be called Track and Trace.'

Morgan giggled, and even Ben broke into a smile.

'Ah, nothing fills my heart with more joy than seeing the two of you relaxing for even the briefest of moments. You look good with smiles on your faces, the both of you. Now, I just want to roll her body and have a quick check underneath her and then I'm done here. You can move Emma to the mortuary when you're ready. I've got a clear morning tomorrow; I should have been in court, but it's been adjourned, so I'm thinking we get started on the post-mortem nice and early around—'

'Nine o'clock.' Both Ben and Morgan spoke in unison, and Declan laughed.

'Yeah, nine o'clock. I keep telling you if you two ever get fed up with being superheroes, you could form a comedy duo and get yourselves on *Britain's Got Not Much Talent*. You're sure to be a big hit with the criminals.'

Ben kneeled down to help Declan move Emma's body slightly to the side. There, lying underneath her, was a large, bloodied knife.

'Well, that was a good decision, wasn't it?'

Declan picked up the large kitchen knife that had been underneath Emma's lower back. Morgan felt a cold shiver. It looked like the kind of knife Shirley Kelly had in her kitchen, although she'd need to compare it to the others. Whilst Wendy brought him a plastic evidence tube to drop the knife into, Morgan began checking the drawers in the kitchen to see if Emma had a set of them hidden away.

She found one small, faded pink sharp knife, the kind for peeling potatoes. The one Declan had found looked like a professional chef's knife – razor sharp and mean looking.

She turned around. 'I think that's the knife we couldn't find at Shirley Kelly's house – the missing one out of the knife block.'

Declan and Ben both nodded.

'Well, I'll let you guys figure that out, but I'm pretty confident that when I do the post-mortem, that blade will fit the wound across her neck.'

They stepped aside to let Declan out of the front door, and he squeezed past them, heavy steel case in one hand, lifting the other to wave at them.

Ben reached an arm around Morgan's waist, pulling her close. 'Come on, let's get to the station. The quicker we deal with Daniel, the sooner we can get home and go to bed.'

The warmth of his hand on her waist even through the paper suit was an instant pick-me-up. She wanted nothing more than to turn and hug him properly, wrap her arms around him and not let go, except to maybe eat the pizza they'd bought hours ago. Instead, she reached down her fingers, squeezing his hand, thankful that they would eventually go home together.

It was all she'd ever wanted from the first moment she'd set eyes on him, and it made her pulse quicken to realise that for once she'd managed to do something right in her life. She'd been played a better hand than poor Emma.

TWENTY-EIGHT

They arrived at the station and went straight to the custody suite to see if their suspect had been booked in. Ben hammered on the grey steel door to be let in. There was a camera above it that the staff behind the desk used to see who was there, and Morgan waved. The lock clicked and Ben pushed it open. There was a racket going on from the desk where arrestees were booked in ready for a stay in a clean, sparse cell. Four officers were tussling with a drunken guy. Jo, the custody sergeant, looked bemused as they all landed in a heap on the floor.

Ben shouted, 'Do they need a hand?'

She shook her head. 'No, any minute now he's going to stop fighting and start crying – it's like clockwork. Happens at least twice a week. This time he's going to end up getting remanded again, because I mean how many times can you breach your court bail?'

Her voice echoed as she suddenly realised it had gone silent. She peered over the desk, lifted her finger up and down three times and then a loud wail filled the air.

Morgan smiled; it was a sad way to live your life but that was his choice.

'See, told you. Are you here for your guy?'

Ben replied, 'Yes. Has he been booked in already?'

Jo laughed. 'Mate, seriously, it's the busiest night we've had all month. Is it a full moon out there? I'm sorry but there are four more of these delightful guests in front of yours. As far as I know, he's parked up outside still in the van. It's going to be some time before he gets booked in. You might want to go home, grab a few hours and then come back nice and early. From what I've gathered, he's going to need a full forensic examination and a solicitor; it's going to take some time before you can interview him.'

Ben looked up at the huge clock on the wall behind the desk. It was almost midnight. They should have finished hours ago, but he clearly didn't want to just go home, not when there was a major crime scene.

'I'll ring you when he's ready to be interviewed – I promise.'

'At home, no matter what time it is?'

Jo leaned over, offering him her little finger. 'I pinkie promise.'

Ben stared down at her finger. It was Morgan who crossed her little finger over Jo's.

'If he doesn't answer, will you ring me?'

'Of course, Morgan.'

She smiled at Jo and turned to Ben. 'We may as well go and grab a couple of hours, get changed, eat something.'

He nodded. 'Thanks, Jo. See you soon.'

Once they were back in the main part of the station, Ben turned to her. 'Are we leaving the body where it is until the morning?'

She shrugged, knowing that he liked to make sure all the forensics had been thoroughly collected, photographed and searched. Yet he hated leaving bodies lying around for hours more than they needed to, preferring to get them safely to the mortuary. This crime scene had turned into a nightmare though, and she thought that it might be best.

'I think we should, then we can go and take another look first thing without all of the fuss and people. It all turned into a big mess; I know that Declan was happy to move her but I think it won't hurt to go back again.'

He nodded. 'You're right.'

He rubbed his hand across his forehead, the exhaustion so apparent, and she realised that he didn't look well; in fact his face was a grey colour that she'd never seen before. Even though she'd given him many causes to look a funny colour, it had never been this one, and suddenly a rising sensation of panic filled her insides.

'Are you feeling okay, Ben? You look...'

'I look what?'

Mads walked out of his office, catching Morgan's last sentence.

'You look like shit, Benno. What's up? If you're coming down with something, keep away from me. I'm going on holiday in three days.'

'Cheers, Mads.'

Morgan grabbed his sleeve and tugged him towards the car park.

Mads's voice shouted after them, 'Bloody hell, give the guy a chance, Brookes – you're wearing him out.'

She turned around and gave him the finger, which set him off laughing. then continued ushering Ben out to his car. He got in the passenger side, and she rushed around to the driver's side.

'I don't feel too good.'

'What's wrong? How do you feel?'

Her heart was racing. She began driving towards the huge security gates.

'Do you need to go to the hospital?'

He turned to look at her. 'No way, I just feel a bit like I'm going to pass out.'

'Low blood sugar – we need to get some food into you.'

'Yeah, probably.' He closed his eyes, leaning his head back against the leather headrest, and she drove as fast as she could to his house.

She helped him out of the car, and he smiled at her. 'I'm not going to die on you – I just need to eat something and have a lie-down. I have a terrible headache.'

'Okay, let me get you inside, then I'll come back out for the pizzas and warm them up.'

He didn't argue; he let her help him in, and she took him to the living room to the huge leather sofa that doubled as a bed whenever either of them couldn't sleep and didn't want to disturb the other. Ben kicked his shoes off, shrugged off his jacket and loosened his tie, threw them all on the chair, then flopped onto the sofa and closed his eyes.

Morgan rushed back out to the car for the pizzas and took them inside. She set the security system once the door was locked, took out some plates then set about ripping into pieces the pizzas that had looked so appetising earlier but now resembled congealed pieces of circular card. After warming a plateful up for Ben, she took it down to him. He was barely awake.

'Hey, just eat a slice to line your stomach.'

He opened one eye as he took the plate off her. 'Thanks, Morgan, you're too good to me.'

She laughed. 'If warming a slice of pizza up is making you that appreciative, I can't wait until I cook you a roast dinner.'

He grinned at her through a mouthful of pizza, chewing with his eyes closed.

'Why aren't you eating?'

'I'm going to – just checking you're okay.'

He gave her a thumbs up, and she realised that she should eat too or the pair of them wouldn't be any use to the investigation.

Leaving Ben to it, she went down to the kitchen and warmed up her own pizza, then sat at the table and tried to eat, but all she could think about was Emma's body lying on her kitchen floor in a pool of her own congealed blood.

After a couple of mouthfuls, she threw the rest in the bin.

She made sure the back door was locked, then went and double checked all of the windows. By the time she'd had a quick shower and put her pyjamas on, she went into the bedroom, expecting to see Ben in bed.

He wasn't.

She went back downstairs and saw his plate of half-eaten food on the coffee table. A soft snore escaped his lips. He was asleep on the sofa. He hadn't even finished undressing. Morgan wanted nothing more than to lie next to him, but she knew he needed sleep, so she grabbed the throw and gently covered him.

Leaving him to sleep, she went up to their bed, threw back the duvet and climbed onto his side, which smelled of his aftershave. She closed her eyes and was back in Emma's house, standing in front of her bedroom mirror. If it had been covered, she would have picked up on the connection sooner.

Morgan had felt a fear like no other when that dark shadow had passed the doorway. How on earth had Emma felt? She'd probably felt silly for ringing the police only to be standing in her kitchen and be attacked by a silent shadow that had crept down from her attic. Morgan shuddered. Where was Ben's loft hatch? She didn't know.

Reaching over, she turned on the bedside light and studied the ceiling. It wasn't in here. She turned the light back off and turned on her side, closing her eyes for around twenty seconds before she threw the covers off again and sat up.

She knew she was being stupid, but she was never going to

sleep if she didn't check his attic. What if these ones were all connected to each other and led down to the flats where Shirley Kelly had been murdered? That could explain how the killer got in and out without opening a window or the front door.

Ben was snoring much louder now, so she couldn't wake him up to help her.

Barefoot, she crept from room to room. He had five bedrooms; one was filled with all her stuff from her apartment. Her books were stacked in cardboard boxes, and what few possessions she cared about were all wrapped in bubble wrap in more boxes.

The hatch wasn't in here, which made her feel better. She had an image now of some bogeyman like Michael Myers hiding amongst her things waiting for the perfect moment to strike. It was at times like this she wished that her favourite reading material wasn't true crime or horror stories.

She crept into the other rooms, flicked the lights on and checked them but saw no loft hatches. Wondering where on earth it was, she realised there was one room left and the bathroom; she didn't remember seeing it in the bathroom and stuck her head inside. No, she was right – it wasn't. That left the last room: the one that used to be Ben and Cindy's bedroom.

She stared at the door and whispered, 'It would be in here. Sorry, Cindy, I'm just taking a quick peek.'

She grasped the handle and pushed it down, reaching in her hand first to press the light switch on and flood the room with light. Stepping inside, she looked up, and there it was.

It was a much bigger room than Emma's. She paused, looking around it. The bed was still there, a sheet of plastic thrown over it. There was also a wardrobe, which ran the full length of one wall, and two tall chests of drawers. She felt like an imposter, like she was in the wrong house.

There was a long stick thing with a hook on the end propped against the wall in the corner and she crossed over to it, grabbing it. For some reason, every nerve ending in her body felt as if it was on fire. She was scared to look but knew that if she didn't, she would never get to sleep. Besides, they had a suspect in custody; there wasn't going to be any dark shadow man lingering up there waiting for her.

An uncontrollable shiver went through her. She lifted the stick and caught the handle on the door. As she pulled it down, she hoped it wouldn't make a racket and wake Ben up.

It didn't – it opened smoothly, and the ladder that was part of it slid down effortlessly.

Morgan peered up into the darkness and whispered to herself, 'You have lost the plot, Brookes.' Still, she took hold of the ladder and began to climb upwards, her phone in her hand, the torch illuminating the way.

Near the top, she saw a pull string. She stepped into the attic, tugged the piece of string and the room lit up.

It was empty – or at least it looked as if was.

Letting out the hugest sigh of relief, she looked around the large space. It was full of boxes, a few suitcases; there was an old-fashioned pram wrapped in polythene, and she felt her breath catch in the back of her throat. Ben had said they'd never had any kids but it looked like Cindy had been pregnant at some point. She felt terrible, as if she was prying, but she couldn't stop herself.

Once she'd checked all the walls to make sure there were no hidden, secret doorways, she looked at the large suitcase nearest the pram. Kneeling down, she blew some of the dust off it and unzipped it. Inside were women's clothes, and she knew they must be Cindy's. There was a photograph album wrapped in a scarf too, and she pulled it out.

Sitting on the floor, she began to look at the wedding photos of Ben and his wife. They looked so young. Ben had a full head of hair; he was muscular and looked dashing in his top hat and tails. Cindy was beautiful – she looked radiant in her full, ballgown-style white wedding dress and glittering tiara. They made a handsome couple. Cindy had had honey-coloured hair, the bluest of eyes and a sun-kissed glow to her skin that was emphasised by the white dress. Morgan was the polar opposite of her with alabaster skin, freckles, green eyes and copper hair. She couldn't see any tattoos on Cindy, not like her – she had them on her thigh, forearms and the back of her neck.

She flicked through the photos, smiling at Ben's obvious discomfort at having so many pictures taken. He looked as if he was being forced to document the day when, really, he'd rather be getting drunk at the bar. That was the Ben she knew; he seemed a million miles away from the one squirming in these photographs.

Realising she didn't want him waking up and catching her snooping, Morgan put the photograph album back, but not before slipping her favourite photo of him and Cindy out. Then she zipped up the case and stood up, satisfied that there was no way anyone could sneak in and out of this attic.

Of course it didn't mean that the houses further down the street weren't connected – that was something they would need to check first thing.

There was a lot to do tomorrow, and as she began to climb down the ladder, a wave of tiredness hit her. She needed some sleep.

Struggling to push the ladder back into place, she gave it one last shove, and it crashed against the hatch. Morgan froze, wondering if she'd woken Ben, but the sound of his snores filtered up and she breathed a sigh of relief.

She tucked the photo into one of the boxes in the spare room. Not sure why – she just felt as if she needed to. Then she turned off the lights and got back into bed, this time turning out the light and closing her eyes, drifting off to sleep in a matter of seconds.

TWENTY-NINE

'Morning.'

Morgan opened one eye, groaning. 'It's not – it can't be. What time is it?'

'Quarter to six. Jo rang. We can go back – the solicitor is on the way.'

The side of the bed went down as he sat next to her. He reached out and stroked her hair. 'Sorry I never made it to bed. I don't know what came over me.'

She grabbed his hand; her eyes open now and fully awake, Morgan carefully studied Ben's face to see if he still looked as ashen as he had last night. It was hard to tell in the darkness.

'You were wiped out – don't worry about it. How are you feeling?'

'Better for some sleep; you're not mad I slept on the sofa?'

She shook her head. 'Well, only a little because you're like a nuclear thermostat with your body heat, which is nice in this cold weather, but no. Why would I be mad?'

He nodded. 'Cindy...' He stopped himself from talking, and she squeezed his hand.

'It's okay – you can talk about your life with Cindy to me.

I'm not going to freak out or feel all sorry for myself. I'm a big girl, and she was a big part of your life; you should be able to talk about it.'

He studied her face, and she smiled at him, nodding. 'So Cindy what?'

'She used to get so mad at me if I'd fall asleep downstairs, if I'd worked a late shift or been to the pub. I think she thought it was a reflection of how I felt about her, but it wasn't. Most of the time I did it so I didn't wake her up. Why should she suffer because of the long hours and occasional piss-up?'

'I suppose she couldn't bear to be parted from you, or...'

'Or what?'

She sucked in a breath, wondering if what she was about to say was too far, was pushing Ben too much, but he needed to know.

'Don't get angry with me, but maybe she was too needy and a bit of a control freak.'

He stared at her, and she instantly regretted those last words, but then he started laughing. 'Yeah, a bit. She was actually when you come to mention it. She liked everything to be done her way, and if it wasn't, my life wasn't worth living.'

'Yet you still loved her, and her loss is one you'll never get over, but it's also okay to move on and be happy. I love you more than anything, but personally if you get pissed as a fart and come get in bed to snore like a pig all night, well I'd rather you took the sofa. I think you're going to realise in time to come that I'm nothing like Cindy and she is nothing like me – we're two totally different people, and it's okay for you to love us both. I don't have a problem with that, Ben. All I care about is that you're not beating yourself up with guilt all the time.'

He didn't speak, reaching down and wrapping his arms around her. Pressing his lips on hers and kissing her with enough passion to make her eyes water. He smelled of mint and

Eau Sauvage; she wanted him more than anything, so she pushed him away.

'Too soppy for this early in the day, Matthews – we have a suspect to interview and a crime scene to process.'

He laughed.

She threw off the covers and jumped up. 'Back off, mister – I need to make myself presentable.'

As she walked past him to go to the bathroom, he grabbed her hand. 'You look sexy as hell in those little shorts and your hair falling over your shoulders.'

'Yeah, you won't be saying that when I'm leaving hair samples all over the crime scene.'

She pulled away and went to get ready. He went downstairs to make breakfast since today was going to be even longer than yesterday. They had an interview, and then they needed to get back to the crime scene and get Emma's body moved to the mortuary, so that Declan wasn't behind with the post-mortem.

When they were both in the car, after a quick breakfast of fried-egg sandwiches and with travel mugs of steaming coffee courtesy of Ben's fancy Nespresso machine, Morgan felt as if she was ready to face the day. Ben didn't look as grey, which was good, but she was still worried about him.

'Hey, I was thinking, shouldn't we go back to the scene and get Emma's body moved? If we don't, it's going to hold Declan up.'

'I was going to suggest that. I think so. We'll give it the once-over in the daylight and then get her moved.'

'Great minds and all that.'

When they turned into Fell Close, they found the street was deserted and much different to the chaos that had ensued last night. There was an unmarked police car at each end, parked in front of the cordon of blue-and-white police tape.

They got out, dressed in the paper suits, gloved up and walked towards the officer in the car, who had his head down.

'Is he asleep?'

'No, I think he's on his phone.'

Ben knocked on the window, and the officer jolted violently, opening his eyes. Ben arched an eyebrow at Morgan. The window went down.

'Sorry, was just closing my eyes for a second. I wasn't asleep.'

'Is the house locked up? Have you got keys?'

The red-faced officer reached down and plucked off a key ring that was looped around his radio antenna, then passed it to Ben.

'I think it's going to be released soon anyway.'

Morgan glanced at Ben. There was no mistaking the two small splotches of red that were growing on his cheeks, signalling he was getting angry.

'Said who?'

'The DCI when he came to take a look around earlier and get the body moved – he said we probably wouldn't be here much longer.'

'What, which DCI?'

'That new one. He was here an hour ago with a CSI from Barrow. They were inside for some time and then he gave the undertaker the okay to move the body. You just missed it – they only left about ten minutes ago.'

Ben turned away, taking huge strides towards the house. Morgan looked at the officer, muttered, 'Thanks,' then followed Ben towards Emma's front door. He opened it and they both stepped inside.

She closed it behind them and whispered, 'I can't believe he's done that.'

Ben was so angry he didn't even speak. He walked through

to the kitchen; there was a bloody outline where Emma's body had lain.

He turned to Morgan. 'What the hell is he playing at? This isn't his decision alone. I wanted to take one last look and make sure I was happy with her being moved, because last night was such a total fuck-up.'

'Maybe he thought he was being helpful.'

He glared at her. 'How? By coming in and taking over without so much as discussing it with the team first? I would have phoned him before making the final decision to move the body. I wouldn't have thought that it was acceptable to just do it without consulting him.'

'What are you going to do? I want to check around before we leave and make sure Emma didn't have a diary or journal somewhere that may be helpful.'

Ben had his phone out and was already scrolling for a number to ring. 'Yeah, help yourself.'

She slipped away, leaving Ben and his rolling waves of anger to his phone call. She ran back upstairs, checking the spare room first to see the loft hatch was closed and a ring of black fingerprint powder around the edges of it. There was no ladder in sight, and no chance of anyone coming out of the attic whilst she was up here without her hearing them.

She checked the boxes, which were taped up and not the place you would keep a diary unless you could be bothered to cut through the packing tape then reseal it every time. There was a chest of drawers, and she pulled each one open; they were empty apart from some odd socks and sanitary towels. This left Emma's bedroom; she went back to where she'd left it last night.

Standing in front of the drawers, she didn't look in the mirror, because even though she knew that the guy from last night was safely in custody, she still felt a coldness seeping through her bones at the emptiness and sadness that now filled this house. It was as if the walls had soaked in the horror that had happened last night, and it was always going to feel an unsafe, scary place instead of a warm, loving home. She wondered if the next person to live here would pick up on these vibes or was that just her? Did her old apartment give off similar vibes after all the horrific incidents that had happened there? She'd almost died but been saved. Poor Emma hadn't been so lucky.

She bent down and looked underneath the bed. Through the carpet, she could hear Ben's muffled voice, and she knew he was raging; privately she thought he had every right to be. Marc had crossed the line by not conferring with him before moving Emma's body.

There was a small, pink, flowery box beneath the bed and a pair of slippers. She tugged the box out.

Sitting cross-legged on the floor, she lifted the lid and peered inside to see a stack of photographs and a black notebook with a quote on it in gold lettering that read: 'She Believed She Could And She Did'. Feeling sad for Emma and the life she'd been living, Morgan picked up the photographs and began to flick through them.

They were of a much younger Emma; she was dressed in what looked like a uniform: black trousers, black shirt, hair in a neat bun. She looked young, in her late teens, early twenties maybe. In the background, there was a blurry house that looked huge. There were photos of her outside with a couple of older women and two men. They all looked very serious and sombre, but there was one where the photographer must have said something that made them laugh, because they were all far more natural and had broad smiles on their faces.

The other photos were of an older couple standing with who she assumed was a very young Emma: her parents. Then a few school photos, but none of Emma with a partner. She kept the ones of her outside the house to one side, then opened the notebook and felt her heart tear in two.

On the first page was a heading 'Bucket List'; she scanned through it and felt sad that Emma had only managed to tick a few of the items off her list. There wasn't much in the book: a few notes jotted down, no diary entries.

She placed the book back inside the box, pushed it back underneath the bed and went downstairs with the photographs that she'd kept to one side.

Ben was in a deep discussion with someone, so Morgan went outside, stripped off the white suit and gloves, then crossed the road to knock on Paula's door.

It was opened by a sleepy teenage girl; her ruffled hair and smudged mascara made her look as if she'd been on a wild night out.

'Hi, Ashley. Is your mum in?'

She nodded, opening the door for her to step inside. Morgan did and followed her into the living room, where Paula was lying on the sofa, the television on mute.

'Well, it's not even seven o'clock – are you here to tell me that it was all some kind of mistake and that Emma is alive and well?'

Morgan sank down onto the cream leather armchair. 'Unfortunately not.'

'Well, is it true you caught the sick bastard that did it? And was it that bloody little weirdo, Danny, from a few doors down?'

'We did arrest a suspect last night, but I'm not at liberty to give you any further details just yet.'

'According to Jen next door, he was marched out of Emma's house in handcuffs and thrown into a van. I bet you weren't giving him a lift to The Dirty Duck, were you?'

'We haven't interviewed him yet so it's difficult to say.' She passed the two photos over to her. 'Do you know where this is or when they were taken?'

'Bloody hell, that's a few years ago – look how young she is there, bless her. I'm not sure. She mentioned she was a house-keeper at one of the big, posh houses when she left school, until the old lady who lived there went into a home, but I couldn't tell you where. I bet if you ask around, someone will recognise it.'

'Thanks. Did Emma have a thing with Danny?'

'No, she's been single for a while after Mick. The only offers she had were from Danny; he goes to the bakery all the time, buys the cheapest thing possible and asks her out.'

Morgan sat forward. 'Did she mention if she thought he was stalking her?'

'God, no, nothing like that. I don't think he's stalking mater-ial, although if you found the little creep in her house, I could be completely wrong. Emma felt sorry for him. She thought he was okay, maybe a bit lonely like her.'

'Then why didn't she want to go out with him, if they were both lonely and seemed to like each other?'

''Cause he was a lot younger than her and she decided that she wasn't into men, told me that deep down she never really had been, was going through the motions but the feelings weren't there, and can't say I blame her; they're a pain in the arse.'

'Not all of them are.'

Paula sat up. 'You're in love. Well whoever he is, I hope he treats you right and doesn't break your heart.'

She smiled. 'Thanks, me too.' Morgan declined to tell her about the run-ins she'd had with various members of the oppo-site sex.

'What about her parents? How can we get hold of them?'

'You can't – they're both in a home in Barrow with advanced dementia. She didn't even bother to visit because it broke her heart that they didn't even know who she was. She was on her own and having a run of bad luck – that's why I tried to help her as much as

I could. Things were a bit tough for her, but it was just a rough patch. I told her it would get better, that it always does. She just had to hang on to see it through. What I didn't expect was some sick arsehole to come and bloody kill her. What kind of justice is that? She didn't deserve to die like that on her own and scared.'

Paula began to cry, sobbing into the sleeve of her dressing gown.

'It's not bloody fair. I can't stop thinking about what she must have felt when she saw him. Did she die straight away, or did he leave her there dying on her own?'

The lump in the back of Morgan's throat made it hard to swallow. 'She didn't die alone. Cain, the officer, held her waiting for an ambulance.'

A loud howl came from Paula, and Morgan moved to sit next to her, wrapping an arm around her. 'He's a good guy. He's devastated about what happened.'

She sniffed. 'Is that the guy we were laughing about? Did he come when she rang?'

Morgan nodded.

'I said to her I wish he'd strip-search me. He's a bit of all right for a copper. Please tell him thank you from me for doing that – it means a lot.'

'I will. If you think of anything, can you phone me?' Taking her notebook out, Morgan wrote her phone number down on one of the Post-it notes she kept inside, tugged the note out and passed it to her, then stood up.

'I'm sorry for your loss, Paula.'

She left Paula sobbing in her living room, and Ashley crying on the stairs, feeling like a piece of crap and went back to Ben, who was sitting in his car waiting for her.

'Are you okay?'

He shook his head. 'No, I'm bloody furious at him and his audacity.'

'Who were you on the phone to?'

'Tom. I rang him to ask if he thought that it was acceptable for him to come in and do that.'

She knew that he must be really upset to bother Tom at home so early when he'd retired. 'What did he say?'

'That the guy's an arse, and even though he has jurisdiction to do that, he should have spoken to me first, not gone above my head. Let's go find him.'

Ben set off in the direction of the station, and Morgan hoped that this wasn't about to blow up in everyone's face, because they still had Daniel Walker to interview before driving to Lancaster for the post-mortem.

THIRTY

1989

He waited for his grandmother to come and punish him, after four hours of lying on his bed reading a copy of Stephen King's *The Dark Half* that he'd helped himself to from the teacher's desk one break time. She'd left it there underneath a sheaf of loose papers, so he'd picked it up when no one was around, pushing it into his bag underneath the PE kit he hated wearing.

He had closed his eyes for a moment. Now he was awake, and his room was full of shadows. His curtains were still open, showing him the night sky was a black void; he couldn't even see a single star, never mind the moon. He couldn't hear the familiar ticking of the ancient grandfather clock out in the hallway, which was strange because it had never been this silent before.

He sat up, scrubbed at his eyes with the sleeve of his jumper and realised he hadn't even swapped his clothes for pyjamas. Standing up, he crossed to the window, staring out onto the gardens that stretched down to the lake. Where was everyone and how come no one had come looking for him after his outburst at school? Well, after his complete meltdown more like. He hadn't meant to hurt that girl – or had he? He couldn't be sure about any of it because the anger had burned through him like a bright, white light, all hot and fuzzy.

He changed out of his clothes into his pyjamas but kept on his socks; the floors in this house were all made of wood and cold to the touch.

He had expected his door to be locked from the outside, but the knob had turned easily, and it opened without a fuss.

There was a small lamp burning on the table at the other end of the hallway near to his grandmother's bedroom chamber. Her rooms were off limits – pretty much everything in this house was off limits. The word crypt echoed inside his mind – wasn't that what the kids had called it? Whatever it was, there were a lot of locked rooms that he didn't have access to, and he didn't know why because there wasn't much in any of them. One day, he'd stolen a master key from Emmie, when she had gone inside the empty room next to his grandmother's and carelessly left it in the lock for anyone to take. He had hidden it well; in his bedroom there was a gap between the windowsill and its casing, and he had put pieces of card in to line it, and it was where he stashed all the small objects he wasn't allowed to have.

He thought back to that day.

Emmie had been furious with him and ran down the stairs as if her hair was on fire to find him. He had been in the library perched on an armchair, a copy of *Oliver Twist* open in his hands.

'Give it back, you little thief.'

He'd given her his best, bemused, *I don't know what you're talking about* look. 'Give what back?'

'You know fine well, you little sod.'

He'd shrugged. 'Sorry, but I don't know at all.'

She'd stepped into the room, closing the door behind her, and looked quite convincingly menacing.

He'd almost been scared – almost.

She'd hissed, 'You've taken the master key, so give it back or I'll get in big trouble.'

He'd shaken his head, then shrugged for good measure. 'I don't know what key you're on about. You probably dropped it. Don't come in here blaming me.'

'Empty your pockets – now.'

He'd rolled his eyes at her, insinuating that she was crazy, but stood up and pulled out the pockets of his trousers, waving the white cotton lining at her.

'You've hidden it.'

'I have not. Now stop bothering me and go do some work. It's not my fault you can't manage to remember where you put stuff.'

It had been difficult not to smirk at her small white hands that were curled into tight fists, and he'd wondered if she would actually have the nerve to hit him. She could try but he wouldn't let her get away with it. His mum had always said to hit someone back if they hit you and it didn't matter if they were a boy or a girl.

She'd stormed out of the library, slamming the door behind her, her footsteps echoing straight down to the kitchen, where she would go and talk about him to Cook. He didn't care. He now had the key and could go anywhere he wanted. No more locked doors for him, and hopefully she'd get sacked for losing it.

That had been over a month ago. She hadn't got sacked, but she had been made to go into the village and get a new one cut out of her own money. He'd wandered around smiling whenever he thought about that, and once everyone was in bed, he'd taken to exploring every room in the house. If he was living here, he deserved to know what was behind all those locked doors.

The reality had been not a lot though. He'd found one room

that must have belonged to his mum because it was painted pink, with lots of white furniture. There was a canopy of sheer lilac material over the bed that still had lots of stuffed teddy bears and dolls sitting on it. Why hadn't she just come home with him when things had got hard and there had been no money for food or heating? He didn't understand. This house was big enough for ten people to live in, yet his gran was wandering around on her own like one of those lonely ghosts out of a Dickens story. Next time he saw his mum, he was going to ask her— no, tell her she should come back.

His feet glided effortlessly across the polished floors, and he slipped down the staircase at the back of the hallway. It was easier to come up and down this one without being seen than using the grand, sweeping one in the main entrance. He half expected to bump into Emmie or Cook, but he wasn't sure what time it was: the grandfather clock had stopped working at six. It must be way past that by now though.

He made his way into the library, where there was a large pendulum clock on the wall, and flicked on the light. How could this be? This one wasn't ticking either and the time was set to six.

He turned off the light and made his way into each downstairs room, checking the mantle clocks and various wall clocks, but every one read six. This was weird. Had there been some kind of magnetic pulse that had wiped all the power out of them at the same time? Maybe the aliens had finally come and taken everyone away, like some sci-fi movie. He didn't know. The only room with a modern clock was the parlour at the front of the house.

He crept on towards it. When he tried to turn the knob, he found it wouldn't move – it was locked.

He stepped away. This was strange. This room had never been locked since he'd come to live here.

Intent on finding out what time it was, and the reason he'd

been locked out of this room, he took the master key from the piece of string around his neck. Taking a quick look around to make sure no one was watching him, he pushed it into the lock, opening the door enough so he could slip through it, then closing it softly behind him.

THIRTY-ONE

Ben strode into the station on a mission. Morgan was torn between following him or lagging behind. Marc was out of order and she fully stood by Ben, but she hated confrontation of this kind. God knows she'd been through enough the last couple of years herself. She wasn't, however, a coward and sprinted after Ben, who was already inside, the back door to the station slamming hard behind him in the wind. She swiped her card, pushed the door open and headed towards the stairs and Tom's office, where she assumed Ben was heading. Cain was walking out of the kitchen area with a mug of something hot in his hands. He took one look at her, put the mug on the countertop and rushed to catch up with her.

'What's happening?'

'Ben's going to lose his shit with the new boss.'

'Why?'

She didn't get to answer, as the sound of raised voices filtered down the remaining stairs. She took the last few two at a time and came face to face with Ben, who was standing opposite Marc.

Cain muttered, 'Oh crap.' And in a couple of strides managed to push himself between the two men.

'What's the problem, Ben? Why are you so mad?'

'You released the body from the crime scene without even speaking to me first. I was going back to take another look.'

'I thought I was helping; I couldn't sleep so I got dressed and decided to get the on-call CSI to come back with me to take another look without everyone milling around as if they were waiting for a bus.'

'Yeah, well that's exactly what I intended to do, but you screwed that up.'

Marc held up his hands. 'I'm sorry, I had no idea. I wasn't trying to go behind anyone's back; I wanted to help, make a good first impression. It looks as if I couldn't have made a worse one if I tried. I'm your boss so ultimately, it's my call, but I guess I should have consulted you first – that would have been the right thing to do.'

Cain looked at Ben. 'You don't want to be taking this outside, do you, because I'm kind of sick of everyone's bullshit at the moment, no disrespect to you both.'

They answered at the same time. 'None taken.'

Ben shook his head, and Morgan could see he was biting his tongue because he *was* his boss, but they worked as a team. He didn't want him turning it into a one-man show to get brownie points. He turned and walked down to his office, leaving Cain, Marc and Morgan all staring at each other.

Marc lowered his voice. 'I really am sorry.'

Cain shrugged. 'You want a bit of friendly advice, boss? I suggest you run your great ideas through Ben and the team. They work hard, have solved more major cases than Vera and if, God forbid, I end up dead, I'd want them working my case. You're the new boy – it's kind of rude to jump in and take over like that.'

Morgan turned away, her cheeks pink with the compliments, to hide the smile that was threatening to fill her face.

'Thank you... Cain, isn't it?'

He nodded.

'I'll remember that. Like I said, I wasn't trying to step on anyone's toes. I'm just trying to keep up to date with any leads and on top of the investigation, so I'd appreciate it if everything was shared with me.' He glanced at Morgan, then turned and went back inside his office, closing the door behind him.

'That was close. How come Benno was that wound up?'

'Tired, stressed, worried about living up to his expectations, I don't know.'

'How about you? Are you wanting to pick a fight with anyone before I try and take five minutes to drink my now cold coffee?'

Her laughter filled the air. 'No, I'm good, thanks. How are you, Cain?'

He lowered his voice. 'I've been better. I couldn't sleep. I kept reliving finding her on the floor like that – you know how it is. Everything you've been through, yet you're still here ready to fight another day. It's not easy, is it?'

She shook her head. 'No, it's horrible, but you did what you could, and her friend Paula said to thank you for being there with her at the end.'

Moisture glistened in the corners of his eyes, and he blinked, nodding.

She gave him a quick hug and made to leave him at the top of the stairs, only to hear Amy shout up, 'What the bloody hell have I missed now?'

Morgan peered over the balcony as she waited for her to get to her level. 'Nothing much apart from Ben wanting to deck him.' Morgan pointed towards the office where Marc was on the phone.

'Crap. A couple of days off and you two are running around causing even more havoc than usual.'

The lift pinged at the end of the corridor and Des stepped out. 'What's this, a team meeting on the hop?'

He headed towards them both, glancing into Tom's office to see Marc leaning against the glass, the phone clamped between his ear and shoulder.

'Who's that?'

'Tom's replacement.'

Morgan headed down towards their office, not wanting to stand around gossiping when he was in hearing distance.

Des looked at Amy, who shrugged. 'Don't ask me, Desmondo – I've been ill.'

'I hate it when you call me that.'

She smiled at him. 'I know you do, but it's your nickname.'

'Sod off, Amy. I'm not your pet chihuahua.'

'Nah, you're too ugly.'

She dashed away from him before he could say or do anything, and followed Morgan.

Ben was inside his office. The rest of them took their seats outside.

'So, what's happening?' Amy asked. 'I saw the news this morning – it said a woman had been found murdered in her own home an hour after officers had attended, and it was being investigated by the Independent Police Complaints Commission, but there was a suspect in custody.'

'Read the log for the full update, but yes, Cain and Amber attended a report of an intruder in her house,' Morgan replied. 'They did a full search, didn't find anyone, but when Cain decided to go back and check on her, he found her bleeding to death on the kitchen floor with her throat slashed.'

'Jesus.'

'It was horrific. Poor Cain, he held her waiting for an ambulance, but she died in his arms.'

'What's he doing in work? He should be at home.'

Morgan shrugged. 'Probably had to come in to speak to the IPCC and to give his statements. He looks awful though, bless him.'

'Who looks awful?' Ben appeared at his office door with a clipboard in his hand.

'Cain.'

'Right then, Morgan, let's go interview the creep downstairs. Amy, Des, it's great to see you both in so early. Are you here for a particular reason? I hope it's not so you can get a flyer and leave early, because quite honestly, you'll wish you'd come in later. We have two murder investigations running and there's a lot to do.'

Des looked away; Amy shook her head. 'I can't speak for him, but I saw the news and figured you could do with me here to help out.'

'How's your cold?'

'I'll live. We can go and start the house-to-house and CCTV enquiries down at Fell Close if you want.'

'That would be amazing, thank you.'

Morgan smiled at Ben. 'I spoke to Emma's friend, Paula, who lives opposite her at twenty-two, before we came here. She'll give a full statement about what happened when Emma rang the first time. She's a bit hungover and very upset about it all, but her bark is worse than her bite. She's nice and had a terrible shock.'

'I'll go speak to her then. Des can carry on with the door knocking.'

Ben was already on his way down to the custody suite. Morgan followed him down.

· · ·

They waited patiently for the door to be unlocked. Jo was putting her coat on as they were let inside.

'What a night. Your guy was clean by the way. Nothing of forensic value – no blood spatters on his clothes, hands or body. No hidden weapon. All the intimate samples and DNA have been taken and are ready to be sent off, but if he slashed the victim's throat, I would have expected them to find traces of blood on him somewhere. I mean he should have been covered. He's waiting for you in interview room A with his brief.'

Ben sighed. 'Thanks. Maybe he had time to shower before we turned up. Task force will tear his house apart this morning and see if they can find anything. Has he said anything?'

'Plenty – mostly that he hasn't done it. He liked her. Why would he kill someone he liked? Over and over to anyone who'd listen. I hate to tell you this, Ben, but, in my humble opinion, I don't think he's your guy.'

'He was caught sneaking around in her house whilst she was dead on the floor, and we were inside it.'

'Morbid curiosity. Or maybe he's just fucking stupid, either one, but I don't think he's a killer.'

'Cheers, Jo.'

She lifted a hand and waved, then disappeared into the back office.

Morgan didn't dare look at Ben. She knew he was pinning his hope on Daniel being the guy, and she wasn't so sure that he was.

THIRTY-TWO

Before Ben opened the door to the interview room, he whispered, 'We need to tie him to Shirley Kelly.'

Morgan nodded. 'We can try.'

He opened the door and she followed him inside, where Daniel was sitting in a pair of grey jogging pants with a matching sweatshirt. His face washed out, his eyes wide, he looked small and scared. His solicitor was next to him, sipping on a cup of coffee from the vending machine. She nodded at them both. They sat opposite them, and Ben placed the file he'd been holding on the table.

'Morning. Should we get to it? I'm sure you want this over with as quickly as possible. Is there anything you need before we start?'

Daniel shook his head.

Ben leaned across and pressed record on the audio system and also the camera which would record everything.

'For the purpose of the tape, this interview commenced at seven forty-one. I'm Detective Sergeant Ben Matthews and this is my colleague, Detective Constable Morgan Brookes. Also present is the duty solicitor.' Ben smiled at her.

'Lucy O'Gara, Rose and Dunning Solicitors,' she supplied.

Ben nodded and continued. 'Could you give me your full name and date of birth?'

'Danny Walker – Daniel Walker – thirteenth of May 1995.'

'Danny, how well did you know Emma Dixon?'

He glanced at his solicitor, who nodded. 'I, erm, she's my neighbour and works in the bakery up town.'

'Were you friends with Emma?'

'Yes, well, I spoke to her every day.'

'On the phone, messaging, in person?'

Daniel was caught between looking down at his hands that he was wringing underneath the table and at the door. Morgan knew he wanted this to be over, and she felt a little bit sorry for him even though he'd scared the shit out of her last night.

'At the bakery. I go in for a pie or sandwich most days.'

'How often have you been inside Emma's house?'

'I haven't – well, until last night.'

'So all the hundreds of samples that were collected and sent off for forensic testing won't place you there. Apart from last night?'

He shook his head from side to side.

Ben leaned forward, resting his elbows on the table. 'Why were you there last night? Creeping around in a crime scene when you had no permission to be there?'

His face, which had been redder than Morgan's hair, drained of all the colour and he looked to his solicitor, who spoke. 'My client wants to help you find the person who killed the victim, but he maintains his innocence.'

Ben looked at her. 'Then he can tell us why he was creeping around a crime scene.'

She looked at Daniel. 'Tell them what you told me.'

'I...' He gulped. 'I'm sorry, I don't know what came over me. I really *like*-liked Emma. You know how it is when you fancy someone. I saw the cops crawling all over her house and panicked. I denied knowing her. I don't know why – I guess I was scared this would happen but it did anyway, so I should have told the truth. Then when you came and told me the attics joined together, I wanted to check it out for myself, and I wanted to make sure Emma was okay. I didn't want to believe that it might be her that was dead.'

'Did you kill her?'

'No. I keep telling everyone: I liked her – I wouldn't hurt her. I'm not sick in the head.'

Morgan spoke. 'I'm sorry for your loss, Danny – it must have been a terrible shock for you. I can't imagine how awful it would be to find out the person you really like has been murdered.'

He looked at her, his eyes watering.

'All we want to do is to find out who did this, who thought they had the right to go into Emma's house and kill her. Did you ever fall out with her? Did she ever tell you to stop bothering her at the bakery?'

'No, we used to have a laugh, and she was never horrible to me.'

'Did Emma have a boyfriend? Anyone who used to go around to her house that you know of?'

'I think she had a bit of an on-off boyfriend, but she'd finished with him some time ago. She told me she was off men for the foreseeable.'

'How did that make you feel? Were you upset about this?'

'Well, I was a bit gutted, but it didn't mean she'd never say yes, did it?'

There was a loud knock on the door, and Cain stuck his head through. 'Sorry to interrupt. Can I have a word, boss?'

Ben glared at him, but Cain was nodding, so Ben stood up.

'Interview stopped at seven fifty. Sergeant Matthews is leaving the room.'

Ben went outside.

A minute later he opened the door. 'Morgan.'

She smiled at Daniel then went outside to where Cain was leaning against the wall. 'What's going on?'

'He's not your man. Amy rang to say she spoke to the woman four doors down from Emma's house as she was on her way out of the house to take her kid to breakfast club. The kid spoke to a man last night on the street when everyone had been told to leave their houses. He said he came out of the empty house, and he asked him his name.'

'What was it?'

'He told the kid he was the bogeyman and if he told anyone, he'd come back to take him away. Poor kid spent all night cowering in his mum's bed too scared to say anything, then started crying this morning when she told him to get ready for school.'

'Christ, did she ask him what he looked like or if he knew him?'

'According to the kid, it wasn't anyone he'd ever seen before.'

Morgan looked at Cain. 'It was dark – would he recognise Danny in the dark?'

Cain held up his hands. 'I'm just the messenger – you need to speak to Amy. She's talked the mum into going back inside the house. They're waiting for you to go and speak to them.'

'Morgan, can you go speak to the kid? I'll finish up here – ask him about Shirley Kelly.'

'Of course.'

Ben went back into the interview room, and she followed Cain out of the custody suite and into the main part of the station.

'Thanks, Cain. Are you heading home now?'

'Soon – I'm just waiting for someone from the IPCC to come and speak to me.'

'You did everything you could. You went above and beyond the call of duty,' she reminded him.

A dark shadow crossed his face and his expression flickered between sorrow and anger. 'Yeah, I thought I had, Morgan. I thought she was overreacting. It sounded so stupid that her cheese was on the wrong shelf.'

'The cheese – she said it had been moved. Did Wendy bag it up, do you know?'

He shrugged. 'I'd assume so, but it all got a little bit crazy, didn't it? I don't think I'll ever forget the look of fear in her eyes as she lay there dying on my lap, Morgan. It's etched there forever. If I get my hands on whoever did this...'

'I know. I'm sorry, Cain.'

'Thanks. Better not let anyone see me losing my shit, eh? Hey, is Ben going to smack the new DCI or what?'

'I think not.'

'Boring. Let me know how you get on with the kid.'

He walked away back to the report-writing room to wait for the next round of questions to be fired at him for doing his job.

Morgan left her car by the police car guarding the entrance to the street and phoned Amy. 'Hi, what number are you?'

'Eighteen – the door's unlocked.'

As she hurried down towards the house, she glanced at the empty house which was directly next to Daniel's. Assuming the killer wasn't Daniel, and they'd used the empty house, they would have had to cross through Daniel's attic, then through three more to get to Emma's.

She shivered – the thought of someone being able to come and go above as they pleased scared her. Passing through people's houses like some kind of ghost that could walk through walls, and he could – he 'd walked through them literally because of those stupid half doors that someone had deemed a great idea when they'd built the houses. What kind of person would even come up with such a way to move around?

She knocked on the door and pushed it open, wondering if it was a good idea to be leaving doors unlocked with a killer still out there.

'Hello, it's me, Morgan.'

'In the living room.'

There was the tiniest hallway with a door that led into the living room. It was the exact same layout as Emma's house, only it smelled of clean laundry. Opening the door, she saw Amy sitting on a sofa next to a small boy, who looked around seven or eight. His mum was in the process of spreading washing out on a clothes maid.

Amy smiled.

'This is my colleague, Morgan; this is Cara and Bailey. Bailey, can you tell Morgan what you told me about the strange guy last night?'

The blonde boy looked Morgan up and down, staring at her Doc Marten boots, rolled-up, slightly ripped jeans, and her eyes, taking in her winged eyeliner. Then he nodded.

'Are you a copper like her? You don't look like one.'

'Bailey, don't be so rude.' His mum glared at him. 'Sorry, I don't know where he gets this from, probably his dad. He doesn't have a good word to say about anyone.'

Amy laughed. 'That's okay. She doesn't, does she, Bailey? Morgan is a bit of a rebel when it comes to her dress code.'

He glanced back at her. 'You look like someone out of *The Matrix*.'

'How would you know about that film, Bailey? I bet your bloody dad has been letting you watch it.'

Morgan stepped in, before Bailey and his mum could start arguing about TV. 'Thanks. It's a compliment, don't worry – I'll take it. So, Bailey, I need to know what you saw last night. Do you think you can tell me what you told Amy?'

He looked at his mum, who smiled at him gently. 'It's okay, you need to tell them what you told me. They're here to protect us – they won't let anything bad happen.'

Morgan sucked in her breath at Cara's words because, yes, they were here to serve and protect the people, but how did you protect them from an unknown threat who had the foresight to sneak around like this killer had? The responsibility weighed heavy on her shoulders, and she found her legs feeling weak, so sat down on the chair, wondering what she was supposed to tell them. That she couldn't guarantee their safety, that they may have to move out to a strange place no one knew about, where they could at least give it their best shot to keep them alive.

'I saw a stranger come out of the empty house; he was standing next to us, but not with us.'

'How did you know he was a stranger? It was dark and there were a lot of people in the street last night.'

He rolled his eyes at Morgan as if to say *are you for real?* 'I'm seven, I'm not stupid. I see everyone in this street every day. Emma goes to work in the cake shop; Paula stays at home – she's always decorating; Ashley goes to school but sometimes she doesn't and hangs around in the little park with her friends, but Paula doesn't know because she never walks past it.'

'What about the man who lives next to the empty house?'

'Danny?'

She nodded. 'Yeah, Danny, do you know him?'

'Yeah, of course I do. He always waves and he plays *Fortnite* and *Call of Duty*, spends all his money in the cake shop. I think he likes Emma and that's why he goes in there, but I don't think she likes him, because he never goes to her house just the shop.'

His mum was watching him, mouth open, eyes wide. 'How do you know all this?'

'I'm a kid – I play out in the street, I see things, and Danny always has a paper bag with the cake-shop picture on the front of it.'

Amy sniggered. 'He's good. What do you want to be when you grow up? We could do with someone like you.'

'Urgh, I'm not being a copper. I want to be a fireman or racing-car driver.'

'Bailey, stop it with the cheek.'

Morgan didn't quite know what to say. 'Can you tell me about the guy you spoke to last night? Are you sure he wasn't from the street?'

Bailey crossed his arms. 'Yes, I haven't seen him before. He was all dressed in black; he had a baseball cap on, and he smelled funny.'

'Like what?'

'Soil. You know when you dig the garden up to bury your toy soldiers and the ground is a bit wet? Like that.'

Morgan knew that as well as soil he was also describing the earthy, metallic, rusty smell of blood. She felt a tingling sensation crawl up her spine.

'What did he say to you?'

'He was hanging around, but he didn't belong here. He looked as if he was trying to hide. I asked him his name.' He stopped talking and glanced at his mum.

'It's okay – tell Morgan.'

'He said he was the bogeyman and if I told anyone I'd seen him, he'd come back and take me away.' His voice broke at the last part of the sentence, and his mum came and sat next to him, putting her arm around his shoulders.

'It's okay, Bailey, we won't let him take you away. He was trying to scare you, but you've done the right thing. We needed to know this; we need to try to find this man – for Emma, so thank you. Did you see where he went? Did he stay in the street and go to the community centre with everyone else?'

Morgan was thinking about Daniel. He had; in fact, he'd been the last man to leave the centre before being escorted home by Ben and Al.

His head shook from side to side. 'No, he walked across the street and disappeared into the back.'

'Would you know him if you saw him again?'

The boy shrugged. 'It was dark. Maybe. I suppose. I know it wasn't Danny though.'

'Can you show me which way he went?'

Bailey stood up, crossed to the window and pointed across the road to the end house next to Paula's.

The hairs on the back of Morgan's neck stood on end as she looked down at Bailey. 'Are you sure it was a man? It couldn't have been a teenage boy, or a girl dressed to look like a man?'

'I think he was a man; I'm pretty sure he was.'

'Okay, thank you. That's great, Bailey – you've been a big help.'

Amy was busy writing down everything he'd said word for word in her notebook. She looked at Bailey. 'Hey, show me how you play that game again.'

He grinned at her and began explaining the rules of *Fortnite* to her. Morgan beckoned to his mum, and they went into the kitchen.

'I don't think that this person would come back, but do you have anywhere you could stay for a week or so, away from this street? Just until we've apprehended him.'

'I suppose we could go and stay at my mum's in Kendal. Do you think it's really necessary though?'

Morgan thought about someone creeping through the attics of these houses whilst everyone was asleep, and being brazen enough to sneak into Emma's house and kill her violently in cold blood.

'Yes, I really do. We don't know what this person is capable of, and I don't want to put you or Bailey at risk. If you don't have anywhere, we can arrange something temporary for you.'

'No, it's fine – my mum would love to have us. But you're scaring me. I thought Bailey was telling tales this morning to get out of going to breakfast club. He hates it – but when he said the guy was called the bogeyman, it freaked me out.'

'We'll have someone watching your house, and we'll wait here whilst you pack some things. I know it's a lot to ask, but I'd rather make sure you're both safe. We can have someone keep an eye on your mum's house as well, and we'll put an alert on the address so if you had to ring the police, it would be treated as an emergency and officers would be there in minutes.'

'Christ, this isn't making me feel any better. You're scaring the crap out of me.'

'Sorry, but we can't take any chances. I'd rather you were fully aware of the situation.'

She nodded. 'I'll go grab some stuff.'

Cara turned to rush upstairs and Morgan followed her. She couldn't get rid of the feeling that she was being watched. That somehow this monster was watching the street and everyone in it.

THIRTY-THREE

Des had agreed that he and Amy would follow Cara to her mum's house in Kendal to make sure no one else did. They drove out of the street first, waiting around the corner for Cara's Citroen C3 to leave.

Morgan left the house at the same time as Cara and Bailey. She watched her throw a couple of backpacks of their belongings into the boot of the car, no suitcases; she had told her not to make it too obvious they were leaving. Then she'd watched them drive off. Bailey had turned to glance back with his toothless grin, and Morgan had returned the smile.

She took out her phone and rang Ben. He didn't pick up.

So she rang Cain, who did. She'd had a feeling he would decide to stick around after the IPCC interview.

'Can't leave me alone today, can you?'

She smiled. 'No, I really can't. Are you busy? Can you go tell Ben he needs to ring me right away?'

'For you I will. Anyone else I'd say no.'

'Thanks, Cain.' She hung up wondering how long it would take him to get to Ben.

She caught movement from the corner of her eye. Glancing

across at Paula's house, she realised someone was watching her from the upstairs window: as she'd looked up, they'd stepped back. Unsure whether it was Paula or Ashley, she waved to let them know she'd seen them. There was a quiet hush over the street, giving it a strange atmosphere. These streets were usually busy. People in and out, cars, people walking dogs; this morning it seemed as if the whole street was in mourning.

She walked across to the house where Bailey had pointed and stopped – better to let the dog try and track whoever this was instead of her stomping all over the scene.

Her phone rang, making her jump, and she realised this case was making her nervous in a way she hadn't felt before.

It was Ben. *'What have you got, Morgan?'*

'A seven-year-old star witness who spoke to our guy on the street last night before he slipped away down the back on the opposite side. He said he knows Danny and it wasn't him.'

'Christ.'

'Sorry, can you get a dog to come and try to pick up the scent and find where he went?'

'Yes. Where's the kid now?'

'I've sent him and his mum to stay at her parents' house in Kendal; Amy and Des are following behind. He threatened that he'd come back for him if he spoke to anyone; I'm not taking any chances.'

'Good – that's the right thing to do. Is he telling the truth? You know what kids are like – they're better storytellers than Stephen King.'

Morgan smiled. 'He's very astute for a seven-year-old, plus he said the guy smelled like earth. Which was his way of describing the smell of blood that clung to his clothes. A seven-year-old wouldn't know that, and he looked pretty scared.'

'I guess Danny is off the hook then, at least for now.'

'I'd say so. Get me a dog here. I'll wait around.

'Another thing I was thinking.' She turned around, walking

away from the houses so she was standing near to the police car with its engine running to keep the PCSO sitting inside it warm. She lowered her voice. 'What if it was a teenager trying to scare her and it all went a little bit wrong?'

'What?'

'Her best friend across the road, Paula, has a teenage daughter – maybe she was jealous of the attention her mum gave to Emma instead of her, and maybe she has a boyfriend who she's talked into doing this because of the jealousy.'

'That's a lot of maybes, Morgan. Is there any evidence to suggest this?'

'No, it's just a theory.'

Ben laughed. 'I'm not disagreeing with you because I know better than to disregard your input...'

'But?'

'Let's see if the dog can pick up a trail. If it leads us to their house then we'll arrest them all, okay. If not, then we're going to need something concrete to tie them to it.'

'What about Mick Oswald? He's connected to both victims?'

'Once Danny has been bailed then I'll get him picked up and brought in. When you're finished there, we need to get to the post-mortem. In fact, I'll come to the scene soon and we'll both travel from there. I'll get someone to come down and wait for the dog handler.'

'Who?'

'Our new boss is very keen to pitch in. I'm sure he won't mind driving me down and waiting.'

She laughed. 'Not too sure about that. See you soon.'

She began to take photos from where she was standing: of the street, Emma's house, the empty house, Daniel's house and Cara's. Turning to the opposite side, she began to photograph Paula's and the space Bailey had pointed to. She was itching to go and take a look where it led but didn't want to ruin the chance of the dog picking up the killer's scent.

A metallic blue BMW X5 roared into the street, slamming to a halt by the white Corsa she'd arrived in, looking as if it could swallow it whole. Ben waved at her from the passenger side, and she nodded.

Marc jumped out, crossing to greet her.

'Excellent work. Any witness is better than none, even if it is a kid.'

'Thank you, but this wasn't down to me. It's Amy you need to thank; she was down here early enough to catch Bailey and his mum getting into the car.'

'I'll tell her when I see her. I get why you all work so well as a team. Back in Manchester it was totally different – they didn't care about who should get the recognition. They'd take it and pretend it was all their doing.'

Ben was standing slightly behind him, his eyes screwed up so much the creases on his forehead looked like deep gouges.

Morgan pointed to the area she wanted the dog to search.

'Bailey said he disappeared around there. I haven't been near – I thought it was best to let the dog have the first access. I'll tape it off if you want so no one can walk down that way.'

Marc shook his head. 'It's okay – I'll hang around and wait for the dog handler whilst you two get off to the post-mortem.'

Ben didn't wait to be told twice and pointed to the Corsa. 'Is that you?'

She nodded then turned to Marc. 'I'm sure you could request another PCSO to come down, save you waiting.'

'I know, but I feel as if I need to make amends for being so stupid and brash earlier. I really did just want to help and lighten your load a little – there wasn't any ulterior motive. I'm not here to make life difficult; if anything, I want to make mine less difficult.'

Smiling, she glanced at Ben, who was already in the car. 'I'm not sure this place is the right place if you're after an easier life. It looks very pretty; it's a gorgeous place to live, but there's some undercurrent running through this area that seems to turn the ordinary people into extraordinary, depraved killers.'

A nervous laugh escaped his lips. 'Surely it can't be like this all the time?'

'I can't speak for before I joined up, but since I've been working, it has.'

He nodded. 'Let's hope I can fit in and be of some use then. I realise Tom's reputation is hard to live up to, but I'll do my best.'

'That's all anyone can do, isn't it?'

She left him standing by the corner of the street, waiting for Cassie the dog handler to arrive.

Ben waited for her to get inside the car before asking, 'What was that about?'

'I think he's genuinely sorry and trying to help. It was an apology for earlier.'

He let out a long sigh. 'Talking about how he wants to fit in?'

'Stop being so harsh and give the guy a chance – maybe he doesn't have an ulterior motive and wants a quieter life.'

His laughter filled the car, it was so loud. 'You told him he'd come to the wrong place, and it was never going to happen, right?'

Morgan dead eyed him. 'Yes, I did. Smart arse.'

She drove away from Fell Close, glad to be away from the street and the unsettling feeling of being watched that was still casting a shadow over her. They needed to get to the post-mortem, but she wanted to stop at Shirley Kelly's flat first to seize the knife block for comparison with the knife found last night.

As she walked into the communal entrance of the flats, she caught the door of number three closing softly and was torn: did she bother the guy who lived there or not? Her feet made up her mind for her, and she found herself knocking on his door.

Taking a step back, she could hear him inside as he began to draw back the bolt. There was a metallic rattle as a safety chain was slid into place then the door opened a crack.

'Hi. Sorry to bother you – I'm with the police and we're investigating a murder in the flat above you.'

'A what? A murder? Oh dear, no. No, there must be some mistake.'

Morgan felt a wave of regret that she'd knocked on this poor guy's door when he was fresh out of hospital.

'I'm sorry. Your neighbour, Shirley, was found dead. Can I ask you when the last time was you saw her?'

She could hear his breathing; it was rapid and he sounded as if he was struggling to speak.

He took the chain off the door and opened it wider, but she couldn't see his face because he was staring at the floor.

He whispered, 'I'm sorry, I don't speak to anyone. I struggle with bad anxiety. I like to keep to myself, and I've just come out of hospital. I can't help you.'

'That's okay. I'm sorry to have bothered you. We have to ask though – you know it's how we work.'

He nodded. Stepped back inside and shut the door, sliding the dead bolt across once more.

Morgan felt bad and went upstairs.

Tina was leaning against the wall outside of the flat, looking down at her phone. She jumped to see Morgan, who smiled at her.

'Is it open?'

'Yeah. Are we almost done here? It's been forever.'

'I think so. Once I've been inside to seize a couple of items, I'll ask Ben if we can release the scene.'

'Thanks.'

Morgan pushed open the door and felt her stomach retch. She'd forgotten about the dreadful smell.

Breathing through her mouth instead of her nose, she tugged on a pair of gloves and went straight into the kitchen.

The knife block was big. She took hold of the handle of one, pulling it out. It looked identical to the one found underneath Emma last night. But why would Shirley's killer take a knife from here to kill Emma? And what did that mean for the silk scarf he'd used to strangle Shirley? It didn't really fit with what she'd learned of Shirley. Had that come from somewhere else?

After bagging up the heavy block with the knives in, she went to have a quick look in the bedroom.

She tugged the curtains open so she could see what she was doing and began a quick search of the drawers and cupboards, then checked the wardrobe. There wasn't one silk scarf amongst her items of clothing, meaning either that was her only one or he'd brought it with him.

Morgan knew that he'd brought it with him – he had to have. So where had it come from?

THIRTY-FOUR

1989

He closed the door quietly, pressing his back against the wood that he felt even through his clothes. It was colder in here than the rest of the house.

After giving his eyes a few moments to adjust to the darkness, he could see that the curtains were all drawn, blocking out what little light the night sky might offer. He could just make out the shape of a new table in the middle of the room – it was long and a strange shape. He wondered if he dared to turn on the light, just for a moment, to see what the time was.

His fingers danced across the wall until they reached the switch, flicking it down. Light filled the room, blinding him momentarily.

Blinking until his eyes adjusted, he glanced at the huge mantle and wondered why the large gilt mirror was covered over. The clock was on the opposite wall, and he turned to see that this too was stopped at six. This was too weird.

He turned to look at what he'd thought was a table, realising it was in fact a coffin. Why was there a coffin in the parlour?

Fear made his legs tremble, and he wondered if he was in some nightmare. Maybe if he pinched his arm he'd wake up in his bed, because this couldn't be happening. Everyone had disappeared, the clocks were all stopped, the mirror was covered, and there was a big coffin in the middle of the room his grandmother served morning coffee and afternoon tea to her guests in.

Swallowing the lump that had lodged in his throat, he edged his way forward, pinching his arm hard enough that he yelped. The fear that this was not a dream and the urge to find out who was in the coffin was too much; he took a couple of steps forward and looked down to see the cold, waxy, yellowed face of his mum staring up at him.

He whispered, 'Mum, Mum, wake up.' But she didn't move. She was frozen in time.

Reaching out, he lowered his hand inside the coffin and gently prodded her in the chest. Her body was hard, solid, as if she was made out of wood. He didn't recognise the screams that came out of his mouth – screams of fear and frustration as he leaned in and began to shake her as hard as he could.

The door was thrown open and he saw Emmie standing there with a look of horror on her face. He turned away and went back to his task, trying to pick up his mum and get her out of the stupid box. He was still making that loud, weird noise but couldn't stop it if he tried. Then Cook was there and they were both staring at him.

She ran at him. 'Stop it, stop it. Leave her alone. You can't do anything with her – she's dead.'

He didn't care what Cook said and carried on trying to lift his mum, pushing his hands under her armpits.

Cook screamed at him, slapping his face at the same time. 'Stop it now – get off her. She's dead.'

The slap was so loud it echoed around the room along with the word *dead*. It seemed to float in the air, taunting him. His fear giving way to anger, he turned to look at the woman who had just slapped him. He wanted to hit her back so hard that she'd die and end up in this stupid wooden box and not his mum.

Then his grandmother swept into the room. Her normally neat bun had been unpinned and her long silver hair cascaded down her back. She rushed over to him, grabbing his shoulders, and pulled him away from the coffin. He was furious with them all, especially his grandmother for letting the staff talk to him the way they did and for not telling him about this.

'Why didn't you tell me?'

She let go of his shoulders, backing away from him, sensing the rage that was threatening to be set free. She motioned for Emmie and Cook to leave them alone.

Cook turned to leave; Emmie hovered.

'Thank you, ladies – I will take it from here.'

They nodded, turned and left. He stood defiantly waiting for her answer.

'There are some things that are too painful to talk about, especially to a ten-year-old boy. I did not tell you because I didn't know how to. I am upset and disgusted by your mother's selfish actions. That she cared more about the rubbish she liked to inject into her veins than her own family is very hard for me to accept. I did not want it to be true. I did not want to have to tell you this, but then again, I would never have wanted you to find out this way. I'm sorry that you did. I was going to tell you in the morning. You had a difficult day without this on top of everything else.'

He felt the anger subsiding a little. She looked like an old woman, frail and broken, in her long white cotton nightgown and her hair unpinned, and he'd never seen her this way.

'When someone in our family dies, it is a long-standing tradition to bring them home. Regardless of what they were like.'

'Why are all the clocks stopped? Why is the mirror covered?'

'It's a Victorian mourning ritual – it's our family tradition and we've been doing it for a very long time. As a mark of respect and to make sure that your mother's soul isn't trapped here on earth, we cover the mirrors. If I had any photographs on display, I would have ordered Emmie to turn them over so her soul could not possess them. But your mother's photographs are all boxed up in the attic. I could not bear to look at them because they reminded me of what she had given up to live the lifestyle that she did. When I die, this is what I will expect to be carried out for me.'

He looked down at the body of his mother. She looked much thinner than the last time he'd seen her, her cheekbones so much more prominent. He wanted to cry. He also wanted to shake her because now she'd left him for good and he was stuck here in this house that was like a crypt with people that he hated.

He felt his grandmother's bony hand on his shoulder.

'Come on – you've had a nasty shock. Let's get you a hot chocolate then tuck you back into bed. Tomorrow we have a lot to discuss – I expect you to be where I can find you. No hiding or running away – you're old enough to accept the burden of your responsibilities.'

Tears welled in his eyes for his mum and himself, but he let his grandmother tug him away from the coffin, and he followed her to the kitchen where she busied herself pouring milk into a pan and heating it up on the cooker. He'd never seen her do anything in here; in fact he'd never seen her do anything apart from read, write letters, and host her friends for tea and bridge.

He sat at the table wondering what would happen to him if she died. What would happen to the house? It was just the two of them now. How did she pay for it all if she didn't work? There were so many questions whizzing around in his head. He squeezed his eyes shut to try and stop them because they were making him dizzy. When he opened them, she was standing in front of him with two mugs in her hand and a packet of biscuits.

'Come – let's get you back to bed. You can drink this upstairs. I think we have both had a very long day, and you've had a terrible shock. Turn the lights off behind me.'

She led the way, carrying the steaming drinks, and he did as he was told, too tired to do anything else.

As he turned off each light, he couldn't stop picturing the cold, hard body of his mum, lying in the dark. What if he took the cloth from the mirror? Would she leave her body and get stuck in there? Every time he looked in a mirror would she appear, her ghost trapped inside of them, haunting him forever?

She took him into his bedroom, put the mug and the biscuits on the table next to his bed. He sat down, and she patted the top of his head.

'I need you to be a brave boy – try to contain your anger inside of you whilst we have your mother downstairs.'

Then she left him, closing the door behind her. He looked up at the heavy mirror that hung above the dressing table and felt cold fingers of fear crawl up his back.

Grabbing the top sheet off his bed, he ran and tucked it all around it. He loved his mum, but he didn't want to see her gaunt, dead face staring back at him from the mirror.

THIRTY-FIVE

Morgan watched as Declan straightened up. She'd listened to Smooth FM for the last couple of hours – lost in a world of sad songs that all seemed to be playing for Emma, as if the DJs knew that they were providing the music to the last stages of her life.

'That's a wrap from me, Susie. I'll let you sew Emma back together.'

Susie smiled. She was prepared and waiting.

Ben turned to Morgan. He looked exactly how she felt: saddened beyond belief.

'He hesitated – that shows me he wasn't sure or confident in what he was doing. I think he'd have preferred a different mode of death, but he went for quick. He wanted it over fast.'

'It wasn't though – it took a few minutes because she lay there bleeding out in Cain's arms.'

'Your boy must have missed him by minutes, maybe less. He made one cut that wasn't very deep and had to go in for a second. He still didn't cause instant death though. Don't get me wrong, if he'd gone deep and pressed harder, it would have been quicker – and he used a smooth blade; a serrated one would have caused more damage. Still painful, horrific, incredibly violent and a terrible way to die. The knife from last night fits the wound like a glove: that is definitely your murder weapon. Are you thinking Emma's and Shirley's deaths are connected?'

Ben answered, 'Yes. Can you give me something that confirms it?'

'Well, did you see that some of her hair had been cut off, same as Shirley? I'd say your man is definitely a trophy collector. Apart from that, at the moment, all I have is that Emma's killer is left-handed; it's harder to tell with Shirley's. So both fatal injuries were neck injuries, we've got the hair, and didn't you say something about the clocks being stopped in both houses, Morgan? My professional opinion is this is the work of the same man, but this is where the dream team takes over.'

Morgan smiled at him. 'Who's the dream team?'

'Really, Morgan? You need your uncle Declan to spell it out to you?'

'Us?'

He nodded.

'Thanks, that's a great compliment. What if we prove that the knife used to kill Emma was from Shirley's kitchen?'

'If you can match this knife as the missing one, well, you're heading for a home run. Now do me a favour and earn that compliment by finding this sick bastard and soon, please, before anyone else ends up on my table.'

She drove back to Rydal Falls in a sombre mood.

'Have you heard from Marc? Did the dog pick anything up?'

Ben shrugged. 'I'm assuming not – he said he'd ring.'

'Have you not got any missed calls though? Your phone was on silent.'

'No.'

'That's a shame. I kind of wanted the dog to go straight to Paula's house. That would have been nice.'

'Not sure how nice it would have been for Paula.'

'You know what I mean. Awful, but nice – it could have given us a solid lead.'

At the station, Ben went in search of Marc, who was nowhere to be seen; Mads was in his office scrolling through his phone so he settled for him.

'All right. Do you know where the boss is?'

'God knows. Might be in custody.'

'Why's he down there?'

Mads looked up from the eBay page he was on. 'What, didn't he phone you?'

Ben's fingers curled into fists. 'No. Should he have?'

'Christ, he's got a death wish that bloke. Never seen someone so happy to dive in.'

Morgan called, 'Ben,' from the spiral staircase, and he turned to look at her.

'Got you under the thumb already eh, ha-ha.'

Ben ignored him, striding towards Morgan.

'He's brought Paula's daughter, Ashley, in.'

'What? Why?'

'Amy said the dog did lead to her house and it sniffed out a pair of bloody gloves; they were by the back door inside a welly that belonged to her.'

He closed his eyes.

'What are you doing?'

'Counting to fucking fifty before I lose my shit.'

'Should we go in, see what he's doing?'

He shook his head. 'I think he can handle a teenager. Where's Paula?'

'Apparently screaming blue murder in the front office, about to be arrested.'

'Right, let's get to the scene. I take it Wendy is there?'

'And Des.'

They both hurried to get out of the back entrance of the station before they were caught up in the ensuing chaos.

'Looks like your hunch was right.'

'I'm not sure I want it to be right. She's only a kid. Would she have the guts to do that? And what motive would she have for Shirley Kelly?'

'Let's bring Mick Oswald in too; he's connected to them both. This is the plan – we'll go see if Wendy has found anything then we'll go find Oswald.'

She nodded, feeling thoroughly miserable at the thought of a teenage girl who had known Emma so well being capable of killing her so viciously.

THIRTY-SIX

Saint Quentin's Retirement Home was set in secluded grounds a short walk from Sizergh Castle on the outskirts of Kendal. Evelyn stared out of the bedroom window to the beautiful rose garden that was nothing but sharp woody stems until the warmer weather would bring out the blooms. She thought back to the times she'd been able to prune her own roses; they had been happier times. Gardening gave her great pleasure; it always had been her escape from life's responsibilities. Watching something grow from a tiny seed she had planted in the ground and nurtured never failed to make her heart sing, and she treasured every single plant.

A line of saliva escaped the corner of her mouth, slowly trickling down her bottom lip and onto her chin. The shame of the state she was in made her cheeks burn and her heart ache with sadness.

The door was thrown open, and she smelled a familiar Dior perfume, which made her feel a little better.

'Blimey, Evelyn, I swear those roses aren't going to come up any quicker with you staring at them all day. Not unless you have hidden, magic powers to unleash a forest of flowers. And I suppose that you don't, because I'm pretty sure you wouldn't be stuck in here – you'd be anywhere you wanted. Wouldn't that be nice for you? Have you ever fancied one of those around-the-world cruises on one of those massive ships? If you do, you only have to say the word; one nod from you and I'll book it – I'll even be your carer if you pay for me. I can't afford a weekend in Blackpool at this rate. What do you say? Should we make plans and run away?'

Angela kneeled down in front of Evelyn and winked at her as she chatted away. Evelyn managed a smile; Angela had patted the corner of her mouth with a tissue before she'd even realised. She would like to spend her last days on a luxury cruise ship. Why had she never thought about that?

'Yesss.' She tried hard to get the words out, but they emerged as a long hiss.

'Was that a yes? Bloody hell let's do it. I'll hand my notice in and we'll be off.'

The door opened and Linda walked in. Evelyn let out a small sigh. She'd rather dream of exotic cruises than what rubbish they were going to spoon-feed her for lunch.

'Stop talking absolute rubbish, Angela. Sometimes I think you're more away with the fairies than the patients.'

Angela pulled a face and whispered to Evelyn, 'Oops, Nurse Misery is here to spoil our fun again.' She emphasised the *again*.

Evelyn wished she could tell that awful woman to bugger off, but she couldn't.

Angela was busy folding washing and putting it away. She turned to Evelyn. 'I suppose we'll have to wait until sourpuss is on her days off and then we'll be out of here.'

Evelyn lifted a finger and pointed to the washing, then her neck.

Angela shook her head. 'I'm sorry, I have no idea where your scarf went. I've checked the laundry, and each time I go into a different bedroom, I check that too, in case it got mixed up. It will turn up – I'll keep looking.'

Linda replied, 'Well good luck with that, Angela. Evelyn, you have a visitor, isn't that nice?'

Evelyn felt her heart sink. The only visitors she ever got were the local vicar or sometimes Emmie popped in. Evelyn's grandson sometimes came. She didn't want to see him though, because he scared her. She looked at Angela, her eyes wide.

'Who's here to visit?' Angela asked Linda.

Angela had read the look on Evelyn's face; the woman was worth her weight in gold.

'Her grandson – he's on a flying visit from work.'

Evelyn shook her head to the best of her ability, which wasn't much and as slow as a snail.

'Tell him to come back tomorrow, Linda, I don't think Evelyn is up to a visitor.'

'I'll do no such thing. Who do you think you are? You can't decide who comes in to see her. It will be nice for her.'

Linda left the room to go and fetch him.

Angela looked at Evelyn. 'How about I give him ten minutes, then I'll come back and kick him out? Is that what you want? He doesn't scare me, and I don't think he's God's gift to women either, like the rest of them.'

Evelyn managed to move her head down slightly – a jerky movement.

The door opened and in he walked. He was no longer the small boy who had been sent to live with her when her daughter had gone off the rails. He was a tall, handsome, smartly dressed man in an expensive suit. He had a bunch of white roses in his hand. Crossing the room in two strides, he bent, kissing her cheek. His cold lips against her wrinkled skin made her shiver inside.

'Grandmother, these are for you. How are you today? You look a little bit under the weather.'

He held the roses in front of her face, then pulled them away, passing them to Angela without even so much as a please or making eye contact with her.

'I'll go and put them in water then, should I?'

He ignored her, pulling a chair across to sit opposite Evelyn. 'Lord I've been busy, very busy. I'm so tired I could crawl into your bed and sleep for hours. How are you? Have you been managing to sleep much?'

His eyes stared into hers, trying to read her reactions and thoughts – the only time she was glad that she had very little speech and movement left was on the rare occasion he put in a visit.

She stared back at him, eyes glassy, wishing that Angela could whisk her away anywhere. It didn't even have to be a cruise.

'You wouldn't believe what they're going to do with the old house. I saw the plans on the council planning portal. Sad really that they're going to tear it to pieces when we have so many happy memories of the old place. You know, you could have signed it over to me instead of letting them sell it. I'd have paid for you to stop somewhere and be looked after out of the proceeds. I still don't understand why you didn't do that; you could have stayed at home and been looked after in your own house with twenty-four-hour carers. Wouldn't that have been nicer than this awful place that always smells of soggy cabbage and piss?'

Evelyn couldn't imagine living in that house with him, alone, with just a carer. She also didn't believe that he would have hired enough of them to look after her. She felt her heart ache. She'd been cold when he'd arrived, not very loving towards him. It hadn't been his fault. It wasn't his fault that his mother had prostituted herself out to that many different men to fund her drug habit that she didn't even know who his father was, but Evelyn had struggled to open her heart at first. But after Kate had died and he'd found her that night in the parlour, she'd tried her best to love him like she should, be more caring, warm and grandmotherly. It hadn't made a difference to him; he didn't care about anything but his dead mother. She should have let the social workers take him away, maybe then he wouldn't have ended up the way he did.

She looked at him. He was on his phone, which was all he ever did when he visited. She had failed her daughter and her grandson, and now look at her – this was the price she had to pay. Frozen in a body that wouldn't do anything she wished and stuck in an old people's home, when she'd had a grand house that was far nicer than this had ever been.

Anger began to build inside her at the injustice of life.

Her grandson looked up as if sensing a change in her demeanour.

'What's up? You look like you're about to burst. Cat got your tongue?'

He started laughing at his own joke. 'Sorry, Gran, that was rude and uncalled for. So, what do you want to talk about?'

This set him off laughing again.

'Maybe I could help you. If you're fed up with sitting here like one of Pavlov's dogs drooling down your face waiting for a bell to ring, I could stop it you know. I could put an end to this misery. Don't tell me that you enjoy your days here, waiting to die? I couldn't think of anything worse. If it was me, I'd beg you to do something about it. What do you say? Give me a nod and I'll make it all go away.'

The door opened and Angela walked in with a small, cut-glass vase filled with the white roses. Placing them on the windowsill so Evelyn could see them, yet not so they blocked her view, she noticed the change in the old woman. Her eyes were full of tears.

'What did you say to her?'

He was looking down at his phone. 'Nothing.'

'Why is she so upset?'

He looked up, glancing at his gran then fixed his eyes on Angela.

'How the hell would I know? It's not as if she's a fountain of conversation. Maybe she's fed up with this place.'

'Maybe she's fed up with you?'

Angela knew she shouldn't have said it, that she had just crossed the line – Evelyn could see it on her face.

He stood up. 'And just who do you think you're talking to?'

'I think you should leave now; your grandmother needs a rest.'

'Or else what?'

He was standing so close to Angela that Evelyn knew she would be able to smell his expensive aftershave, count the buttons on the white cotton shirt he was wearing.

Linda walked in and stared at the pair of them, standing off against each other.

'Angela, please go and help Bill; he wants the toilet.'

Angela left the room, but not without glancing at Evelyn and noting the terror in her eyes.

Angela made her way to the lounge, where Bill was banging his fist against his walking frame. She couldn't get the image of the old woman's terrified eyes out of her mind. She didn't care how well off he was or what job he did, Evelyn's grandson was an arsehole.

THIRTY-SEVEN

Wendy was leaving Paula's house as Morgan and Ben arrived.

'Clean as a whistle.'

Ben asked, 'No bloody clothing, forensics, dead bodies?'

She shook her head. 'I've videoed, photographed, searched, paying extra attention to the bathroom and the teenage girl's bedroom. Nothing. I mean there's plenty of dirty pots, crisp packets and the usual crap stuffed under her bed but nothing that screams "I just murdered my mum's best friend".'

'What about the garden?'

'I've printed the metal catches on the gate; the wellies are bagged up to be sent off; the gloves were seized earlier and are ready to be sent off too.'

Morgan pointed to the house. 'Can I go in?'

'Suppose so. I don't think there's much else I can do with it. I'm not sure what Marc wants.'

Morgan left her talking to Ben on the front step and walked inside. She wasn't a psychic by any means, but she trusted her gut feelings and she wasn't feeling anything in here. Except for maybe envy at how clean and homely everything was.

She went upstairs to check the two bedrooms and bathroom. Ashley's room was probably the messiest in the house, and even that wasn't as bad as her own teenage bedroom had been. She looked out of the window that faced Emma's house. She'd seen Ashely watching her – or at least someone from Ashley's window – but that would just have been morbid curiosity, wouldn't it?

She headed downstairs to the kitchen and let herself out into the tiny back garden. Anyone could have hopped over the fence and dumped the gloves in the wellies, then been on their way.

There was a narrow back lane along this side, with a steep banking full of overgrown brambles down the embankment that caused a barrier between the lane and the railway line. She let herself out of the gate and walked along until she found a gap big enough to squeeze through between the bushes. Her sleeve caught on a sharp branch of brambles and she let out an 'Ouch' but carried on.

It was a tight squeeze but once she was through, she stood on the other side and sighed. He could have gone in any direction – along the tracks, across the tracks; he could have doubled back and headed away from this area back into the main street.

After going back the way she came, she found Ben was waiting in the car for her; the CSI van had left.

'Been for a nice walk? You've ripped your jacket.'

'No, I was checking out the back lane. There's brambles all over the back. It's also a perfect getaway; if you squeeze through the gap, it leads down to the train tracks. I don't think it was Ashley.'

'Christ, Morgan, will you make up your mind? One minute it's her, the next it isn't.'

'I just said wouldn't it be nice and easy if it was, but come on, in all reality, if she'd cut Emma's throat she would have been covered in blood. There's none in the house; plus she doesn't have a boyfriend and that kid Bailey said it was a man, wearing dark clothing and smelling of blood. It has to have been a guy, and he's escaped right from under our noses.'

'Rub it in a little bit more – it's fine.'

'So, what does that leave, boss?'

'Mick Oswald – we need to find him.'

Ben squeezed the bridge of his nose with the tips of his fingers. 'You give me a migraine, Brookes.'

'Not on purpose. I want to catch him before he does it again. We know he's connected to both Shirley and Emma, but if there's anything at both scenes to tie him to them, we need to figure out whether he's on some kind of mission to kill off his friends or picking random women.'

'You're right. There's a couple of things they both have in common: they're both single and living alone, oh and they both drank with Oswald. It's time to bring him in.'

'What are we waiting for?' Morgan asked.

'I knew you were going to say that.'

'What about Paula and Ashley?'

'Let the boss deal with them. He's going to be tied up for a while with that mess, so let him be the one to pick up the pieces.'

Morgan didn't disagree with him; this was a mess but hope-fully they would find Mick without too much fuss and get him booked into custody before anyone else was killed. They had trusted him far too easily when they'd spoken to him yesterday; he was a convincing storyteller.

They reached his house in minutes. She parked the car a little way up the street so they could watch the house for a few minutes.

'Should we call for backup? Maybe see if Al's on duty and get him and the team to come do this?'

Ben turned to look at her. 'When did you become so

responsible?'

She grinned. 'Since my entire world is sitting next to me, making plans to put himself at risk. I'd rather we took precautions.'

He leaned over and kissed her cheek, before quickly moving back. 'I'm flattered – you've got me right here.' He clutched at his heart. 'But are you also saying that I'm too old and past it to be able to handle bringing Mick Oswald in, because if you are then I'm also a little insulted.'

'I don't mean it like that. For all we know he's a killer, and I love you more than anything, Ben.'

A soft smile played across his lips. 'I love you too. Are you beginning to understand the torture that you've put me through so many times now?'

She shrugged. 'Technically, it was never my fault, you know. It just kind of happened when I didn't expect it, which is why I think we should get some backup – you know, just in case.'

'I agree with you, but I don't want to wait here for hours while he escapes out the back door. He might not even be home. There's a good chance he's at the pub.'

Morgan knew this, of course she did, but she'd put it out there, and if it all went wrong then at least it wasn't because of her.

They got out of the car and walked towards Mick's house. The old, battered boat in the front garden was a good hiding spot for evidence. They needed to get it lifted and see what was underneath.

The front door was ajar, moving ever so slightly in the wind.

'I don't like this – something feels off.'

Ben rolled his eyes at her and growled, 'Don't say it.'

She didn't; she let him knock on the door. The force of his blows pushed it open enough that they could see a figure on the floor.

Ben immediately slammed it open, pulling a pair of gloves out of his pocket and ran inside.

She did the same.

On the floor was Mick Oswald, bleeding heavily from a head wound, blood pooling around him on the floor.

Morgan pulled her radio out of her pocket and asked for an ambulance to the address.

Ben was bending down next to Mick, feeling for a pulse.

'Is he...?'

His head shook. 'No, there's still a strong pulse, but he's unresponsive.'

'Should we put him in the recovery position?'

'He's breathing; it's shallow but he's managing, and I don't really want to move him. Stay with him whilst I have a look around.'

Straightening up, Ben squeezed past her in the narrow hallway and ran upstairs.

She looked down at Mick's pale face and felt bad for him. If they'd waited in the car, he'd have probably died here on the floor all alone, just like Shirley. She looked around to see if there was a clock stopped or any mirrors covered. Emma's mirrors hadn't been covered, but maybe the killer had been disturbed by Cain's arrival.

She stepped over Mick so she could get into the living room, but there was no clock in there. She then manoeuvred herself back over him and into the messy kitchen that smelled of tobacco smoke. There was an old, grease-covered clock on the wall, but it had stopped at eight o'clock and had probably been like that for months, if not years. She checked her watch just to make sure and saw it was only two in the afternoon.

Sirens echoed in the street, and she crossed back over Mick to go outside and wave the ambulance in the right direction, just as Ben came back downstairs.

'Nothing much up there. Junk really. He has a thing for old

computers. There's a room full of those ancient monitors and keyboards.'

She was standing on the front step waving at the paramedics, who had stopped the ambulance in the middle of the street.

'Probably just as well, seeing as how we don't have a search warrant.'

Ben smiled. 'I want to know where Morgan is. Who are you? What have you done with her?'

They stepped to one side to let the paramedics in; there wasn't enough room for two people in the hallway, never mind four of them.

'What happened?' one of the paramedics asked.

'No idea. We came to speak to him and found him like this. We've only been here since we phoned for your good selves to come.'

'Who are you? Friends? Family?'

Morgan realised that she didn't recognise either of the two women who were working on Mick, which made a change: usually Nick, who was the friendliest paramedic she knew, was on duty when she needed help. If she didn't recognise them, they wouldn't know who she was either.

'Police. Well CID. Well CAST now. This is my boss, Ben Matthews. I'm Morgan Brookes.'

The other woman turned to look at her. 'I've heard all about you, Morgan. Isn't it usually you bleeding somewhere?'

Morgan didn't know whether to laugh or be offended. She settled on a smile and shrugged.

Ben, on the other hand, looked as if he was ready to explode on her behalf.

'How bad is he?'

'He's not responding well at the moment – hard to say. We need to get him to A&E pronto.'

She turned back to help her colleague work on Mick for a

little longer. When he had lines in, and his head was bandaged enough to slow the bleeding, she went out to the truck to get the trolley. There was barely enough room to manoeuvre, but they managed to get him on the trolley and out to the ambulance, leaving behind a mess of wrappers, empty packets and an unfortunate trail of blood from the trolley wheels that led out to the ambulance.

'There goes our crime scene.'

'Life and limb, all that jazz. Why do you think someone attacked him?'

Ben was staring after the ambulance as it took off, lights and sirens flashing.

'Who knows? Drugs? Revenge? Maybe he did it himself out of remorse because he's our killer.'

'There's no obvious weapon to hand, so probably not.'

He smiled at her. 'She was rude to you. Are you okay?'

'She did have a point though, and yes, I'm fine. I have tougher skin than that. Years of being a coppertop at school have served me well against that kind of thing.'

'Were you bullied because of your hair?'

'I wouldn't say bullied full-on, no, but I was always referred to as ginge, ginger nut, Duracell, you get it.'

He shook his head. 'Not really – you have the most beautiful hair. Jealous or idiots, I'd never have let anyone speak to you that way.'

She felt heat begin to thaw her frozen insides. 'Well, you know, sticks and stones and all that. It didn't bother me too much. I suppose that's why I turned into a bit of a goth – I was already different; I had nothing to lose.'

A police van turned into the street, and she nodded. 'The cavalry's here – they can scene guard until CSI arrive. Are we going to the hospital or sending an officer to stay with Mick?'

Amber and another male officer Morgan didn't recognise

got out of the van. Ben nodded at them both as they joined the conversation.

'Up to you. I don't care who does what, but I need someone to scene guard and someone to follow the ambulance to the hospital to stay with Mick Oswald.'

Amber peered past Morgan's shoulder to see the large pool of blood. 'I'll follow the ambulance. Scotty will scene guard, won't you?'

Scotty looked as happy to scene guard as he would be to jump in a tank full of great white sharks.

'Yeah.'

Amber turned and walked back towards the van, and Morgan looked at Scotty.

'You better get your hat, and have you got a jacket? Because it's going to be cold waiting outside here for hours.' She smiled sweetly at him, watching as he realised he'd just been given the crappiest job out of the two.

He jogged after Amber to get his hat and coat.

Ben lowered his voice. 'Is it me or are all these young kids about as enthusiastic as a death-row convict going to the electric chair?'

Morgan sniggered a little too loud. 'That's a terrible metaphor, but yes, I think you're right – they don't make them like they used to.' She realised she was comparing herself to them, when she'd joined up only a few years ago. She was keen, ready to protect and serve, and proud to be doing it.

'Come on, Brookes – let's get back to the station. I need to wrap my head around what a gigantic mess this all is.'

They waited for Scotty to come back. He had a scene guard logbook in his hands, his hat was pushed firmly onto his head and his thick padded jacket was thrown on over his body armour.

THIRTY-EIGHT

As Ben drove down the main street, Morgan realised she needed to eat. She was hungry, and even more than that she needed coffee.

'Let me out here. I'll go get us some lunch and walk back.'

'I'll wait for you.'

'No, it's fine. I need a bit of fresh air, and I could do with nipping in the post office for a couple of envelopes. Can you manage without me for ten minutes?'

He started to laugh. 'I don't think I can, but I'll have to learn to.'

He stopped the car and let her out; she blew him a kiss.

There was a queue at the café, so she decided to go to the post office first.

She browsed the envelopes, picking up a couple of padded ones, and went to queue at the counter. When it was her turn, the woman who she'd seen a few times when on enquiries smiled at her. She couldn't remember her name and looked at her name badge, which read 'Mary'.

'Hello, lovey. How are you keeping?'

'Busy, you?'

'Not as busy as you.' She lowered her voice. 'I can't believe it about Shirley and Emma – it's just awful.'

Morgan hadn't seen the paper, but she doubted that they'd released Emma's name so soon. But they lived in a small town where gossip and news spread like wildfire, so she wasn't overly surprised.

'It's sad – terrible. Do you know which house Emma used to work at? Mick said it was called Armboth Hall, but I couldn't find it when I did a quick search?'

Mary leaned as close to the glass as she could, her lips almost kissing it, and whispered, 'I do, and to tell you the truth, I'm a bit scared. I can't sleep and keep looking over my shoulder in case whoever it is comes after me next.'

Morgan felt the hairs on the back of her neck stand on end and goosebumps rise on her arms. 'What do you mean?'

'Well, we all used to work at the big old house by the lake. It was called Armboth Hall back then, but it's been empty for years now and I think they changed its name quite some time ago, although I've heard there's some fancy writer living in it now.'

'Where is it and how long ago did you all work there?'

'On the outskirts of Keswick and, let me see, ooh, be a good twenty years now. I didn't work there for very long. I came along near the end in the last couple of months before the old lady went into a home. She's probably dead now, bless her. Look at me holding you up. I better let you get on, but do you think I should be worried?'

Morgan nodded, trying to digest the information she'd just been told. Glancing behind, she saw there was now a long line of people waiting for her to hurry up.

'I need to speak to you, Mary. Can you get someone to cover for you? I'll buy you coffee.'

Mary lifted her head and peered over her glasses. 'My

husband should be back soon. Why don't you wait for me at
The Coffee Pot and I'll be there as soon as I can?'

Morgan held her debit card against the reader and nodded.

Once she was done, she turned around and walked past the
line of people, all of them watching her with great interest. Her
heart was racing – this was the connection they'd been looking
for. If they'd worked together years ago, maybe it wasn't Mick
Oswald they should be looking at – although someone had hit
him over the head, so what was that about?

The queue at The Coffee Pot had gone down, and there was
one table left in the corner. Morgan shrugged off her ripped
jacket, placed it on the back of a chair, sat her envelopes on the
table and went to the counter. She ordered two cheese savoury
baguettes to take away and three large lattes; she asked for
coconut syrup in hers, feeling as if she needed a sweet pick-me-
up. She felt jittery and wasn't sure if it was the thought of
uncovering some great secret that might just blow the case
open.

That done, she sat at the table, took out her phone and
googled mansions near Keswick, but before it could load, the
door opened and a flushed Mary rushed in and sat at the table.

'Where did they all come from? It's as if someone dropped a
coachload off. Sorry about that.'

'Don't be sorry – you're doing me the favour and I really
appreciate it. I got you a latte – is that okay?'

'Oh, you little darling that's perfect. Thank you. Right,
where should I start?'

'At the beginning, please. You said you worked with Shirley
and Emma. Could you tell me where?'

She sipped her latte and nodded. 'Armboth Hall it was
called originally. You wouldn't know it. I don't think Rydal Falls
police cover that far up. I think they changed its name to Lake-

view House, or maybe they didn't, but it was a big mansion, really, kind of set back against the fells yet near to the lake.'

'It sounds amazing.' Morgan thought about the photos she'd found under Emma's bed of her outside a grand house.

'It does, but in reality it wasn't. It was too big for Evelyn. She was the lady who owned it, and she lived there alone for a very long time after her husband died. Her grandson was brought to live there one day because his mother was a drug addict who was neglecting him. He was a strange boy. I didn't see much of him because of the incident with his mother, and then not long after that, Evelyn had a stroke and needed care. She was looked after at home for some time but eventually didn't want to stay in the house and was taken into a private nursing home. We were given notice by the family solicitor and that was that. The four weeks' notice was spent packing up the house. Boxing everything up. I think the house stayed empty because Evelyn didn't want to sell it – at least not until she had to. Private care is expensive and the money eventually dwindled away.'

'What is Evelyn's full name, and can you tell me about her grandson? What was the incident you mentioned?'

'Evelyn Reynolds, and her grandson was Mark Ralph or Ralph Mark. I can't remember now, and anyway she always referred to him as the boy. Shirley or Emma would have been able to tell you more. They said he was a nightmare, always very angry, always in trouble, but it was when they brought his mother's dead body home that the real problems began.'

Morgan was scribbling notes down. She looked up and stared at Mary. 'What?'

Mary leaned forward, her elbows on the table, and lowered her voice.

'His mum got herself in lots of bother with the police. She was on a downward spiral, she overdosed, and Evelyn, despite distancing herself from her, did what she was expected to do.'

'What?'

'Well, she brought her body home until the funeral and had her laid out in the parlour. This is according to Shirley, who was a real gossip and quite good fun until the drink took hold of her. Well Mark or Ralph, he found her in there – no one had thought to tell the poor kid his mother was dead, and he was found trying to drag her out of the coffin.'

Morgan felt her heart tear in two for the boy who'd had to deal with such horror. 'Did they get him help?'

'Evelyn got him all sorts of help. It didn't make any difference. He started acting stranger and stranger. Got himself kicked out of school for beating up a girl. He stopped coming out of his room throughout the day. He ended up going to the family plot in the grounds of the house one night with a shovel and dug his mother up. They found him with her in the outhouse. God, it makes me shudder, the thought of it.'

'What happened to him?'

'Got carted off to the loony bin and probably put into care when they let him out; actually I have no idea what happened to him.'

Morgan felt the horror of the situation settle over her. If this kid had an obsession with his dead mum, through no fault of his own, maybe he was killing the only people who'd known him and let him down.

'Do you think Evelyn could still be alive? Would she know where he is?'

Mary shrugged. 'I couldn't say, flower – it's been a long time.'

'Do you know which home she's in?'

'Now then it was a fancy private one... near Sizergh maybe? I think it's changed its name a few times, but they might be able to tell you if she's still alive, but I wouldn't pin your hopes on it. She was in her seventies when she got taken into it. She'd likely be in her nineties now. What about me, do you think I should leave town or something, because if this person is killing the staff who used to work there, I might be next?'

'In all honesty I don't know. Do you live above the post office?'

She nodded.

'It will have an excellent security system. I can arrange for someone to keep an eye on it. If it was me, I would probably go away for a little break. Could you do that? Could you get someone to run the place for a week?'

Mary smiled at her. 'I could try. My sister usually does that for me when we go on a break, but I wouldn't want to put her in any danger by default. I'll be okay – I'll tell Donald he can't leave me on my own. He's enough to scare anyone away.'

'Make sure he doesn't, and I'll arrange for an alert to be put on your flat so if you had to call, it would be prioritised. Thank you for coming to speak to me, Mary – you've been very helpful.'

'What about you, flower? Make sure you don't put yourself in any danger either. I've read the news stories; I don't know how you're still standing.'

'Thanks. I'm made of strong stuff.'

Mary picked up her coffee and walked out, turning to wave at Morgan.

Her phone began to vibrate on the table, and Ben's name flashed across the screen.

'Are you okay? Did you get lost?'

'No, it was busy. I found out some very interesting stuff that relates to the investigation. I'm on my way back now – I'll fill you in.'

She stood up and looked around the café, which had emptied since she'd been talking to Mary. There was a guy on his own sitting at a table in the window on a laptop all dressed in black. Normally she wouldn't blink an eye because she was also dressed in black and always was, but she still couldn't shake the feeling of being watched that had been lurking around her since she'd discovered Shirley's body.

Ending the call, she grabbed the coffees and brown paper bag containing their lunch and began the walk back to the station, glad of a chance to clear her head and try to make sense of what was happening. She needed to find out if Evelyn Reynolds was still alive and where her grandson was.

THIRTY-NINE

Morgan walked into a full office; the whole squad was there, even Marc, who was perched on the corner of the desk she usually sat at. Ben had been busy – there were photos of both Shirley and Emma tacked on to the white board. Below it there were lists, and Mick Oswald was on both of them. There was also a custody photo of Mick on there; underneath were Shirley's and Emma's names. It looked like it all sewed up neatly. She passed Ben his baguette and latte, then sat at her desk.

'Glad you made it back before the end of the shift, Brookes.'

She turned to Des, fixing her stare on him. Only certain people were allowed to call her Brookes; he needn't think he could start doing it.

'Morgan to you, and you're a fine one to talk, Des – takes you longer to get your lunch than you spend solving crimes.'

Red patches flared on his cheeks, and she felt a bit mean.

Ben lifted his hand. 'Children, behave – we have too much to do for you two to be bickering like preschool kids. I'm just waiting for Al to join us then we'll start.'

Morgan opened her mouth to speak when in rushed Al, the

mug he was carrying sloshing hot coffee all over the front of his shirt and trousers. Amy passed him some tissues to blot himself with.

'Right, I'll go through what we do have then anything else you can add to it if I've missed it off.'

She opened her mouth again, and Marc stood up. 'Let's get this clear: I'm very grateful to you all for your hard work.'

Ben was staring at him in amazement. Amy glanced at Morgan, flicked out her fingers and mouthed, 'Boom.'

'Sir, that's great but—'

'But we need to get this solved. We have two murders and one mutual suspect who has now been found this afternoon with a serious head injury, unconscious and bleeding at his house. You and Morgan found him – do the injuries look self-inflicted or was he attacked, and if so, by whom? Who would have a reason to do this to him?'

He picked up a white-board pen, uncapping it. 'Answers on a postcard, please.'

The air in the room was charged, full of unseen bolts of electricity, and she knew it was just a matter of time before something happened.

She stood up.

'There was no weapon to hand that we could see, but he had a significant head wound; it would take a lot of force to the back of his head. I don't think it was self-inflicted.'

'You don't think it was or the evidence suggests it wasn't – which one is it, Morgan?'

'There was no evidence, sir. There wasn't a weapon anywhere in plain sight, nor did it look like he had fallen and hit his head on anything, therefore it's highly likely whoever did this took it with them.'

'Right, good. So where does that put Mick Oswald as a suspect if someone tried to kill him too? Does he know something or is he connected? I've looked on his intelligence records and he's a low-level drug dealer. Is there a possibility this is nothing to do with both murders and more to do with the criminal element?'

His phone began to vibrate in his pocket. He took it out and glanced at the screen.

'Sorry, I need to take this.'

Then he was out of there, leaving them all staring after him as the door slammed shut.

Ben sighed. 'Right, where were we?'

Amy replied, 'Is he for real? Does he not know he can't just bounce in and take over when it suits him then disappear again? We don't even know anything about him. Is he a good inspector? Has anyone got the gossip yet?'

'I think he's trying to help. What I don't think he realises is how much he's getting on our tits.'

Morgan held up her hand. 'I have some information that is probably going to blow all of that out of the water. I'm not saying Mick isn't or couldn't be involved...'

'But?' Ben was staring at her. 'Is this why you took forever to get lunch and my stomach is complaining more than Des's?'

She nodded. 'Mary from the post office asked me if she should be worried about the two murders. I asked her if she knew about the house Emma worked at and why she was worried. She said that over twenty years ago she worked with Shirley and Emma at one of the old lakeside mansions. Armboth Hall, perhaps later known as Lakeview.'

Everyone was staring at her.

'Well, the old lady who lived there, Evelyn Reynolds, had a grandson who was a bit odd – apparently none of the staff liked him, and then he barricaded himself in one of the outhouses.'

Ben stepped closer. 'Why?'

'With his dead mum's body; he dug her out of the family plot.'

'Jesus, where is he now?'

She shrugged. 'I'm not even sure of his name. Mary said it was Ralph Mark or Mark Ralph. He got taken away to a mental institution. I don't even know if Evelyn is still alive.'

'Amy?'

'I'm on it – give me a minute.'

Ben smiled at Morgan. 'I should make you walk into town more often.'

'Ha-ha, funny.'

He turned to write on the board. *Mark Ralph , Ralph Mark, Evelyn Reynolds.*

'What was his mum called? Do we know?'

'Found her. Or at least I've found Evelyn. Wow, look at that house! It's amazing – looks like my dream home.'

They all crowded around Amy's computer. On the screen was a black-and-white photo of a typical Lakeland mansion, built out of slate and limestone. Standing in front of it was a tall, smartly dressed woman, her hair in a bun. She was a scary-looking woman.

'You wouldn't mess with her, would you? She looks... What's that word?'

'Austere?' said Morgan.

Des looked at her. 'What does that mean?'

'Strict, severe, gives the impression that she doesn't take fools lightly. I bet she was a harsh woman to work for.'

'Look at you with your big words, Morgan.'

'I read a lot; you should try it sometime, Des.'

Ben reached his hand out, placing it on the small of Morgan's back where no one could see. 'Let's me and you go and pay a visit to Lakeview to see if Ralph is still there. Amy and Des, you try and find out what happened to Evelyn, please. If you manage to locate her, I want you to go and visit her immediately.'

They replied in unison. 'Yes, boss.'

'If our new inspector wants to know what's happening, tell him you're going to speak to Mick Oswald's next of kin.'

Morgan looked at Ben questioningly.

'I just need to do this my way, okay, without him jumping in feet first and taking over. We'll fill him in later.'

She wasn't judging him. She'd done her fair share of not being open and honest with Ben about leads and enquiries; she was just surprised to hear him this way.

'Don't say it, Brookes – you are a bad influence on me.'

She laughed. 'Let's go. Apparently there's some famous writer living there now. Let's hope it's not Ralph. Could you imagine if he took his childhood experiences and turned them into a novel Stephen King would be proud of?'

She was smiling, but deep down she was thinking that this was exactly what it could be. There was a good chance that Evelyn's grandson was a deeply disturbed individual – unless he'd worked through his issues whilst in hospital and now lived a relatively mundane life, of course, but somehow she didn't think this was true.

The more she thought of it, the more certain she was they had their killer. Now they needed to find him.

FORTY

All good things must come to an end and now it was time to take her home. That was life; it was how it was supposed to be. You live then you die – there wasn't anything more to it. He'd saved her for last because he'd wanted her to know what he'd done; he wasn't sure if the care staff would even let her see a newspaper or whether she still had the mental capacity to read one.

The house had been sold for a steal a few years ago. If he'd had the money, he would have snapped it up, but unfortunately he hadn't. He had a plan though; they'd only sold it because her funds had dried up to pay the nursing-home fees, so once she was dead, the proceeds of the sale would go directly to him. There was no one else left – he'd made sure of that. If she'd got all sentimental and decided to leave those two bitches Cook and Emmie something, well they were no longer around to receive.

He'd realised Emmie was only a few years older than him when he'd started tracking her down; she'd seemed older when he was a kid. She must have gone straight to working at the hall from school. What a miserable life.

Killing them hadn't just been about the will but about

how they'd helped his grandmother to keep him from his mother. Oh he had hated them for years. Turns out he shouldn't have worried too much about them though, because they were both living sad existences that couldn't have been much fun. In a way, he'd helped them out by removing them from the miserable lives that they'd been living, much the same as his grandmother. Sitting in a chair by a window, drooling and mumbling for twenty years, was hardly what you would call enjoying the last years of your life; it was barely an existence.

He'd received a phone call from Linda, the nursing supervisor, to say his gran wasn't well. He smiled. Gran wasn't a name he'd ever called her in his youth – it had been Grandmother and nothing less.

He looked in the mirror: clean-shaven, face scrubbed and moisturised, aftershave on, check, check, check, always giving the impression of a well-put-together man. You never let them see you with your guard down; it just wasn't done. He'd been taught well until that night that everything changed.

If he managed to pull this off, then there was one last person he was going to be paying a visit to. That stuck-up little bitch Tamara, who had made his life a misery on the school bus and in the classroom. He knew that she was now called Tammy and worked in a hairdresser on Main Street; he knew that she'd only been married for a short time before her husband had left her and that she'd been on her own for the last three years.

He knew a lot of stuff about a lot of people – he was good at that. He was good at finding out information, seeking out facts and then storing them until he needed them. He would enjoy watching her die this time for the sheer pleasure of it and not out of necessity.

Strolling up the drive to the nursing home, it reminded him of the hall. Lately he couldn't stop thinking about the hall. All those dark thoughts that would float through his mind that he'd never given much time to had begun to hover in the same place and never move on.

He was let in by Linda, who looked as if she was having a terrible morning. He felt a tiny bit bad for her because it was about to get a whole lot worse.

'Mr Reynolds, thank you for coming. I'm sorry to call you out, but I think you need to see her for yourself. She's not been well since the last time you were here, but today she's very agitated. We had to give her a mild sedative in the night. She keeps pointing to the photograph of her house. It's all very sad.'

'It's heartbreaking, Linda, it really is. She was always such a strong, independent woman and a huge part of my life. I wonder if it would be too much for her to take her for a drive to see the old place? It might make her feel better if she could see what a terrible state it's in now. It's been left abandoned for all these years – the windows are gone, it's all boarded up and the gardens that she so lovingly tended are all overgrown.'

'I don't think that would be a good idea, if I'm honest – it might upset her even more. I think she'd be better to remember it as it was. Maybe you could take her a walk in the grounds, if you wrap her up and talk about the good times before she had her stroke.'

A loud screech from the opposite end of the hall sent Linda waddling off in that direction.

He headed down to his grandmother's room and walked right in. As annoying as Linda was, she was right – his grandmother looked frailer than ever tucked up in the bed.

'I have a surprise for you. Let's go home.'

Her eyes opened wide, and she tried to jerk her head.

'Oh, don't be like that. Linda doesn't think it's a good idea either, but do you know what? I think Linda should keep her fucking nose out of business that doesn't concern her. Now let's get you wrapped up and out of this stinking shithole. There's only so much piss you can withstand before it fills your nose and your pores.'

He crossed the room and grabbed a large towelling dressing gown off the peg by the bed, then pulled off her covers and swung her legs around, so she was sitting up. She was shivering, her body shaking with either fear or cold. He didn't really care.

He wrapped the dressing gown around her, then opened the wardrobe door and pulled a thick, black woollen coat out. He knew this coat; it was her funeral coat – she'd worn it to his mum's funeral. There was a small, diamanté Chanel brooch pinned to the lapel – or there would be if some thieving little bastard hadn't stolen it.

As he put the coat over her, he saw a glint of something sparkly. It was still there – wasn't that something? He really hadn't expected that.

Next, he pulled a pair of thick bed socks over her feet, then put her old lady slippers on.

'There, that looks okay. Sorry about your scarf – I had to borrow it for something important, but you'll be fine without it. We just need a wheelchair now.'

He disappeared back into the hall briefly – nowhere near enough time for Evelyn to shuffle towards the emergency bell – and walked back in with a chair.

'Come on – no time to waste. There's some emergency down the other end. I think old Bill has croaked it. Let's get you out to the car.'

He grabbed a hat off the shelf and placed it on her head, then put his arms under hers and swung her round into the chair where she let out a 'Urrgh'.

He tipped her back and pushed her out into the corridor, where all the activity was focused on a bedroom at the opposite end of the hallway.

No one gave them a second glance. He made his way to the front entrance and pressed the green door-release button on the wall. Then the door was open, and they were outside on the driveway.

He pushed the chair towards his car. His 4x4 was a bit too high up for Evelyn even on a good day so he opened the back door then scooped her up and practically threw her in. He was going to leave the wheelchair, then decided it would come in handy and save him exerting himself when they got to the house.

He opened the boot, folded the chair up then threw it inside, slammed the boot shut and got into the driver's seat.

He glanced in the rear-view mirror at the terrified face of his grandmother. 'Hey, you don't need to look so scared. You're finally going home after all these years. Won't that be wonderful for you? Isn't that what you've always wanted?'

Then he started laughing and drove away from the nursing home before someone realised he'd just stolen their longest, most loyal resident and some poor bastard's wheelchair.

FORTY-ONE

Morgan had googled Lakeview House, which was situated right at the far end of Thirlmere, before they'd set off, and found an old listing for it on Fine and Country Estate Agents. It had ten bedrooms, four bathrooms, a drawing room, dining room, library, parlour and its own lake frontage. Ben was driving, and she let out a sigh.

'What's wrong?'

'Nothing, it's just this house is amazing – or it was amazing. It's a bit of a wreck now. Imagine living in a house with ten bedrooms and your own library.'

'Nice, but the cost to keep it would be extortionate. Would you live there if you could?'

'In a heartbeat. Imagine wandering around with your books tucked under your arm and going for a picnic by the lake whenever you wanted.'

'It's not a Disney film, Morgan,' he said as he turned into the overgrown driveway then slowly drove along the bumpy road until the house came into view, with its boarded-up downstairs windows and long tendrils of ivy creeping along the outside of the wall. 'In fact, it's more like a bloody horror movie.'

Morgan didn't think so, she loved it even more in person. There were no cars parked out the front.

'I thought you said there was a writer living here?'

'That's what Mary said.'

They got out of the car, the slamming doors echoing loudly in the air.

'Imagine living here as a kid. How cool would it have been?'

'Terrifying.'

She smiled at him. 'But you live in a house that's pretty big for a guy with no kids.'

He glanced at her. 'Yes, I do, but I was supposed to have a tribe of kids to fill it until it all went spectacularly wrong.'

Morgan's hand cupped her mouth. 'Oh, Ben, I'm sorry – I wasn't thinking.'

He laughed. 'In all honesty, I don't think I really wanted them: too noisy and far too messy.'

He strode off towards the front door, and she would have kicked herself in the pants if she could for being so insensitive.

He raised his fist and hammered on the huge, somewhat dilapidated, oak door and waited.

'Just in case someone is home.'

She left him there and walked around the perimeter of the property, in complete awe at the size of it. There were over-grown box hedges that had once lined a formal garden. What she was looking for was the private cemetery plot and the outhouse, but she couldn't see either of them.

She got so far and then had to turn back; the brambles and gorse had run wild, and it would need a rotavator to get any further.

Walking back, she could see the lake against the backdrop of the fells. The dark, mottled greens against the navy of the water was stunning. There was a wooden jetty that she could imagine sitting on and paddling her feet on a balmy, summer's evening.

Ben shouted, 'Dead end, come on – let's get back and see if there's anywhere else we should be checking.'

She walked back to the car, where he was already getting inside. Turning around for one last look, she knew that if she'd been given the chance, she would have looked after and cherished this house until the day she died.

Ben headed back to the station; Morgan was staring out of the window.

'Hey, what's up? House envy?'

She laughed. 'Yes, I suppose it is. Not just house envy, but how do people have the kind of money to own properties like that in the first place?'

'Well, I can tell you now they don't work for the police, that's for sure.'

She laughed. 'Are you telling me I'm in the wrong job?'

'That depends on what you want out of life. If you want a millionaire lifestyle, you're going to need to find a millionaire because I'm never going to cut it unless I win the lottery.'

She reached out her hand, placing it on his leg. 'No amount of money is worth trading you for – I love you.'

'I love you more than you could ever know, Morgan, and no, I don't think you're in the wrong job. Look at all the cases you've solved, the killers and criminals you've helped put behind bars to make the world a much safer place. I mean I'd suffer far less heartburn if you decided to take up a different vocation, but it wouldn't be you.'

She laughed. 'I suppose it wouldn't.'

She didn't speak the rest of the way, but there was a longing deep down inside her for a life she could never have, and she needed to push it back down to where it belonged, buried deep inside of her, because she had no right to let it rule her life.

FORTY-TWO

Amy had passed Des a list of nursing homes with their phone numbers next to them. 'Start phoning around and ask if there's an Evelyn Reynolds there, and I'll try and find the grandson.'

'They won't tell us that.'

'Yes, they will. Tell them you're a detective and working a major investigation. You're not asking for her bank account number – you just need to know if they have her or if she used to live there. It's basic legwork. Christ, you don't even need to leave the office – just use that charm of yours and see how far you get.'

He flipped the finger at her, and she gave him two back.

'I need a coffee; do you want one?'

He shook his head.

She walked down to the small kitchen area and switched on the kettle, wondering if Marc wanted a drink. He hadn't been back since he'd abruptly left the office over an hour ago.

She walked to his office and knocked on the door. There was no answer, so she pushed the door open and stuck her head inside.

There was no sign of him, but his aftershave lingered in the air. She had to admit he smelled pretty good.

Looking around to see if anyone was watching her, she realised that there was no one around and stepped inside. Not quite sure what she was doing, she walked over to his desk. If she got caught, she'd just say she was repaying the favour from when she'd caught him snooping in Ben's office.

His desk was clear of anything exciting, not even a dirty coffee cup. There was a photograph frame on his desk. She picked it up: there was a woman and two teenage girls smiling for the camera. It didn't look like the kind of photograph an amateur photographer would take. In fact... She looked closer. It was the kind of picture you saw on websites or catalogues advertising hiking gear. She was pretty sure this was either cut out of a magazine or printed off a website – it was weird. She put it down quickly, in case he caught her snooping, realising she was overstepping the line.

She slipped out of his office and back to the kitchen area.

'How are you getting on?' She placed a mug of coffee on the desk in front of Des, who was shaking his head. He ended the phone call.

'Not very good. do you have any idea how many of these places there are?'

'Give me some, I'll do the rest and you take over searching the systems for a Ralph or Mark Reynolds. What do you think of the new boss?'

He shrugged. 'Not sure. Up to now a pain in the arse. Why are you asking?'

'I don't know, he just gives off a weird vibe, and he's got a picture of his wife and kids on the desk, but it doesn't look like one.'

'No, what does it look like then, a loaf of bread?'

'Don't be stupid. It looks like he's cut it out of a magazine.'

Des started laughing. 'Jesus, Amy, maybe they're models or maybe they were in a magazine, it doesn't mean anything, or maybe he's such a good photographer that's what it looks like when he takes a photo. If that's the case get him to do you a new one for your Facebook profile, so you don't look like you've been stung by a wasp.'

'And maybe you shouldn't be such an arsehole. I'm just saying, and where is he? He disappeared ages ago, one minute he's leading the investigation all fired up and the next he's missing without a trace.'

'You and Jack want to switch it up a bit, stop watching all those thrillers on Netflix and give the comedies a go for a change.'

She shook her head at him.

The phone began to ring on Morgan's desk, and she reached over to pick it up. 'CAST'

'It's Amber, I'm at the hospital and can't get hold of Ben or Morgan. The guy I'm here with has come round a little, if they want to speak to him. Can you let them know?'

'Will do, thanks.'

She rang Ben's mobile, figuring Morgan was probably driving. He usually let everyone ferry him around.

'Yes, Amy, are you ringing to tell me you've found Evelyn or her grandson?'

'Not, yet. Amber rang to say Mick Oswald has regained consciousness, if you want to pay him a visit.'

'That's something. One less body to worry about. Cheers – we'll head there now. The house was empty or at least no one answered.'

'Hey, before you go, where's the boss?'

'No, idea. What do you want him for?'

'Nothing, just wondered where he'd disappeared to.'

'Your guess is as good as mine.'

The line went dead, and she put the phone down. Something was amiss, but she couldn't put her finger on it. She knew it was none of her business and she should be concentrating on finding Evelyn, but something wasn't right.

FORTY-THREE

The hospital was busy, but Amber must have been waiting for them because she appeared out of a set of double doors and waved them forward. They followed her through the busy accident and emergency department to a cubicle with the curtain drawn. Mick Oswald lay on the bed, hooked up to a blood pressure monitor, his face ashen, but he managed a small smile when he realised who Morgan was.

'Hey, Mick, glad to see you're awake. How are you feeling?'

She pulled a chair up next to his bed. Ben hung back with Amber.

'Better for seeing you.'

She smiled at him. 'Bless you. What happened? Can you remember?'

'Not really. I know I was getting ready to go out but that's it.'

'Did you let anybody inside your house?'

'No, don't think so. It's a bit fuzzy, and I feel a bit queasy if I'm honest.'

Morgan reached up and patted his hand. 'I bet you do –

that's a nasty head injury. I have to ask you: did you do this yourself?'

He smiled. 'No, I can tell you that one for sure. My arms don't bend that far back, and to be honest with you, if I was going to top myself, I'd do it a far less painful way.'

'Why would someone want to hurt you? Do you owe anyone for drugs? Beer? Have any gambling debts?'

'You missed sex off that list. No, I know I've been a bad lad in the past, but I don't do any of that now – too old for a start.'

'How well do you know Emma Dixon?'

'Don't tell me she did this. I would never have guessed that in a million years.'

Morgan turned to look at Ben, then back to Mick.

'No, she definitely didn't, Mick. I just want to know how close you are to her.'

'We were seeing each other for a while, but then that interfering old cow, Shirley, told her I was bad news and then we weren't. I really like Emma, she's nice and easy to get on with – never any dramas with her.'

'Were you angry with Shirley because of that?'

'Too right I was, but not angry enough to kill her, if that's what you mean.'

'Why did you not mention this when we spoke to you last time? And have you heard about Emma?'

He stared straight into her eyes, and she could see fear inside of them. She felt bad – no, not bad, terrible because this never got any easier.

He tried to shake his head. 'Argh, that hurts. Look I wasn't going to admit I'd had a bit of a falling-out with Shirley. You'd have thought I killed her and I didn't. I'm telling you now it wasn't me.' He clamped a hand to the side of his head.

He closed his eyes, and she glanced at Ben. He nodded at her to continue and suddenly she didn't want to be here, passing on bad news. She wanted to be anywhere but sitting next to

Mick Oswald in hospital, the beeps and vibrations distorting the air around them, the smell of blood and antiseptic making the lining of her stomach crawl.

He opened his eyes and looked at her again.

She looked down towards her feet, took a deep breath and met his gaze.

'I'm sorry to tell you this.'

He held up a hand. 'Then don't, love, please don't. I don't want to know what you're going to say.'

Ben stepped closer. 'I think you know, Mick; we're only doing our job. You have a right to know.'

Tears filled his pale blue eyes, and he looked back to Morgan. 'She's dead, isn't she?'

'I'm sorry, yes she is.'

They began to flow freely down his cheeks, leaving clear tracks through the dirty brown patches of dried blood on the side of his face. They gave him a few minutes, his eyes squeezed shut.

He finally opened them.

'How and why? Where did it happen?'

'She was murdered in her house.'

He swallowed loudly. 'Have you caught whoever did it?'

Morgan answered, 'Not yet.'

'You think I did it. I didn't; I wouldn't. I can guarantee you this though, I will kill whoever has done this, if I find out who it is, so you better get a move on before I'm allowed out of here.'

'How did the person who attacked you get into your house? Was the front door locked?'

'I don't know – probably not. I don't have anything worth taking.'

'Apart from your lifestyle and the various criminals you associate with, can you think why anyone would want you dead?'

'Nothing comes to mind.'

'Could you tell us more about when you worked at Armboth Hall?'

'I told you everything last time. I worked there occasionally when I was younger – that was a lot of years ago, love. I helped out in the gardens, but I mainly worked at the church or cemetery.'

'Doing what?'

'Grave digging. Back-breaking work that was, I tell you; we never had no fancy diggers back then.'

'Did you ever dig a grave at the hall?'

'Yes, I did just the one, and after that awful incident never again. They had a private burial plot in the cemetery. When the kid went nuts and dug his dead mother up, she was moved there and put into a specially built crypt. Suppose it was the safest thing to do. Who knew he'd go that level of crazy? Sad really – he was only a lad.'

The curtain opened and Morgan recognised the fiery doctor who always told them off. Her eyes were blazing with anger at all three of them.

Ben whispered, 'Time to leave.'

'Who told you it was okay to come in here and question my patient?'

She was staring at Amber, who looked down at her boots.

Morgan stood up. 'We're leaving. Thanks, Mick, take care.'

'Yes, you are,' the doctor said.

Ben squeezed past her; Morgan looked at her. 'Sorry, but it was very important.'

'Come on, Doc – they're okay for coppers, even if they have just broken my heart.'

The doctor clamped her lips shut so they were nothing more than a thin line.

Morgan and Ben made their escape, leaving Amber to face her wrath.

. . .

Once they were out of the hospital and almost back at the car, Ben asked, 'Do you think he's telling the truth?'

'Yes, I felt sorry for him. Someone tried to kill him and then we told him the woman he loved had been killed. You can't fake that kind of emotion – at least I don't think so.'

'I'm not so sure – I wouldn't rule him out just yet.'

'It has to be something to do with that house. All of them are connected to it some way or another. I have an idea: why don't we call at the primary school? They might remember the grandson. It's not every day you get a kid dig up their dead mum.'

'Be my guest.'

Morgan drove to Priory Grove; it had probably changed a lot since then but there was one person who hadn't.

'Are you coming inside?'

He shook his head. 'Not unless you force me to.'

She shut the door.

As she hurried through the gate, her eyes fell on the patch of tarmac where her old school friend, Brittany Alcott, had bled to death after throwing herself out of the staff-room window. There was a small bench there with her name on it now, and a large tub of brightly planted flowers. Blinking away the tears, she hurried towards the large doors and pushed her finger against the buzzer.

'*Yes.*'

'It's Detective Constable Morgan Brookes.'

The door clicked, and she pushed it open, stepping inside, not quite expecting to see Sandra sitting in her little office behind a safety glass screen given that the school day was over but relieved that she was.

'Officer Brookes, how nice to see you – or should we be worried?' Sandra laughed, and Morgan smiled back, letting the slip go. It didn't matter how many times she corrected the woman, she still got it wrong.

'Nothing for you to worry about. I'm trying to trace someone who may have been a pupil here over twenty years ago. Would you have any records that go as far back as that?'

She was nodding. 'Me – I'm the records; I was here then. Who are you looking for?'

'A pupil called Ralph or Mark Reynolds we think.'

She came around, opening the internal doors so she could step through them.

'Mark Ralph – the kid that dug up his dead mother?'

Morgan nodded; everyone had heard about him but her. 'Yes.'

'He was a strange boy, you know. I felt sorry for him when he first got here, so quiet and having to live in that big old house with Evelyn, who wasn't the warmest of people. Oh no, she was as frigid as the air that blows down from the fells on a cold winter's day.'

Morgan wondered how much of this was the truth and how much had been fabricated by the village gossips, but she didn't interrupt.

'He came here after he'd been taken off his mum. She was a druggie and had been leaving him on his own to fend for himself. I don't think Evelyn quite knew what to do with him. She'd only ever had Kate and she went off the rails as soon as she hit puberty. Some kids are that way inclined, aren't they? You give them the world, and they take it and throw it all back in your face without a second thought.'

'That's true.' She didn't particularly agree with Sandra, but she wanted to know everything.

'Well, he never settled in, not really. I think he was isolated and mixed up by all accounts. He adored his mother, even though she never fed him and left him alone to fend for himself.'

'What happened to her?'

'It was the drugs – gets you in the end. She was injecting – they found her keeled over the kitchen table with a needle sticking out of her arm. But Evelyn was a stickler for family traditions, and despite her not speaking to her for a couple of years, she had her body taken up to the house and she was laid out in the parlour. Well, no one thought to tell poor Mark, and he stumbled across her body in the night. I don't think he ever got over it. Shirley told me that he was trying to drag her out of the coffin. Urgh, it gives me the creeps just thinking about it, but you have to feel sorry for the boy, don't you?'

'What happened to him whilst he was here?'

'Attacked a young girl one day, pulled out a bloody big clump of her hair. The teacher, Mr Atkinson, threw him on the floor he was so angry with him. It was awful. I can honestly say we haven't had an incident of that magnitude since. Apart from poor Brittany that is, and little Charlie, but she wasn't in school when that evil man took her.'

Morgan realised that this small school had had more than its fair share of tragedies.

'Is Evelyn still alive, do you know? I'm trying to find her and Mark.'

Sandra's eyes opened wide. 'The last I heard she was in that posh nursing home on the outskirts of Kendal, might be Saint Quentin's. It's a private one. I think she's still alive. She was a stubborn old bird. She's probably still hanging on. I'm not sure about Mark though. I don't think she had anything to do with him after he got taken away. Sorry, after a few years it was old news – I lost track.'

'Don't be sorry – that's really helpful.'

She left Sandra wondering what was with all the questions and rushed back to Ben.

.   .   .

He was sitting there with his tie loosened and the top two buttons of his shirt undone. He had a black suit on today and with his recently shaved head, he looked a little bit rough around the edges but as gorgeous as ever. She wondered if he was unconsciously mirroring her dress sense, or if it had been the last clean suit in his wardrobe.

She filled him in on Sandra's gossip, and he began typing the name of the nursing home into the search bar on his phone. Seconds later, he was typing the postcode into the sat nav.

'Come on, what are you waiting for?'

She began driving, following the directions, but she had a rough idea of the area where she was heading.

She just hoped that Evelyn was still alive and able to give them the information they needed.

FORTY-FOUR

He stared at his grandmother in the rear-view mirror. Her face was slack on one side and taut on the other, her eyes were wide with terror, and he didn't know if he should feel bad for her or not. He was doing her a favour; she was going to live forever if he didn't put an end to it, and surely that wasn't much fun when you were stuck in a body that you couldn't control. He knew he would hate it and be grateful for someone to come along and put a pillow over his face to put him out of his misery. She knew where they were heading. He hadn't meant to let it slip earlier, spoiling her surprise. He could tell by the look on her face she was getting stressed out with him.

'Isn't this nice? How long is it since you've been here? I'm sorry, I should have brought you much sooner, but it's been hard, you know. So hard trying to keep up this façade of being a normal person when the voices inside your head have much different ideas. How I keep a job the way I do is beyond me. You must be a little bit proud of me. I turned out better than you imagined, didn't I? Just give me one little nod instead of staring at me like I'm Hannibal Lecter.'

He laughed. 'You do know who he is right? Or do they only

let you watch reruns of *The Golden Girls* and *Cheers* in there? Although I'm not a cannibal – even I draw the line at that. I mean blood smells awful when there's a lot of it. Not as bad as decomposition though – you have no idea how bad my mum smelled when I dug her up. I could taste and smell her for days after that night. She used to smell of that cheap body spray – Charlie I think it's called. Not when I broke her coffin open, oh no – that had all gone. But she was still beautiful and still my mum. They should never have taken me away from her. We didn't have anything, but we were happy. Look at you, you had more than you could ever want or wish for and were as miserable as sin. How about that for irony? You were kinder to the staff than to me. I was a kid – I needed someone to tell me everything was going to work out.'

He slammed on the brakes as he passed the overgrown entrance to the drive, and she jerked forward.

'Oops, sorry about that. You really let the old place go to the dogs. Look at the state of it – you'd never guess that a once beautiful house full of crap memories was hidden behind the brambles, nettles and long grass.'

———————

He began reversing then turned into the drive, and Evelyn noticed a glint of silver – a Parker pen wedged into the leather seat just out of reach. She began to stretch out the fingers on her lame arm with her good hand, doing her best to push it along so she could try and knock it towards her. The strain of it made tiny beads of perspiration break out on her forehead, but she didn't stop – she kept on nudging her hand towards it.

The house came into view, and she tore her gaze from the pen to look at it. He was right: it was nothing but a wreck now. What had she been thinking? Leaving it this long. She had spent years holding on to it for what reason? For it to come to an end like this?

She had known he was troubled from the very moment the social workers had brought him to her doorstep. How could he not be – living the way he had been, watching his mother bring men home and have sex with them to get her next fix? She realised now that she could have changed all of this; she could have brought Kate home sooner and tried again to get her off the drugs; she could have loved him better. Instead, she'd shut herself off after her husband's death. Kate hadn't been there for her, so she hadn't made the effort to be there for her, and now Shirley and Emmie were dead and she knew it was because of her bad decisions. She had known he'd hated them as a child, but she could not have known he would have harboured that hatred deep inside him until now.

She had heard the nurses talking about the murders outside her room as she lay there, her blood chilled to the bone, terrified of what might happen next.

The car lurched to a halt outside the house, the sudden movement dislodging the pen, sending it rolling towards her hand. It took every ounce of strength she had to pick it up, but she did with her good hand, pushing it deep into her curled-up fist and hoping to God that he didn't notice it. She had made her peace with death and was ready to go when her time came, but under no circumstances would she die at the hands of a madman, whether he was her grandson or not.

When God decided to take her, she would go, but not this way.

He got out of the car and went to get the wheelchair out of the boot, and she looked down at her curled-up fist, satisfied that he'd be too busy to even notice the tip of the silver metal pen peeking out of it. The door was opened, and the cool air hit her. It was always cool by this house unless it was a baking-hot summer's day.

He grabbed her and lifted her out effortlessly, as if she weighed nothing, then dropped her into the chair.

'It's a good job there's no one home. Did you know the people who bought it sent a fancy writer from London to look after it until they could start to renovate? Who'd have thought? She's gone back. I heard her telling that woman in the post office she needed to go home for some important meetings, so we have this place to ourselves. Just like old times – won't that be nice?'

He pulled a large key out of his pocket and inserted it into the lock.

It opened, and Evelyn realised that after all this time, she was finally back in her home and, this time, she wouldn't ever be leaving it.

He pushed the door open, ran back down the steps and began to jerk the chair and her backwards up them, banging the wheels against each granite step, sending shockwaves through her body.

Inside the grand hallway, it was dark, but it wasn't as bad as she'd expected. A myriad of memories flooded her mind. It hadn't all been doom and gloom. She'd loved this place and had spent all her life here, laughing and hosting parties until Arthur had died, leaving her alone. She wondered if he was still here, wandering the rooms, waiting for her to come home. That thought gave her a warm rush of heat that filled her heart. They'd been happily married. He'd have loved to have filled the house with children, but it had never happened. Kate had been their only child.

A sharp pain replaced the warmth inside her heart. She wished she could relive her life and make it right. Give Kate and Mark the happy endings they deserved, instead of this madness that had led them all down a dark, shadowy path into the darkest depths of hell.

FORTY-FIVE

The nursing home wasn't that dissimilar to the house they had visited earlier: long sweeping drive, huge house built from Lakeland slate and limestone, formal gardens – the only real difference was that it was like looking at a before and after. Oh and there was a small duckpond in the grounds. No Lake Thirlmere, but she could see how Evelyn would enjoy it here, even if she only occupied a single bedroom. There were a couple of nurses in uniform out with patients and why not? The day was pleasant.

'If you manage to put up with me long enough that I reach this age, then you have my permission to suffocate me if I become a burden.'

Morgan laughed. 'Don't be awful – it's not that bad.'

'No, wait till we go inside.'

She rang the doorbell, and a woman dressed in a smart suit came to open it.

'Can I help you?'

'I hope so, I'm Detective Constable Morgan Brookes and this is my colleague, Ben Matthews. We've come to visit Evelyn Reynolds.'

Ben gave a slight nod, and she knew he was impressed; she was far better at wording things than he was.

'Is she expecting you? Oh dear, I hope this isn't bad news for her – she's been a bit under the weather.'

Morgan had to stop herself from fist pumping the air. 'No, nothing like that. We're just interested in getting some background information about her family home.'

'Oh, that's very interesting. Come in – I'll take you down to her room.'

They followed the woman – who introduced herself as Linda – inside and were pleasantly surprised at how fresh it smelled. Morgan had been expecting worse, and by the relief on Ben's face, he had been expecting horrific.

Linda signed them both in, and they followed her down a long corridor, past the entrance to a huge room in which there were an assortment of chairs containing residents all waving their arms in the air.

'Chair aerobics – we like to keep them as active as possible, and they really enjoy it.' She lowered her voice. 'It's the men who are more enthusiastic. I can't possibly think why.'

Morgan looked at the young woman leading the exercises in her skimpy gym clothes and smiled. She had a pretty good idea.

Linda stopped outside a door. 'Evelyn is a very lovely lady; I don't know if you'll be able to get much out of her. She had a massive stroke years ago and lost most of the use of her left side. She can move her right, but her speech never really recovered. She understands everything you say – her mind is still as sharp as ever. She will blink or nod, sometimes she manages a word or two, and on a good day, she can use her right hand to write.'

She knocked on the door, gave it a few seconds then opened it slightly.

'Evelyn, you have some important visitors – is it okay to bring them in?'

There was no reply, no sound or anything. She pushed the

door open wide, stepped inside and looked at the empty bed and armchair next to the window.

'Oh, she may be in the bathroom. Please wait here.'

She went inside, knocking on a door next to a chest of drawers. There was no sound from there either.

Opening it slightly, she muttered, 'Oh...' then turned to them and pointed to two chairs. 'If you take a seat, I'll go and find her – maybe one of the nurses has taken her out for a walk.'

Then she was gone, striding down the corridor in search of Evelyn.

Morgan turned to Ben. 'Where is she?'

'How would I know? Maybe she got fed up and went to join in with the exercises.'

She looked at the photographs on the dresser. There were a couple of wedding photos that had been taken outside of the house. Evelyn was wearing the most beautiful white silk and lace wedding dress, encrusted with pearls. Her husband was wearing a naval uniform, and the pair of them made a handsome couple.

A nurse rushed through the door, her face pale. She checked under the bed, in the wardrobe, and flung the bathroom door wide open to make sure Evelyn hadn't fallen in there and been missed.

Linda joined her, along with another two nurses.

'Where is she?'

'Polly, go check the lounges; Angela, go see if anyone has taken her outside. Didn't her grandson come to visit earlier? Has he signed her out of the book and taken her for a drive?'

Ben stood up. 'Have you lost her?'

The nurse, whose cheeks were burning, nodded. 'I'm afraid it seems that way. She can't be far – she can't walk. Her grandson has probably taken her out, although he's never done that before.'

'Do you have CCTV?'

'Yes, oh God, yes we do.'

'Do you want to let me and Morgan take a look at it? We can help. If he's left the home without letting anyone know, we can start a search. We also need as much information on her grandson as you have, please. Name, address, contact number.'

'Of course – thank you. This has never happened before. I don't know what's going on – he's probably just taken her for a walk.'

She kept repeating herself, and Morgan glanced at Ben. She doubted he was out strolling with her. Was this what it had all been leading to? Had he been killing the people who had done him wrong – or that he perceived as doing him wrong as a child, making them pay for his suffering and his mum's death? It seemed that way.

They followed her to a large office situated behind the reception desk. Morgan grabbed the book she had signed minutes earlier, running her finger down the page. Her finger paused on a name four above hers: Mark Reynolds.

She showed it to Ben.

He was already phoning Amy.

'Amy, everything you have or can find me on Mark Reynolds, please, now, and can you and Des get your arses here?'

'*Where?*'

'Saint Quentin's Retirement Home. Evelyn Reynolds has been taken from her room by Mark Reynolds.'

'Actually, we're nearly there. We were already coming; you beat us to it.'

The nurse replayed the black-and-white camera footage from the last hour. There was a tall man in a smart suit. He kept his head down, making it difficult to see his face. But there it was: he came towards the entrance pushing Evelyn in a wheelchair.

'Oh Lord, where is he going with her and why didn't he tell someone? He hasn't even signed her out of the book.'

'Where was everyone?'

She pointed to another camera where a flurry of staff were in and out of a room. 'We had a sudden death down the opposite end of the corridor, and everyone was down there.'

'Do you have cameras outside?' Morgan asked.

'It's offline. We're waiting for the guy to come fix it.'

'Do you know what kind of car he drives?'

Her head shook. 'Might be a BMW. Actually I have no idea what make, but it's a big 4x4. Sorry, that's not much help, is it?'

Morgan rushed out of the front door to the parking area outside. She had to grab her radio out of the car. They needed patrols to flood the area now and begin searching for Reynolds, although it would be a lot easier if they had his number plate and an idea of the car he was driving.

A plain white Corsa turned onto the driveway, and she waved at Amy, who was on her phone. Des waved back then parked the car.

He got out of the car, and she realised that they could take over here, freeing her and Ben up to go out searching, which was what she desperately wanted to do. Amy got out of the car and ended her call.

'There are quite a few Mark Reynoldses. None with a local address though; the nearest one is Preston. I've checked with the hospitals. There have been no admissions either.'

'What car does he drive?'

'Mini Cooper.'

'The nurse thinks he could drive a BMW. How many of those in the area?'

Amy laughed. 'Morgan, are you having a laugh? This is the Lake District. BMWs, Porsches, Land Rovers and Mercedes are the cars of choice; there's probably thousands.'

'I know that: I mean any registered to a Mark. He may have given them a real name but changed his surname.'

Amy shrugged. 'I'll try, but there's one Marc we know who drives a BMW.'

Morgan felt a little light-headed. 'No, it couldn't be him. Could it?'

'Stranger things have happened. It might explain why he's so weird; and I'm pretty sure that picture on his desk is cut out of a magazine. It's probably not even his wife and kids.'

'Crap, I hope not. I don't think I could take it again.' She was thinking back to Taylor, her tutor, her colleague – who she'd thought was her friend until he'd tried to kill her.

She jogged back inside to where Ben was still trying to get the CCTV clearer.

'Amy's here with Des – they can take over. We need to talk, and I think we should go back to the Lakeview House and see if he's gone there. It's the only place that makes sense.'

He looked at her, read the concern etched across her face and stood up. 'Okay.'

No arguments.

He spoke to Linda. 'We need everyone to keep out of Evelyn's room until we've found her, okay? Just in case. Is that possible or do you want me to put someone outside of it to guard it?'

'Oh no, we don't want a police officer standing outside. It would upset the residents. I'll lock it up now and tell everyone it's out of bounds.'

'Thank you.'

Morgan was already out of the door; he was close on her heels. She didn't stop to talk to him and tell him what was going on, just kept on walking until she was in the car's driver's seat, and he was next to her.

'What's happening? Why are you freaking out?'

'I'm not freaking out – well maybe a little. Amy said there

are no Mark Reynoldses in this area and, somehow, I came to the conclusion that he might have a false surname on his driving licence. All we have to go off is that he might drive a BMW and be called Mark. Amy pointed out that we know a Marc who drives one and that's why I'm panicking. It's like the Taylor thing all over again, and I think we need to go back, because that's the perfect place to take her. I think he took her home.'

'Whoa, that's a big jump from possibly drives a BMW to being our new DI, Morgan. I'm not ruling it out, but that's not really even a thing, is it? He's only just moved here, and if Mark Reynolds has been in and out of mental hospitals most of his life, he's not going to have been able to get into the job, let alone make detective inspector. Sorry, I don't particularly like the guy; I find him overbearing and sneaky, but he doesn't give off any crazy Norman Bates vibes. However, we should go back and check the house – that's a good call, but I'm letting Control know where we are and asking for patrols to be aware of our location, so they can get some of the Keswick patrols to meet us there.'

He was right, of course he was – she was freaking out, but it didn't stop her fingers from gripping the steering wheel so tight that her knuckles turned white.

FORTY-SIX

There was no missing the entrance to the drive leading to the
house this time. She drove into the driveway a little too fast for
the overgrown, pothole-filled track and the car was rattling.
When the house came into view, she saw a metallic blue BMW
parked outside, very similar to the one the boss drove.

Ben groaned. 'Oh shit, here we go.'

Then Marc was there waving at them, his tie loosened, his
sleeves pushed up to his elbows, looking more than a little
frazzled.

He was running towards their car, and Morgan said,
'Should I run him over?'

'No, God, not yet – let's see what he has to say first.'

Ben jumped out; she followed. He kept his distance from
Marc.

'What's going on, boss? Why are you here?'

'I heard you tell Control where you were heading, and I
wasn't far away, so I thought I'd come back you up. This guy
sounds dangerous. I thought it might be safer if there were three
of us. I've just had a snoop around and there's a BMW parked
around the back.'

Morgan glanced at Ben, who nodded. 'Thanks, that's great. Should we go and check it out?'

He turned to Morgan. 'You wait here, okay; you can guide the patrols if they can't find it and call for backup if we need urgent assistance.'

Her heart was in her mouth. She didn't want Ben going anywhere out of her sight with Marc because she didn't trust him at all. She managed a nod, and Ben smiled at her, his eyes pleading with her to do what he'd asked.

She watched as they began walking towards the side of the house. Where was Evelyn? There was a good chance she was inside. Torn between wanting to follow Ben and having a chance to check out the house, she decided to see if she could get inside and find her.

As they rounded the corner, she ran to the steps and pushed the door with the palms of her hands. It opened a little, and she slid through the gap into the cool darkness of the house. She gave her eyes a few moments to adjust to the gloom, then stepped into the huge entrance hall, taking in the beautiful grand curved staircase.

She turned on her phone torch, shone it around and sighed; the house was desperately unloved but absolutely magnificent.

Thankful there was no dead Evelyn on the floor, she stepped forward towards the tall grandfather clock beside the stairs and shone the light on its face. The hands were stopped at six, and a sinking feeling inside the pit of her stomach told her they were already too late.

She checked the clock on her phone and found it read six forty-five. Mark's mum had been in the parlour when he'd found her body, and she was looking around, trying to decide which door might be the right one, when a dark shadow fell across her from behind.

She felt herself being yanked off her feet and then dragged towards a door nearby by her hair. The pain was excruciating, and she began to claw at the big hands that had tight hold of her. Once inside the room, her attacker picked her up off the ground, and she screamed, 'Ben.'

She was thrown against the wall with such force there was a loud crack as her bones crushed against it. Her head, which was still painful and swollen after the attack by The Travelling Man, hit it with such force that it made the room swim, and she felt herself losing consciousness.

Just before she passed out, she saw the figure of an old woman in the corner of the room, huddled in her wheelchair, whimpering, and she whispered, 'Evelyn?'

Morgan had no idea how long she'd been unconscious, but it couldn't have been long. She kept her eyes closed, trying to figure out what to do. Her radio was in the car, and she'd dropped her phone when he'd grabbed her in the hallway. She could hear Evelyn making those terrified whimpering sounds, and she wanted to tell her it was okay, they were here to save her, but Ben was outside somewhere, oblivious to what was happening in here.

Opening one eye, she saw their captor hovering over the wheelchair. He reached down and tugged out the bands holding Evelyn's long silver hair in a bun. Her hair cascaded down over her shoulders, and he began to stroke it.

'You always had the most beautiful hair, like strands of molten silver. Did you know I used to watch you brush it each night, before bed? You would sit in front of your mirror with that big gold hairbrush and just smooth it down over it, again and again.'

He grabbed a handful of her hair and took a pair of scissors from his pocket. The loud snip of the blades as he cut a large chunk from it echoed around the empty room. He held it up in the air to examine it.

'This will make a lovely addition to my collection.'

Morgan watched him, realising that the man was insane. It was hard to see his face in the shadows, but she knew he was grinning.

Then he turned and strode towards the door and disappeared out into the hallway.

She sat up, a wave of nausea hitting her, but she forced herself to move. She needed to find a weapon, something to protect them with.

Crawling on her hands and knees, she searched everywhere but couldn't find a weapon; the entire room was devoid of anything she could use. Reaching Evelyn, she grabbed hold of her cold, frail hand, and squeezed it.

'It's okay, I'm a police officer. I won't let him hurt you.'

Evelyn jerked her head down once. Reaching out her right hand, she stroked Morgan's copper-coloured hair, which had escaped from the topknot it had been fastened up in, wisps of it framing her pale face, which now had a large purple-and-black bruise flowering against her porcelain skin, where her cheekbone had connected against the wall.

Evelyn whispered, 'Beautiful.'

They heard his footsteps coming back towards the room, and she grunted, 'Ralph.'

And Morgan realised that she knew who this was: the man with the bad nerves who lived below Shirley Kelly. She'd spoken to him and felt sorry for bothering him. But all this time it had been him.

He stormed back in, his face a mask of fury at the pair of them sitting there so close together.

'What do you think you're doing? Get away from her now.'

Morgan stared into Evelyn's watery pale blue eyes and nodded once. Then, turning to face him, she pulled herself up, so she was standing upright. 'I'm not going to let you do this, Ralph, so you need to know that you're under arrest.'

He started to laugh. 'For real? You're a bloody copper, you came knocking at my door asking questions that I didn't answer, and you're going to put your life on the line to protect that withered old bat? And they have the cheek to label me as crazy.'

'That's what I do – it's my job, so yes, I guess I am willing to do that, but what are you willing to do? Why are you doing this? Whatever your problems were, they're in the past. You're a grown man – you can't take your fucked-up memories and keep reliving them over and over. At some point you need to let them go. My colleagues are outside, and any second now this place is going to be swarming with armed officers.'

He stared from her to his grandmother then back at her.

'Unbelievable, but I like that – it's a pretty good speech. I'm not ready to let go of anything yet, but when I'm done, I might feel different. I doubt it though – I've been holding on to this childhood angst for a very long time. Just ask my psychiatrist – she'll tell you that I have this really big issue with letting go.'

He was fast.

He darted towards Morgan, and she ducked, but he caught her by the hair again, dragging her away from Evelyn and towards him. Her eyes burned with the pain of her hair being torn from her scalp. She was facing him, and he was practically holding her up on her tiptoes by her hair. Her right leg kicked out, and she managed to connect her Doc Marten boot with his kneecap – so hard that his leg gave way. His knee buckled and he let go of her, but stumbled towards her. She didn't have time to move, and he fell into her. She didn't see his fist coming towards her, but she felt his knuckles connect with the side of her head. Everything went grey as she fell to the floor, white-hot lightning forks of pain filling her head.

She could see the clock in this room. He walked over to it and stopped it at six. She wondered if this was the time of death that would be recorded on her post-mortem report, if she didn't stop him.

Loud banging on the front door echoed around the entrance hall, and Morgan thanked God that Ben had finally arrived.

Panic on his face, Ralph turned to her, growling, 'Stay down and you won't have to die. This isn't your fight. I have no quarrel with you, if you let me do what I need to do.'

Turning away from her, he limped across the room to his grandmother. He leaned down, wrapping his hands around her neck.

Morgan screamed as loud as she could, hoping to draw Ben to them as quickly as possible.

Forcing herself to stand up, she wavered as the room swam in and out of her vision and swayed towards the man, unable to walk straight. She watched as Evelyn raised her right hand. It was curled into a fist. Morgan saw the glint of something metal clenched between her bony fingers, and then whatever it was she was holding was rammed with all the strength she could muster straight into his left eyeball.

Morgan heard the squelch as his eyeball popped – and the scream that came from his lips was louder than anything she'd ever heard. He stumbled backwards, releasing his grip on the old lady's neck, and fell to the floor, clutching his hands around his eye.

Morgan grabbed the handles of the wheelchair, leaning against it for support, and pushed Evelyn out of the room, down towards the front door, where Ben was shouting, 'Morgan', over and over again, and kicking at the thick wood.

'I'm okay, we're okay,' she shouted back and turned the key into the lock.

The door was pushed open with such force that it slammed against the wall inside, making it vibrate.

Ben and Marc were standing there, and she had to squint her eyes against the light streaming in because it was so gloomy inside.

He rushed towards her and pulled her close.

'Your face. I heard you scream, and I thought I'd lost you.'

She felt wetness on her cheek and realised he was crying. Morgan held him tight and whispered, 'You can't get rid of me that easily.'

He covered her head in kisses. 'Thank God.'

'Meet Evelyn, who's the baddest bitch you ever met. She's just put Ralph's eye out with a pen. He's in there crying like a baby.'

Marc and Ben ran towards the parlour as two police vans screeched to a halt and Cain came running out of one, two officers getting out of the other.

'Christ, Morgan, you did it again. You almost caused old Benno to have a coronary, and I choked on my egg mayo sandwich when he put the call out for backup. I kid you not, I was driving whilst choking to death; it was a close call.'

He nodded towards her bruised and swollen cheek. 'Bet that hurts like a bitch. Well done – you saved the day again.'

She shook her head. 'Actually, I'd like you to meet Evelyn – she saved the day. She put a pen straight through Ralph's eyeball.'

Morgan turned to her. 'You're a badass, Evelyn – you know that, right?'

Evelyn was smiling, but her eyes were watering, and Morgan leaned down. Wrapping her arms around her, she hugged her tight.

'What do you say we get out of here? I'll take you home and we can have a cup of tea? Let the boys in blue sort this mess out and we'll go and get warmed up.'

'Please.'

Morgan manoeuvred the wheelchair down the steps, careful not to jolt it too hard. The woman was shivering and looked so frail she hoped the shock of all of this didn't make her heart give out.

Cain smiled at them both, then disappeared inside.

After opening the car door as wide as she could, Morgan placed the chair next to it, then leaned down, slid her hands under Evelyn's arms and lifted her gently into the front seat, buckling her seat belt across her before shutting the door.

'Hey, where are you going? You know the drill, Brookes. You need to get checked out at A&E.'

Turning, she smiled at Ben. 'I'm okay – I'm taking Evelyn home.'

Marc stepped around Ben. 'Oh no you're not. You can't drive. Did you lose consciousness? You clearly have a head injury. I won't allow it.'

She glared at him, but he carried on walking towards her. 'Get in the back of the car. Ben can handle this. I'm taking you both to Saint Quentin's – if you won't go to the hospital, we'll get one of the nurses there to clean you up whilst we're getting Evelyn settled.'

Even Ben, who'd been watching with a look of mild horror on his face, smiled, nodding in agreement, and Morgan climbed into the back of the car, doing as she was told.

Maybe their new DI wasn't such an arsehole after all.

FORTY-SEVEN

The staff at the home rushed out and retrieved Evelyn from the car, whisking her inside to get her checked over and safely settled in her bed. Marc got out of the car and opened the back door for Morgan, who was beginning to feel as if she'd been on the worst bender of her life and was now suffering the hangover from hell. He reached out his hand to her, helping her out.

Amy, Des and Angela came running out of the door to meet them all. Angela took one look at Morgan and said, 'Oh my, we need to get you inside now and I'll sort your head out. Shouldn't you go to the hospital?'

Amy was shaking her head. 'What did you do now, Morgan?' To Angela, she added, 'She won't go.'

'I hate them. If you could stick a plaster on it, that would be great. And I didn't do anything – Evelyn is the one who saved both of us.'

Angela smiled. 'If you're sure, I'll do my best. Thank you for finding Evelyn and bringing her back. Is she hurt?'

'No, shook up and probably a little in shock, but she's tougher than she looks. She stabbed her grandson through the eye with a pen.'

Amy muttered. 'Fucking hell. Nice one, Evelyn.'

Angela gasped. 'What? Why? Did he do that to you?' She was pointing to the bruises on Morgan's face and the cuts on her head.

'Yes, she saved both of our lives.'

Clearly unable to process everything, Angela kept shaking her head. She turned to go back inside, and Marc looped his arm through Morgan's, helping her up the steps.

Amy arched an eyebrow at her but followed Angela inside.

Morgan did think about shrugging him off, but she had the worst case of vertigo ever and was grateful for his support.

When she was sitting inside the medical room on the bed waiting for Angela to come and sort her head out, Marc knocked on the door.

'You can come in – I'm not naked or anything.'

He came in, and she thought that he looked a little sheepish.

'Glad to hear you're not – that would have been embarrassing. Are you okay? Do you need anything?'

'I'm good, thanks. You know, me and Amy thought that it was you – that you were Evelyn's grandson.'

His eyes widened. 'Why would you think that?'

'You drive a BMW, you keep disappearing, and you're both called Mark.'

'Oh, I can see why you might think there was a connection, but absolutely not. I know I haven't made the best impression – in fact I've made a huge mess of it all – but I'll let you into a secret: I didn't actually want to move here. I was transferred because of a bit of bother in Manchester. I had an affair with another colleague; we were both married and, well, you know how it goes: one of us had to leave. I left my entire life back there; my wife doesn't want anything to do with me, and my kids are horrified with the way I've treated their mum. This is between us by the way – plus I know I've been acting like a dick, but I promise I'm getting my act together.

'You did great, Morgan. I'm sorry we weren't there to help you. We saw a ramshackle stone building up the fell and thought he may have been up there.'

She nodded. 'That's okay – we all make mistakes. Look at me – I'm the queen of them. I hope you manage to work things out with your wife.'

'Me too. I doubt she'll have me back, but thanks.'

Angela walked in wearing a plastic apron and gloves.

He stood up and smiled at her. 'I guess I'll leave you ladies to it.'

When he was outside, and the door was closed, Angela said, 'He's a bit dishy, isn't he? Smells good too. I do love a man who wears nice aftershave and dresses smart. It makes all the difference, and that guy you were here with earlier was a bit tasty too. Maybe I need to get a job working with the police if the eye candy is that good.

'So are you going to tell me why our poor Evelyn had to stab her own grandson in his eyeball, or do I have to try and guess?'

'It's complicated, but you deserve to know that he's the suspect in two murder investigations and, trust me, you definitely don't want to do this job.'

'It's always the quiet ones, never said boo to a goose, always polite. Just goes to show, doesn't it. He hurt you. Are you sure you're okay, flower?'

Morgan smiled. 'Trust me, this is just a couple of scratches and a bump. I'm fine – I've had much worse.'

Angela stepped closer. 'Well, this might sting. Are you ready?'

'Always.'

Angela laughed and began dabbing the cuts and abrasions on Morgan's face with some cotton wool soaked in antiseptic.

There was a knock on the door, and Angela shouted, 'Come in.'

The door opened and Ben walked in, straight over to where

Morgan was lying on the bed. He bent down and kissed her cheek. Angela winked at Morgan.

'You were saying I wouldn't want to do your job; I'd say you get some pretty good perks.'

Morgan laughed then took hold of Ben's hand and squeezed it, glad to see everyone was here and accounted for.

Angela finished up, using adhesive strips to hold the cut together on the side of her head.

'Well, I'll leave you for a moment. When you're ready, I'm sure we can manage to get you all a hot drink. I'm just going to check on Evelyn.'

Morgan swung her legs off the bed and tried to stand up. The room swam a little, and she felt as if she'd drunk two bottles of wine. She swayed, and Ben was instantly there by her side, one arm around her waist.

'I think I should get you home.'

'Where is he?'

'Cain was escorting him to Lancaster Infirmary. Nowhere else would take him with that pen sticking out of his eye. I can't believe she did that – it must have been so hard for her.'

'I think she did it for me, for Shirley, and for Emma. I'd like to go and thank her properly before we leave.'

Ben walked her down to the room they'd been shown into a couple of hours ago.

Angela came out. 'You can nip in for a minute, but she's shattered, bless her.'

'Thank you.'

Morgan turned to Ben. 'I can manage. Wait out here.'

He nodded and leaned against the wall.

She knocked gently on the door, then opened it and stepped inside. Evelyn was propped up in bed. She had a clean set of pyjamas on, and her hair was neatly pinned back up into a bun.

Evelyn smiled at Morgan and patted the side of the bed for her to sit on.

Morgan didn't need telling twice and stumbled towards her, glad to sit down but cautious not to crush her. She looked so frail. Morgan picked up her hand and held it gently.

'Thank you for saving my life – you were so amazing. It must have been so very hard for you. I don't know how you did it.'

Evelyn reached up and stroked Morgan's face. 'You're amazing too.' The words were slow and not very clear, but enough so that she understood exactly what the other woman was saying.

'Well, that makes two of us – what a team. You have the most beautiful home; I fell in love with it the minute I set foot on the grounds. In case you're worrying about him, he's okay. He's gone to Lancaster Infirmary with two of our officers. He won't ever be let out again, Evelyn – he's a danger to society.'

Evelyn let out a long sigh, then pointed to a notepad on the bedside table.

Morgan picked it up and passed it to her, along with a pen.

She held it whilst Evelyn bent her head and wrote a note with her good hand. When she was finished, she pointed to it.

Morgan turned it around and read.

If you ever have the time to come back, I'll tell you all about my house.

'I would love that; I'd love to hear all about it. I promise next time I have some time to myself, I'll come back and see you.'

Evelyn squeezed her hand, and Morgan squeezed it back. Standing up, she leaned forward and kissed her on the cheek.

'I'll leave my phone number with Angela. If you ever need me, tell her to ring me.'

The frail old woman in the bed nodded, a smile on her face that warmed Morgan's frozen insides.

She waved at her as she left and knew that without a doubt, she'd be back here to visit Evelyn. She reminded her a little of her Aunt Ettie; she needed to visit her too.

Evelyn was tougher than she looked, just like her. Somehow, she had a feeling that the pair of them had been destined to meet up, and she liked the thought of that a lot.

A LETTER FROM HELEN

Dear reader,

I want to say a huge thank you for choosing to read *Sleeping Dolls*. If you did enjoy it and want to keep up to date with all my latest releases just sign up at the following link. Your email address will never be shared, and you can unsubscribe at any time.

www.bookouture.com/helen-phifer

I hope you loved *Sleeping Dolls* and if you did, I would be very grateful if you could write a review. I'd love to hear what you think, and it makes such a difference helping new readers to discover one of my books for the first time.

I love hearing from my readers – you can get in touch on my Facebook page, through Twitter, Goodreads or my website.

Thanks,

Helen

www.helenphifer.com

facebook.com/Helenphifer1

twitter.com/helenphifer1

ACKNOWLEDGMENTS

I'd like to thank my wonderful, amazing editor Emily Gowers for her never-ending support. Emily, I'm so privileged and proud I get to work with you and grateful beyond belief that together we make such a great team. Thank you xx

A huge debt of thanks to the rest of the amazing Team Bookouture, who work so hard behind the scenes to bring these stories to life. I'm so thankful that I have the most amazing publishers who work tirelessly to make my dreams a reality.

A huge high five to the amazing publicity team, especially the gorgeous Noelle Holten for all her support with each new release. The whole team are just amazing, and I'm so privileged to have you all on my side.

I'd like to say a big thank you to my colleagues, who I've worked with over the years at Cumbria Constabulary and who have inspired many of these characters. Especially my old sergeant Paul Madden, who often reminds me he was actually an inspector by the time he retired; Al McNulty for letting me pick his brains; Claire Benni Benson for being the most amazing CSI who literally brings more life into the police station than the entire force put together with her wonderful sense of humour (if you live in Barrow and see the Easter Bunny or Santa riding around on a motorcycle, then it's more than likely this absolute legend); Sam and Tina, who pop up occasionally, my long-time best friends and the queens of scene guards; and my darling friend Cathy Hayes, who is no longer with us but was the light of our working lives and the source of many outbursts of laughter that often got us into trouble and is missed every single day.

Thank you to Sarah McArthur for letting me pick her brains, I really appreciate it.

I'd also like to pay a huge debt of thanks to the wonderful bloggers and reviewers who read these stories and give me so much support. You're all such kind, gorgeous people. There are too many to remember so if I've accidentally missed you, please give me a nudge and I'll make sure I honour you in the next book: Donna @green.witch.lincs, Nikki @nikkie.the.mermaid, Jenn from @injennslibrary, Dawn @Hampshire booklover, Vik @littlemissbooklover, Melanie @melanies_reads, Marnie @onceuponatimebookreviews, Lynda @lyndas_bookreviews, Mary @kuhlreads, Raine @rainenutreads, Claire @lipgloss-gal3101, Leona @leona.omahony, Beth @bethlizbooks, Lisa @the_thriller_post, John @johns_bookshelf, Julie Loves Reading @Julie476, Elaine @elaine_sapp65, Beverley @BookloverBEV.

A huge debt of thanks goes to my wonderful readers – without you, all this wouldn't be possible. You are just amazing; you have no idea how much you warm my heart and make me smile on the days when it's hard. I bloody love each and every one of you for always being so supportive and making me laugh. I wish I could squeeze you all; instead I'll raise a glass to you all and hope you know how deeply loved and appreciated you are. You make the world a much brighter, happier place. Book people are the best people.

I'd also like to thank the many Facebook groups that are so supportive, especially The Friendly Book Community.

A special thank you to Gabby Secomb Flegg and Jo Ripley for inspiring me to meet my goals and shoot for the stars. What a ride the last twelve months have been. I couldn't have done it without you both.

Thanks to Lucy O'Gara for allowing me to pick her brains and use her name in this story.

A huge thank you to Paul O'Neill for his surveyors report as always – it's very much appreciated.

Lastly, I would like to tell my family I love them all very much. I hope that one day you might actually read these books – hahaha only kidding. I still love you all even though you don't. I know you're all just waiting for the Netflix series to happen and save you the hassle. Keep praying guys 😊 xx

Love Helen xx